YOUTOPIA REBORN

A "Youtopia" Novel
by

Joseph Rein

YOUTOPIA REBORN
Youtopia – Book 2
Copyright © 2024 Joseph Rein

FIRST EDITION SOFTCOVER
ISBN: 1622536436
ISBN-13: 978-1-62253-643-6

Editor: Lane Diamond
Cover Artist: Kris Norris
Interior Designer: Lane Diamond

EVOLVED PUBLISHING™

www.EvolvedPub.com
Evolved Publishing LLC
Butler, Wisconsin, USA

Printed in Book Antiqua font.

Books by Joseph Rein

YOUTOPIA
Book 1: *Youtopia*
Book 2: *Youtopia Reborn*
Book 3: *Youtopia Infinity*

Roads without Houses: Stories [Press 53, 2018]

Dedication

For Mom and Dad:
my greatest champions.

Chapter 1

On the day Youtopia creator Sonya Young disappeared, Lane received a bizarre voicemail from an old friend. No, not a friend, more than that—a once-lover who, like all the other loved ones in his life, he'd lost when he'd entered Youtopia.

With his phone buzzing in his pocket, the circle of quasi-strangers surrounding him leered his way. Phones were silenced during Gatherings. He knew this. The incessant buzz interrupted a newcomer named Martin, or Mark, or some other M-name man with shocks of corkscrew hair and a look of pure despair, a first-time attendee who, Lane could tell, would never return.

Lane rose. He immediately regretted attending this Gathering, a *Midnighter* as the Reintegrators fondly called them. These were meetings of the desperate, those drowning in the harshness of the real world. In Youtopia, they all had lived as royalty in the frantic bliss of their own minds. It was all about them, all for them. Now, with Youtopia dismantled and its successor, Youtopia Reborn, only accepting minors, Lane and his fellow Reintegrators were reduced to rehabilitation rooms like this one, trying in vain to make sense of a promised world reneged.

Standing above the circle, Lane felt even taller than usual, gargantuan. The heat of the group's attention sent his pulse racing. Breathe—he needed to breathe.

He unpocketed his phone as it finally stopped buzzing, and held it up as though presenting evidence to a skeptical jury. "My mother," he said, though in truth both his parents had been gone for years, since before his Immersion. In the moment, he could think of no better lie. "Not a good situation."

The handful of regulars nodded. They sympathized. Mantra One in the Handbook for the Family of Anonymous Reintegrators: *Other people's needs are just as important as your own.* For instance: when Lane's mom needed his help, Lane needed to oblige. A simple concept, learned and preached throughout childhood, and yet, for Lane and others still struggling with Reintegration after two years, it remained one of the most difficult ones to grasp.

Henrick, the group's leader, shot Lane a sharp look. He alone in this group knew Lane was lying. "We understand, Lane," he said through tight lips. Lane and Henrick's acquaintanceship predated Youtopia — with no family, in his desperation to name an Observer, Lane had asked Henrick — and Lane had since called Henrick in desperation more times than he cared to admit. "Please take your call in the hallway."

Lane exited the hotel's small conference room and looked to his phone. The call came from a 612 number — Minneapolis, from his college days. Not a number his phone recognized, though that wasn't uncommon, since he'd lost all his contacts when he Immersed. Thankfully, the caller left a voicemail: forty-nine seconds, suggesting more than just a robocall or a wrong number. He opened it with no idea what to expect.

The sound started hard, a patchy cacophony of voices, likely bar patrons. Five seconds passed without a distinct voice. Five more. It seemed off, impossible even, to have been accidentally dialed by someone without his number. But then suddenly, at 0:21, roughly halfway through the message, a woman's voice appeared: "Laney."

Piquant, pitchy, her voice rented his foggy mind. It rang intimate bells, in real life and in Youtopia — the indefatigable, indomitable Serena Yarborough.

The message ran, but he missed it completely, adrift in that hazy space between memories real and memories Youtopian. Separating the two remained one of the hardest challenges. Mantra Five: *Accept your Youtopia past as real only for yourself.* In this instance, in his Youtopia, Lane and Serena had maintained a fantastic, mutually unexclusive relationship for years, when in reality they had broken up entirely before his Immersion, and not pleasantly. The woman he believed he knew was not the woman calling him now. The real Serena was extravagant, flamboyant, prone to mishaps both accidental and intentional. A voracious liar, even when — especially when — there seemed little reason. She lied when the details were either so inconsequential, or so obvious to refute, that her only recourse was to double-down and push harder. "I lived in Paris for a year," when she couldn't name a single Parisian landmark outside the Eiffel Tower. "I was born polydactyly," without a single scar on either hand. Hearing her voice took Lane back to those outlandish but ultimately harmless fibs, often delivered at the bars they frequented together.

He replayed the message. "Laney. Remember that time? With the card sharps and the Greco-Roman wrestler?" Her voice sounded desperate. Lane tried to attach meaning to these descriptions, but he couldn't immediately conjure the memory. "Remember what I said about my mom?"

She abruptly cut silent at 0:31. Male voices rushed behind her, all carrying distinctive, almost violent tones.

Then she shouted, "That bitch!" and Lane's whole body shuddered. Nearly ten seconds passed. At 0:43, she lowered her voice and whispered something to him in a conspiratorial tone. The words were utterly washed away by the commotion behind her.

"No no no," Lane said, just as Henrick exited the conference room and approached him.

"Hey man," Henrick said. "What's going on with you?"

"Everything's fine," Lane said. He clutched his phone in his hand like a secret, like Henrick had just walked in on some intimate moment. "Just need to jet is all."

"Not anything to do with drugs?"

"Jesus, no." Then he added, "You know I don't do that."

Henrick nodded, his wispy, thinning hair swaying like wheat stalks atop the field of his head. He was the one with the drug problem — pale and thin, his body was withered from oxycontin, ketamine, fentanyl, whatever helped him climb closest to a Youtopian peak. He stayed clean lately, Lane knew, because of his responsibilities to the group. Lane fought the urge to call out Henrick's petty projection.

"All right," Henrick said. "Care to tell me what it is, then?"

Lane hesitated. "I don't think so."

Henrick shot an exaggerated sigh. "Lane, buddy, we've been through this. You're here at a Midnighter. Then you lie to the group about your mom? Obviously, something's up. I can only help you if —"

"I know," Lane interrupted. He pushed back his shoulders, stood tall. He had half a foot on Henrick, more. "But we're allowed a little fucking privacy, right?"

Henrick squinted. Of the group, Lane was the even-keeled one, rarely quick to anger. That he pushed now probably told Henrick more than if he'd just remained quiet. "Mantra Seven, Lane," Henrick said. "Maybe the most important one."

"*Youtopia is lies. We must be the truth,*" they said together, though Lane felt the dripping dogma in their words. He felt like some freaky cult member under a hypnotic spell.

He shivered away the eerie feeling. "I'll be back on Wednesday."

"Or earlier, if you need us," Henrick said. "I'm always on call."

"I know. Thanks."

Lane darted out. The night air had cooled only slightly, the high July heat still hovering over his northern Indiana town like fog. He immediately called Serena back, waited for her to pick up, for the inharmonious din to rush into his line. She had something to tell him in that lost whisper. She had some answer for him—but to what question, he didn't know.

His phone rang and rang. She never picked up.

He listened to the message again, trying to make out her final words. He reminded himself of Mantra Two: *Recognize that everything you're experiencing now is completely real.* He tried to make sense of Serena's sudden need for him, of his sudden, insatiable need for this call, of his need for Midnighters and Henrick at all. He tried to make sense of himself.

***

He checked his phone—2:51 a.m.—before knocking on the questionable door before him. It was far too late. He needed to go home, to get some sleep before his full day at work. He needed not to be standing here, in a seedy apartment building on the upper west side, about to make the desperate decision he'd been fighting against since his Reintegration. He'd learned about smugglers of a Youtopian-like experience—*Immis*, they were called on the street—from one of FAR's sketchier members, a woman named Cuomo who didn't last a month. "It ain't the real thing," Cuomo had told Lane after offering up the name of her dealer, "but it's as close as we're gonna get."

In his jeans pocket, he rubbed at the folded bills—$1,000 in hundreds—that it would cost him for the next two hours of near-Youtopia euphoria. Nearly a quarter of his diminishing savings. As with everything, Lane had done his research on Immis. The experience included an astronaut-style helmet that submerged the senses into a dream-like state, but even if the helmet were of the highest tech, it wasn't what caused the steep price. No, that was for the small dose of KaliSerum, the drug that allowed the helmet's sensory stimuli to reach down from the brain to the chest, the fingertips. The miracle drug presented the only way for anyone not in Youtopia Reborn to approximate the experience, the only way he or anyone could approach the highs of near-Immersion.

- 4 -

Lane needed to turn around. Since Cuomo had introduced him to Rickie, the Immi dealer, one night at a bar, he'd envisioned himself standing here at Rickie's door, like a drug addict begging for his hit. He felt equal parts exhilaration and dread. Rickie hadn't yet answered. He was probably not home, or asleep. All Lane needed to do was turn and walk away. But then he heard a chain slide, and the door creaked open.

Rickie stood in a stained-red bathrobe. He flashed Lane a toothy smile, as though Lane had just reached the end of some inevitable road. With his hunched back and wispy mustache, Rickie resembled a subterranean creature peeking his head above the surface.

Without a word, Rickie stepped aside. Reluctantly, Lane entered.

The second he stepped foot in the apartment, he recognized his mistake. The inside fared worse than its outside, with threadbare couches, a scorched burn mark up the wallpapered north wall, and newspaper on the floor full of animal shit. No helmet, no bed. Perhaps Rickie had it all hidden in a back room—but then, nothing in the apartment bespoke the kind of place where someone made a thousand dollars per visit.

Rickie locked the door behind them and then pressed into the doorframe with obvious intent. As if on cue, three men in matching rust-colored tank tops stepped out from the hallway. Their bodies were emaciated, their chests sunken hollows. They could have been triplets, identical aside from the pistols pointing prominently from two of their belts.

Lane instinctively stood tall. "You're making a mistake," he said, hoping they believed it more than he did himself.

The tanktopped trio fanned out around Lane. He kept his eyes on Rickie, but tuned into his peripherals, keeping all four in sight. His calves pressed against one of the couches, almost sending him into it.

"I don't think so," Rickie said. He still hadn't left the doorway.

Then, as if to punctuate Rickie's point, one of the triplets pulled his gun and approached Lane with vacant eyes. The gun danced flimsily in his hand, as though he'd never used one before. With a forceful enough swing, Lane could have easily knocked it out of his hand. These men were all three quarters his size, and maybe, if he got a hold of one of their weapons...

But no—the flippant gun was a diversion. Lane turned just in time to see the butt of the other pistol surging at his temple. He jerked backward, the glancing blow striking his lip and sending shrieks of pain into his jaw.

He ducked down, bracing for another blow to the head. Footsteps pounded toward him.

"All right! All right!" he shouted to stave off the next attack, his arms pushing against his ears and tunneling his own voice in his head. "Take it. Take it all."

Silence. He slowly peeked up, pulling the billfold from his pocket. The four scant men surrounded him like vermin. One of them ripped the cash from his hands.

"Check him," Rickie said.

As the one triplet kept his gun trained on Lane, the other two knelt and dug through his pockets, their hands pushing and probing like hungry, aggressive snakes. They turned up his keys, his cellphone, and a few other small bills.

Rickie took the phone and keys, holding them up for inspection. "A Chevy guy," he said, pocketing the keys. "Not no more."

The triplets sniggered as they filed into a row. Lane felt the heat of anger rise in his chest, followed quickly by a melancholic exhaustion, a wish to be anywhere but here.

Rickie looked at Lane's phone. "Shit! When you get this? Before the freeze? Cuomo said you were the real deal." He threw the phone back at Lane, hitting him in the chest. "Get the fuck out of here."

Lane stood, the anger again rising with him. "Is this Immi shit even real or—"

The gun cracked down again, this time on the crown of his head, sending bursts of brilliant light into his vision. The pressing, pulsing pain immediately surrounded his whole skull. He felt warm blood clumping his hair.

"Piss off," Rickie hissed, "and be happy you're alive."

Lane limped to his feet. Standing over Rickie, he felt sodden, powerless. To the sound of the trio's laughter, Lane stuttered out the door, his jaw and head aflame, his old knee injury singing from his leg. And though Rickie was right—he should be happy to come out of the sabotaged deal alive—he couldn't help but feel a deep, disdainful dread.

***

9:33 a.m. and his phone buzzed again, this time cutting into the Nina Simone record he always listened to on his earbuds while stretching. He felt the phone's vibration in his throbbing lip, as though the triplet was striking him anew. He'd barely slept, but the time provided him a strange comfort: he superstitiously, stupidly, believed in the fortunes of three. He was six-foot-three; his favorite basketball memory was his triple-double against Belmont. He had completed his bachelor's degree in journalism in three years. His first national expose on Reintegrator prescription overdoses—picked up by the Washington Post and others—was first published on March 3rd. Something about the successive threes felt providential, like something that would have happened in Youtopia—in a perfected, corrected world. Not the world he was in now, with a splitting jaw and headache and a feeling of foreboding no meditative stretching could shake.

He pulled out of his forward bend and looked to his phone, expecting Serena from the same 612 as before, but it was only his boss Millie.

"When are you coming into the newsroom?" she asked in her low-pitched, overly pleasant voice.

Newsroom, he nearly laughed to himself. Millie insisted on calling it that, even though the Huntington Weekly Beacon resided in nothing more than a low-rent office building in the old district, next to a textile front office, an Amazon pallet shop, and an abandoned DMV.

"On an assignment," he lied. "Be in soon."

"I'm not calling to reprimand you," Millie said. Her voice surrounded him through his earbuds, guttural and powerful, belying almost every other aspect about her—her age, her small stature, her benevolent nature. "I've got to cover last night's Bermuda, and I need someone to prep for the game tonight."

A Bermuda. Their slang, referring to a scoop that both arrived out of nowhere and loomed so large and all-encompassing that it consumed and devoured all other news stories—stories like early Covid-19, Russia's invasion of Ukraine, Michael Jackson's death.

"Don't tell me you haven't seen it?" Millie said. When Lane didn't answer, she continued. "Go ahead. I'll wait."

Lane pulled up his browser, where he saw the accumulation of his common search sites, the Weekly Beacon but also CNN, BBC, the Times, ESPN, Idagio, Spotify, and a jazz forum titled *Big Beats*. On the BBC website, the dark bold headline flashed onto his screen:

YOUTOPIA REBORN CREATOR SONYA YOUNG ABDUCTED FROM HER CALIFORNIA HOME

Lane's body tensed. A year and a half of FAR teachings had preached this response into him. Look away. Treat Youtopia Reborn like a lit stove burner, hot to the touch. Youtopia had been a paradise of the individual mind—a place where Immersers had followed their unconscious, prurient desires to their farthest ends. And then came the murders, the unsolved mystery, and the eventual shutting down of Youtopia. They pulled the plug, lifted all half a million people, like Lane, whose lives transformed instantly from dream to constant struggle. Many committed suicide. Some, like Henrick, persevered through countless programs and meetings. Many dealt in the underbelly, stealing VR experiences like Immis to get as close to Youtopia as possible.

It would have been easier, Lane always thought, if Sonya Young had simply blacked out the experiment, buried Youtopia deep in the ground, never to return—if *nobody* could have it. Then why, only a year later, did she find it wise to reopen its doors only to kids? Why should they have what nobody else could?

Lane and another Reintegrator murmured briefly about it once before a meeting, and a third snitched on them. Henrick made a great show of the issue that day, dismissing their natural curiosity as jealousy, as Youtopian desires that only led to ruin. "You're not a child," he said. Then, his voice uncharacteristically rising, "And you're not Sonya Young! So you don't have a fucking say, do you!"

Lane had felt inappropriately chastised and nearly walked out, until he remembered all the times Henrick had saved him in early Reintegration. All those anxiety-stricken nights he might not have gotten through.

"We need to get beyond Youtopia," Henrick had said, his voice subdued, shaking his hanging head. "We need to look to our *future*."

And yet, this abduction felt like proof, vindication, though of exactly what, Lane couldn't say. Sonya Young had to be one of the most difficult people in the world to abduct. Forget Henrick and FAR—as a journalist, Lane needed to read the story out of simple due diligence to national news. Still, he scrolled the article with the guilty pleasure of a young boy stumbling on his dad's old magazines.

"Whoa," he said.

"Yeah," Millie said. "And look, Lane, I've thought about it, and I won't put you anywhere near it. I promise. But that means you've got to cover the game for me."

The game was local Legion baseball against Homestead, a cross-town rivalry that Lane normally would've dived into headfirst, pulling stats and storylines and personal angles with which other local reporters didn't bother. It was how he survived post-Youtopia: he lived in the minute details. Story assignments, jazz playlists—he did everything with obsessive, pinpoint focus. He needed to stay sharp, and yet he couldn't imagine another balmy Tuesday night stuck on hard bleachers. He didn't want to suffer the beer and banter, the cloying parents hoping for stands full of college scouts. He would absorb statistics and mannerisms and reactions, only to lionize a bunch of kids who were more likely to blow out their knees than gain fame beyond high school.

Lane breathed deep into his lungs. He wanted to stop himself, and yet he heard himself say, "I don't know if I told you this, but today's the anniversary. Of... you know... my parents."

Another lie. This one at least was adjacent to the truth—it was nearing the half-anniversary—but a lie nonetheless. They were piling up, his disconnections from the truth. Precursors, FAR would say, to a nosedive.

"Oh, Lane. I'm sorry."

"I know. It sounds like an excuse, but... I just—"

"Say no more. You know what? Forget the game. I'll put Musky on it."

"Thanks," he said. "I really need it."

"But back on it tomorrow, yeah? Your review is coming up next week, and I want to be able to tell the truth when I say Lane Samson is on top of it."

"Can do, boss."

He returned to his stretching, keeping his body tuned to its pressure spots, its points of weakness. After five minutes of cat cows and crescent lunges, his forehead glossed with a subtle sweat. He stripped down to his underwear, taking off even his socks, something he rarely did except to shower. When he'd first Reintegrated, some of the biggest challenges had been physical: rebuilding atrophied muscle, yes, but also dealing with new, inexplicable aches and soreness. His right knee stiffened with any misstep, recalling the ACL tear that shattered his high school basketball limelight. His skin was plasticine, the hairs growing in odd patches on his back and shoulders foreign. He'd been Immersed for two years, and yet it felt as though he'd aged ten.

He finished sitting crosslegged, pushing his knees as close to his apartment carpet as he could manage. As he lowered his head, he briefly saw, on the bottom of his foot, his minute tattoo—S402051, his former Immerser number. This badge followed him everywhere, a permanent reminder of the choice he'd made. Some of his FAR cohorts had paid to have them removed; others, like Lane, simply tried to ignore them, to cover them up as best they could. Few, if any, wore sandals.

He showered and left his apartment on foot, where immediately the dense summer heat brought back his sweat. Mid-nineties, forecasted to get even hotter, a sign that July would outpace even their record-breaking June. He took deep, swimming breaths, noticing how few people were outside. Serena's call, Sonya Young's abduction, the heat—it all jumbled his mind, all blaring wind instruments with no steady percussion, no baseline. Ten blocks down, he turned on Wasson toward the industrial park and the only man he could think of to help him sort it out: Quinn Argyle.

He crossed the small strip of parking in front of Q&C Entertainment. As he opened the door, he expected to feel the rush of artificial cool air, but inside was even hotter. A desk with no receptionist greeted him even though the company, as far as he knew, was doing just fine. He hadn't spoken to Quinn—another high school friend, his entrepreneurial one, who started his own business straight after graduation—in months, but at that time, Quinn made his clientele and prospects sound far better than an empty room without air conditioning. Lane approached the desk and rang an old-time service bell. Moments later, through the door, his face buried in a tablet, an energy drink in his other hand, Quinn entered.

He had the look of a vagabond, his thick black hair askew, his beard grown all the way to his chest, but he was as close to a mastermind with technology as Lane knew. He rubbed his eyes, looking as tired as Lane felt. But when he saw Lane, he smiled.

"My man!" He hugged Lane without compunction, and Lane felt the body heat radiating off him. "It's been, like, what? A year?"

"Not that long," Lane said.

"Feels like it, though. Doesn't it?" Quinn noticed Lane's swollen lip, his hangdog expression. "Aw shit, man. Tell me the other guy got it at least as good."

"Unfortunately, no." Lane tried to smile, his lip burning. "I like what you've done with the place."

"Still an asshole." Quinn downed the rest of his drink, then placed his hands behind him, the pose Lane remembered him in most, as though ready to espouse shrewd wisdom. "This place, my friend, is a capital sinkhole. Nobody visits storefronts anymore."

"Except me."

"Except you. You're old-school. You're a journalist, for Pete's sake."

"That's why I'm here." Lane took out his phone and retrieved the voicemail. "Think you can make this out?"

He pressed play. The voicemail ran as he wiped at his forehead with his sleeve. Standing before Quinn, freed of his own obsessions, Lane heard even deeper contrasts in the voicemail, Serena's shouts louder, her murmur quieter, the message ever more buried.

When the message ended, Quinn said, "Sure this has nothing to do with..." He pointed at Lane's busted lip.

"One hundred percent sure."

Quinn circled his finger. Together, they took in the message five times. Quinn clicked his tongue after the last.

"Have to ask the obvious question," Quinn said. "You've tried calling her back?"

"She hasn't answered."

"Mmmm-hmmm. And this woman, you and her were a thing once, I presume?"

"Not in a long while, no."

"Another question I gotta ask then—you stalking her?"

"Shit, no."

"I'm kidding, man! You could use some sleep."

Quinn swiped Lane's phone from his hand. "Retro. Cool." Before Lane could protest, Quinn flensed its case, its backing, and assessed its bared carcass like a coroner. He pushed on a small crack and a compartment flipped open. "Kept these babies shut up in the crib. Ah, the good old days."

He went to his front desk and unlocked one of the bottommost drawers. From it, he retrieved a mash of cords intertwined like tangled jungle vines, lifting them in a ball and spinning them. When he found the right one, he pinched it and violently shook the rest to the floor. He stabbed one end into the innards of Lane's phone, and the other into a sleek gray MacBook he pulled from another locked drawer. His hands moved dizzyingly fast, with practiced precision.

"The background noise won't give us grief. Not our culprit." Now in his element, Quinn's fingers typed with assurance. "Well, okay, so it *is* technically the culprit, but not the *predominant* one." He said the word slowly: Lane imagined him winking. "We cut too low and we lose her voice. Too high and all those guys in the back want in on the party. Oh, shit—did that touch a nerve? She's probably still in love with you, buddy. They all are." Quinn swiped a finger across Lane's phone. "Good sir, do I have your consent to access the file?"

A large red oval dominated his screen, the words *I Agree* starkly in its center. Lane pressed it.

"Sweet. I now know your full porn download history, you freak." He squinted at Lane. "I'm kidding. Maybe." He raised his hand and theatrically hit the return button.

Lane's message played, with force, through Quinn's laptop. Serena's voice gained a crisp edge. They waited in anticipation through twenty, thirty seconds of the message, but when they got to the end, to Serena's whispers, it sounded as obfuscated as before.

"Damn. A long shot, but would've saved some headaches. Let's try door number two."

On the screen, Quinn opened and closed browsers advertising various noise reduction apps. "Freebies are for suckers. Do less than my programs, and they want you to sign away a kidney."

"Is there anything stronger?" Lane asked. "Like maybe on the dark web?"

Quinn leaned back and craned his neck, his beard folding against his shoulder. In a mocking formal voice, he asked, "What, my good sir, do you know about the dark web?"

"Absolutely nothing."

"Yeah, me neither." He turned back to his screen. "No, this we can get on the one percent. We just need..." He typed and closed screens, typed and closed, until he finally stopped on one, the page of which was laid out in black with neon green writing. It looked like something from *The Matrix*. "Yes. Here we are. The Real Deal Holyfield."

Lane watched him scroll, open the Terms of Use page, squint through fine print. He came to the bottom of the page, then let out a sharp, shrill whistle.

"What?" Lane asked.

"Okay, so this is top of the line. CIA-level stuff. If this can't do it, it can't be done." Quinn leaned back again. "But they want *five hundo* for the program."

"Five hundred dollars?"

"And that's only for the *trial period*." He shrugged his shoulders. "Hot damn. Microsoft's got nothing on these fools."

Lane thought of his stolen car, the thousand dollars. He thought of the weeks and weeks of work just to make up for his losses. "Can you work around it?"

"You mean steal it."

Lane shrugged.

"Lane, my boy, in my line of work, there's a fine line between *can* and *will*. I present to you said line."

Sweat dripped down Lane's lips, stinging in his throbbing wound. "But you're sure it'll work?" Lane asked.

"Yes?" Quinn shrugged again, not the motion Lane wanted to see. "One way to find out."

Lane sighed. The heat of the room weighed on him. Five hundred dollars was outrageous for what they were asking. He was going out on a limb—one that FAR and Henrick would advise him strongly against—and for what? To hear what Serena said to him? To feel a connection—any connection—to the real world? Part of him believed Serena had something important to say. That she needed him. The truth was he needed her more.

"I'll give you fifty," he finally said.

"Fifty? I'm a businessman, Lane. You just offered a textbook raw deal."

"You get to keep the program. You can play around to your heart's content. I need it for one message."

Quinn went silent, which Lane knew was a good sign. He leaned on his journalistic instinct and said nothing more. Teasing out a favor from a friend was no different than teasing out information from a source: appeal to their benefit. Let silent moments linger.

Then, when necessary, push your motives as their own.

"Come on, Quinn," Lane said. "You're as curious about this as I am."

"That I sincerely doubt." Quinn shifted his weight. "Ahhhhhh. Shit. You gotta sweeten the pot somehow. I'm gonna need a three pack of donuts from the Marathon down yonder."

"You're kidding."

"White frosting long johns. Sprinkles, no filling. I'm deadly serious here. Any filling and the deal's off."

Lane smirked. "I'll even throw in another energy drink for good measure."

Quinn returned the smirk. "You sly bastard. Let's chase the white rabbit."

He ushered Lane through a narrow hallway to the back office. The space was a small, densely-packed room covered in wall-to-wall electronics, with LED screens stacked like cake layers and cords dangling like errant frosting beneath them. On plastic folding tables resided a massive switchboard and countless mixers and an aging electric keyboard. Quinn extended his arms like a lord presenting his dominion.

"What dreams are made of."

He then flipped a master switch on the wall, and the room sprung to life. Screens populated with sports and recycled news and midnight programming: Cubs highlights and *Law and Order* reruns and anchors covering the Sonya Young abduction, all silent. The screens flashed strobe-like, adding to Lane's already-blossoming headache. Quinn ignored the lights, accustomed to the discordant mess, but Lane couldn't focus. He was about to tell Quinn to shut the screens off when Quinn plunked down into the lone swivel chair and extended his palm.

"I believe we agreed on fifty."

Lane dug deep into his pockets, retrieving a crumpled twenty and a handful of singles. He flattened them as best he could, then handed them to a bemused Quinn.

"I'll get you the rest later."

"My sweet lord. Years fly by and somehow you never change."

Quinn opened his laptop. The program took five minutes to download, another five to set up, and another five for Quinn to play around. All the while, the screens around them flashed images of Sonya Young's multimillion-dollar glassine home in California, surrounded by police tape and swarming black SUVs.

"Gotta admit, this thing is pretty sweet. Intuitive." Quinn full-screened a black-backed grid, over which various colored, jagged lines scribbled as the message played. They looked like racing heartbeats on a monitor. "Worth the price? Hells no. But then again, what is these days?"

The vertical line of the timestamp surged forward. "See, that's her," Quinn said, pointing at the highest line, a thick purple mountain cascading over all others. "The rest we can cut down. Hopefully."

At the grating pause in Serena's message, the audio cut out. The timestamp halted. Quinn leaned in. "Well, shit. That's new."

He opened a different window of elaborate code. At the screen, he yelled, "I don't know what the fuck you mean!" as though shouting at an incompetent employee. He wiped the first file and reuploaded it. They watched the same bumps and valleys, the same kick when Serena laughed her high-pitched squeal. Then, at the silence, it froze again.

"What's the problem?" Lane asked.

"Might be it can't distinguish the different ambient strains. Getting all jumbled up, like a smudge on a CD. Remember that? If only we could breathe heavy on it, wipe it down."

"Can you just skip over the silence? We only need the end."

Quinn pursed his lips. "Not a bad idea."

He highlighted the first forty-one seconds of the message and excised them. Then he ran it again. When Serena screamed, "That bitch!" they both visibly jolted.

"Ah ha! We're in business, Lane man. That's Mister — what was it? Thirty-two on the ACT?"

"Thirty-three, but who's counting."

The shortened, obscure message played to its end. The graph on the screen contained twenty lines, maybe more, including the thick and then abruptly thin purple thread of Serena's voice.

"This is where it gets cool," Quinn said. "Like this, see?" He grabbed one of the lower threads, pumpkin orange, and isolated it. He played back the audio, the rattling sound of a cocktail shaker. "Martini, Mr. Bond? Or this." A fire-engine red line produced the brusque voice of a man singing Fleetwood Mac lyrics. "Eerie, isn't it? Think of the surveillance implications. Anything you say with your phone in your pocket could—"

"Quinn... Can we?"

Quinn shook from his reverence. "Right. So Professor Plum here..." He pulled the thread. "This baby should be our lotto ticket."

He hit play. Her shout didn't jolt them this time. The sibilant s's and sharp k's came through clearer, but not loudly enough to distinguish her words.

"Here. Let me just..." Quinn went to the switchboard next to him and turned multiple dials. A static hum reverberated through the room. "Here she blow."

"That bitch!" Serena hollered into the room, from behind and before and all around Lane. The shock hit him, as though he was back in some random Minneapolis bar, with Serena circling him like a confetti storm— like New Year's Eve, champagne in plastic flutes, a shimmering silver dress.

That was it.

Suddenly, the memory rushed back to him—the wrestler, hitting on Serena right in front of him. Card players in the corner, never looking up from their game. Ryan Seacrest on every television, in Times Square faux-jubilation. Serena in a top hat, a silver dress with a plunging neckline.

"Want to know the craziest thing about me?" she had asked.

"I know all the crazy things," he replied. "No room for more crazy."

"Oh yeah? How about this." She leaned in, gave her eyes a covert shuffle, then whispered, "My biological mother founded Youtopia."

"Serena."

"I'm serious. My mother is none other than *the* Sonya Young."

"Serena," Lane repeated. He looked straight at her as, around them, the bar began its countdown to the new year. "Not now."

She returned his stare with sharp eyes. "Tell anybody and we both might end up dead."

The lie was so preposterous, bigger than any other she'd ever given him, and so his only reaction was to laugh. She had just stared in reply.

Quinn slapped Lane on the back. "Yes! We got it!" He raised his hands in triumph. Then, turning somber, he said, "Sounds serious, man."

Lane had missed the message, lost in his memory. The haphazard tide of that New Year's Eve, of Serena claiming Sonya Young as her mother, was getting mixed-up with the message, with Young's abduction. It was all a mingling of instruments with no rhythm, like kids attempting jazz — no harmony, just discord.

Then Quinn backtracked and played it again. The message came through clear. "That bitch!" followed by a seemingly endless pause. Then Serena's whisper, low and yet as pure as that New Year's Eve in the bar:

"Help me, Lane. They're coming for me next!"

Interlude: Overheard at the Fat Toad

We're at a dimly lit bar, sports-themed. Paneled walls are decaled in posters across the Midwestern professional sports map: Denver Broncos and Kansas City Chiefs and Green Bay Packers, Minnesota Twins and St. Louis Cardinals and Colorado Rockies. Here is a place of non-affiliation, of geographic uncertainty. Anyplace USA.

Behold the Fat Toad. The mid-thirties bartender exudes machismo, his beer barrel arms draped in sleeve tattoos. He surveys the scene like the appraising overlord of this domain, his begrimed kingdom.

Patrons spatter hightops and booths. Soon will commence a poker tournament, or bar trivia, or a meat raffle: something to reel in the faithful on a Tuesday night. Chatter surges in sudden crescendos.

Time: After midnight.

At rise: Seated at the bar, a woman, early 40s, heavy makeup and long legs, fiddles with the gaudy rings on one hand. She appears a bit bored. She sips a murky yellow concoction garnished with a pineapple wedge, smokes a slender cigarette with all the affectation and simpering innuendo of Anne Bancroft's Mrs. Robinson.

The man next to her is younger, by a decade we might say. He wears a shirt buttoned all the way to the top, pale skin. He has Dustin Hoffman's foppish haircut and disaffecting eyes, looking very much like a recent graduate.

Flatscreens on the wall play a visual symphony of sports stations, a cornucopia of contests past and present. NFL football, La Liga soccer, collegiate lacrosse, you name it. The screen directly before our couple, however, emits a muted Fox News. The red-faced host prattles silent above the ticker:

SONYA YOUNG KIDNAPPER LEAVES HARROWING MESSAGE: "REBORN FOR ALL OR REBORN FOR NONE"

Glenda paws her drink. Her attention bandies about the room. The Graduate eyes the news. Note his intent. Glenda sure does. She taps her glass, shimmies her shoulders in unsuccessful attempts to pilfer his attention back to its rightful owner.

GLENDA: I can hardly believe it! Can you Pook?

GRADUATE: ...

GLENDA: *(Hits him on the shoulder)* I mean, it's just so unbelievable, isn't it?

GRADUATE: What?

GLENDA: The goddamned moon landing! *(Points emphatically at the screen) Reborn for All*, huh.

GRADUATE: It's that movement.

GLENDA: The what-ment?

GRADUATE: *(Scrolls on his phone. Hands it to Glenda)*

GLENDA: Mmm-hmm, yep, blah blah blah... *(Recites)* "...founded by Ohio native Nini Gunderson... belief that all citizens, ill or healthy, young or old, deserve equal access to Youtopia Reborn. Prominent vocal figures for the movement include famous actors, athletes, US Congresspeople, and the American Nurses Association."

GRADUATE: There you have it.

GLENDA: That's dumb.

GRADUATE: People have believed worse.

GLENDA: No, I mean, if people want this thing so bad, just copy it, right? This is America, for Christ's sake. There could be a hundred of these joints.

GRADUATE: They've tried. *Reborn Lites*, they're called. Ninety-nine percent are identity scams. As for the legit one percent, I hear Reborn's legal team shoots them down before they can take flight.

GLENDA: Well, that headline's dumb too. *(Nods at screen)* They're missing the juiciest parts. I read that the kidnapper left one of those Russian nesting dolls on her bed. Unstacked, like a kid was playing with them. *Creeeeepy.*

GRADUATE: Kidnappers usually are creeps.

GLENDA: And those beastly Great Danes of hers! Must've drugged them something good.

GRADUATE: Poor dogs.

GLENDA: Tell me about it! I'm just shocked someone got in. These billionaires, Bezos and Zuckerman and the like... they just seem, I don't know, untouchable.

GRADUATE: Ask Sam Bankman-Fried about that.

GLENDA: Who?

GRADUATE: Nevermind. Honestly, Glen, I haven't given it much thought.

GLENDA: Oh, please! Don't play coy with me. (*Looks around. Leans in close, rubbing a hand on his chest*) Ain't nobody watching us here. No wiretaps in the speaker system.

GRADUATE: You have a phone, don't you?

GLENDA: Stuffed in my pocket! (*Reaches down to his crotch*) Speaking of pockets, you got something in here...

GRADUATE: Jesus Glen, take it easy. We just left the motel.

GLENDA: Oh, forgive me for wanting you. I feel sooooo bad for you. You know, back in my day —

GRADUATE: You had fifty men lining up outside your door.

GLENDA: And *they* wanted *my* attention. *They* wanted to talk to *me*.

GRADUATE: You want to talk? Okay, here goes: that woman had it coming.

GLENDA: What a horrible thing to say!

GRADUATE: You asked. Don't get mad if you don't like my answer.

GLENDA: How did she deserve this?

GRADUATE: All those invincible billionaires you admire? They make the world worse. Sonya Young made the world worse.

GLENDA: Not to those kids she didn't.

GRADUATE: (*Finally turning to Glenda*) That's a crock of horseshit propaganda and you know it.

GLENDA: Like hell it is! You know, for a self-proclaimed genius, you can be such a simpleton. There's terminally ill kids in this world. Unwanted kids born to parents who won't support them. They don't just disappear when we ignore them. Who's going to take them in? You?

GRADUATE: Is that what this is about? You wish *you* could have gone into Youtopia Reborn instead of getting ditched by your deadbeat dad?

GLENDA: (*Grabs his wrist*) Don't. Don't you start. I will slap you so hard, Mr. Arm Tatts back there will feel it.

GRADUATE: ...

GLENDA: I'm not talking about myself. Those kids deserve a better life.

GRADUATE: Of course.

GLENDA: Sonya Young didn't provide that?

GRADUATE: Maybe. All I'm saying is, why those kids and not others? Why only kids anyway? Why does Sonya-Almighty-Young get to decide who's in and who's out? She's just some software programmer with—

GLENDA: *Genius* software programmer.

GRADUATE: A programmer with an idea. And all of a sudden, *she* decides who gets the good life and who doesn't.

GLENDA: Oh, Pook. Is this about Arthur?

GRADUATE: Of course it is! But me too. You. Everybody.

GLENDA: *You* want to Immerse in Youtopia?

GRADUATE: Well, it'd be nice to see the Huskers back in the national championship conversation in my lifetime. That sure isn't happening in real life.

GLENDA: That's it. That's the dream.

GRADUATE: It's not just those *Reborn for All* fanatics. Do you know how many lawsuits have been filed against Sonya Young? This kid is *too close* to maturity, that kid isn't *sick enough* to make their arbitrary cut. How many have died waiting on the courts to force her to do the right thing? How many could have been saved?

GLENDA: Oooo, keep going. You sound like that movie, the black-and-white one about the Holocaust... Liam Neeson?

GRADUATE: Schindler's List.

GLENDA: I like him in Taken. Go ahead. Say, "I would sacrifice anything for her," in a sexy baritone.

GRADUATE: *(Takes a long drink of his beer)* Bottom line is, Sonya Young is gone, and probably dead. And I say good riddance.

GLENDA: *If* she really got abducted at all.

GRADUATE: Oh, no. Stop right there.

GLENDA: What?

GRADUATE: I will not follow you down your Youtube flat-earth rabbit hole bullshit.

GLENDA: The earth is round, yes. But Sonya Young stolen from her house by some mysterious mastermind thief? *That* sounds flat-earth. I have a theory.

GRADUATE: And here it comes...

GLENDA: *(Points a gaudily ringed index finger)* One: Sonya Young abducted from her California home, one out of how many that woman owns? Twenty? More? People say even her highest-ups can't track her movements. Suddenly some kidnapper can? That does *not* pass the sniff test.

GRADUATE: All you're suggesting is that someone close to the woman abducted her. Which is, by the way, how a vast majority of abductions work.

GLENDA: So let's say they did know. How'd they cut off all bajillion levels of security that woman must have? She designed alternate universes, for heaven's sake. You're telling me there's just one wire to snip? Poof, cameras gone?

GRADUATE: Technology fails. Especially Sonya Young's. What do you think happened with the Youtopia murders?

GLENDA: *(Flicks a second finger, ring even more outlandish)* Two: the timeline stinks something rotten. Sonya goes home for a long weekend. No appointments for days. Days! This from a woman who breathes work. *(Points her middle finger, tawdriest ring of all)* Three: what's the motive here?

GRADUATE: Message seems clear to me.

GLENDA: Let's say you want the *Reborn for All* crap. Why *steal* the damn woman? Does she seem the type to give into demands? Tell me that woman will crack. Bitch is like granite.

GRADUATE: See, this is your problem. You assume you know someone because you saw them on TV once. The news only gives you what the person wants you to see. And the tabloids give you BS. Remember that story about her supposedly having a daughter she put up for adoption? Turned out it was just some hack TMZ temp trying to make a name for herself.

GLENDA: Oooh, maybe that one was true too. Hey, maybe the long-lost daughter kidnapped her!

GRADUATE: This is unhinged. You're starting to sound like your brother.

GLENDA: *(Pauses. Blinks back tears. Reaches back and SLAPS him across the face, the bar turning toward them)*

GRADUATE: *(Rubs at his jaw — the rings smart. A weighty pause. The bar slowly turns its attention away, all except Mr. Arm Tatts, ready to pounce at the Graduate's first wrong move)*

GLENDA: I will fucking walk right now. I told you never to do that.

GRADUATE: All right, all right. Let's just relax. Let's talk about something else. Anything.

GLENDA: No. That was an incredibly hurtful thing to say. So now you're going to sip your little IPA and listen to my closing argument.

GRADUATE: All right, Glen. Deal the final verdict.

GLENDA: *(Extends her thumb now, ringless, creased with age)* Sonya Young is in legal trouble. Those lawsuits you mentioned? Piling up. What's the best way to get out of trouble? You go full-on Nick Fury! It's how they ended Dexter. That Hugh Laurie doctor show. Christian Bale in the third Batman. Fake your own disappearance and you're home free!

GRADUATE: Give me one example when that actually happened. In real life.

GLENDA: Well, shithead, if it did, would we know about it?

GRADUATE: *(Mockingly stands to leave)* Want to see a real disappearance?

GLENDA: *(Grabs him forcibly by the waist)* Oh no, you don't. We've got that motel room for the night. And I'm getting my goddamn money's worth, pretty boy.

Chapter 2

"Allow me to officially welcome you to the Reborn Cradles Minneapolis! We are thrilled to share our mission with you today."

The concave movie screen engulfed the room, broadcasting a vast skyscape with brilliant clouds of white. The spokeswoman dissolved onto the screen, the effect disconcerting, like watching dandelion spores return to the stem. The woman smiled, her wide face feeling unnaturally close, bearing down on Lane in his front row seat.

He'd arrived at the building well before the tour, armed with his ID and press badge and, most importantly, the paperwork proving he was truly a Reintegrator and therefore entitled to one of the few reserved seats for Youtopia Reborn tours. Officially, he was not on assignment—in another lie, the silky threads of them now accumulating into a tangled web, he told Millie that the Sonya Young abduction had opened old wounds, and that he needed this visit to gain some closure. He spent $250 on a plane ticket he could hardly afford, another $75 on a deposit for a rental car, and now masqueraded as just another visitor, a simple, curious observer interested in Youtopia Reborn's inner workings—not someone desperately trying to connect the scattered dots of this story, of his life.

After digitally signing his name on numerous disclaimer forms, Lane was ushered with a group of fifty straight to this mini-theater off the lobby. Last in line, he ended up between a heavyset man and an older woman in the dead center of the room. A prolonged wait followed, with only instructions flashing across the giant screen to pass the time. He got the distinct feeling of the pre-ride safety protocols for some theme-park rollercoaster—buckle up, remove loose clothing, keep arms in the cabin. Enjoy the ride.

After five minutes of squirming, Lane pulled his phone and rechecked the texts he'd sent Serena before his flight. *Got your call* and *You sounded a bit stressed out* and *I can come visit if you need...?* His attempts at nonchalance belied the frenzy he'd felt after fleeing Quinn's shop. He had immediately called her back half a dozen times on the way to his apartment, getting nothing but a ringtone. On social media, he scoured the profiles of friends and friends of friends, looking for any current posts that might've tagged or mentioned her. He hastily created Instagram and TikTok accounts just so he could connect with people from college who might still be in contact with Serena. Few replied; one, a former rec basketball friend they called Needles, said he ran into Serena a few weeks ago but hadn't talked to her since. *We should catch up!* Needles said before going dark.

Next, he'd pulled every directory in the Twin Cities metro area, finding three Serena Yarboroughs, two of them in upscale Edina and Minnetonka, making them unlikely matches. For the third, an apartment just off Uptown, Lane called the building's landlord under the guise of a long-lost sibling looking to reconnect. The husky-voiced woman seemed skeptical, and though Lane pushed all the charm he could muster—softening his voice, playing on made-up childhood nostalgias—the woman didn't budge. "Can't help you," she had said before hanging up.

Desperate, Lane had checked for cheap flights to MSP. In his mind, he approached the locked gates of FAR recriminations—*you're frantic, acting on impulse, believing it will all work out. This isn't Youtopia!*—and barreled right through them. He booked his ticket for the Reborn Cradle tour the next afternoon. And that morning, he stood at the foot of Serena's apartment building.

The burnt-red brick of the faded building radiated the morning heat. The buzzer at the front door read simply *S.Y.* He pushed it, hoping against hope that he'd hear her voice. When he didn't, he waited near the stoop, pretending to busy himself on his phone. Some ten minutes later, a bald, middle-aged man exited. Lane put the phone to his ear.

"Yeah," he said to nobody, giving a knowing head nod to the man. "I know—they never work. Someone just let me in. I'll be right up."

He stole into the silent hallway. The floors creaked with his footsteps. At Serena's door, he knocked softly, then with more force. The door was old, locked only at the knob. Lane shot glances up and down the hallway, then pulled his driver's license from his pocket, attempting to jimmy the thin plastic between the side jamb and the strike plate. This trick had worked twice for him in college, when he'd locked himself out of his own apartment. Serena's door had similar give, was warped just enough that he might get it. He was being impulsive, crazy even, but he just felt, he *knew*, that something inside Serena's apartment would—

The front door of the apartment building slammed shut. Lane shot the ID back to his pocket. The bald man had returned, slowly approaching Lane. Lane turned, stooped his head, and passed the man with as much nonchalance as he could muster. The man eyed him until he slipped away.

As he'd marched toward the thick of Uptown, his heart thundered in his chest. What the hell was he doing? Trying to break into her apartment? Hunting her down like the creep Quinn accused him of being? And yet, something here was off—his journalistic instincts told him so. The seeds of the nascent story planted in his mind: Sonya Young's abduction was somehow tied to Serena, a woman nobody knew existed, a biological daughter hidden for nearly three decades. If true, this was potentially the biggest story of Lane's life—his own Bermuda. His blood had raced with the hot adrenaline of his near-criminal behavior. With shaky hands, he had ordered an Uber to take him to the Reborn Cradles.

He squirmed in his theater seat. They were compact, with a short back, not built for men his size. Then he felt a pat on his shoulder.

"Excuse me, sir?" He turned; the squat woman behind him glowered. "I can't really see the screen."

Lane fought the urge to reply that he would have taken a back seat, if the shorter people like her hadn't instinctively occupied them like insecure kids on a bus. If this were Youtopia, plenty of those seats would have been available. If this were Youtopia, he could have turned to the woman and...

He sighed, gave the woman a half-smirk, then slouched down, way down, until his chair held more back than backside.

"I hold this distinct privilege for a reason," the spokeswoman beamed from the screen. "If you don't know already, my son was one of the first Immersers in the original Youtopia."

With that fact, the woman's name came to Lane: Jeanne Haskins, her son Oscar one of the original six Immersers. Like Lane, Haskins was a Reintegrator herself. Her bleached hair spouted atop her head as though escaping an unseen fountain. Her face was covered in heavy makeup and taut, botoxed skin. The gold chain around her tanned neck held a massive diamond pendant—being the spokesperson for Youtopia Reborn was, it seemed, a lucrative gig.

Suddenly, the tone and tenor of the video jilted. Haskins's skin looked even more tanned, its creases hardened. The sky tinged a darker blue. "Before we begin," she continued in a subdued tone, "I must ask that we observe a moment of silence for our beloved leader, our visionary, the one who made all things possible. To Sonya Young: may authorities recover you soon. You are irreplaceable."

The older woman beside Lane dropped her head in prayer, her fingers reddening in gripped fists. Someone behind him coughed.

"Many argued," Haskins continued, "that we should cancel the very tour on which you will embark. But we at Youtopia Reborn all agreed that Sonya would simply not stand for it. *We rise to every challenge*, she is fond of telling us. And so we rise together."

The video glitched, reverting back to the original, chipper Haskins.

"Most of you are familiar with Youtopia. To start, the answer is yes: Reborn shares many of its predecessor's characteristics. Yet Reborn is also what the name suggests: a rebirth, a renewal. If Youtopia is the mother, then Reborn is her perfected daughter."

The skyscape behind Haskins dissolved into the halls from which they had just entered. As she talked, her static body floated backward into the compound. She wore a black seersucker pantsuit and tall heels. Her cheery, painted face, the echo of voices behind her—it all had the eerie feel of a revenant coasting through a polished, corporate underworld.

Her body coasted before a large conference hall. At circular tables, gangs of men and women in lab coats conversed before 3D, incredibly lifelike projections of small children. The kids jumped and played in holographic splendor. The scientists seemed poised to simply reach out and touch them.

"In this tour, you will have the privilege of experiencing the inner life of one of our very special Youtopia Reborn Immersers. We know— it's why most of you are here! But on the way, you may see live researchers in this very facility, conversing, hypothesizing. Making a fantastic discovery, maybe?"

The heavyset man on the other side of Lane pushed his elbow across the armrest, causing Lane to squeeze even further into himself.

"From the outset of Reborn, we recognized the vast potential of these children's unconscious minds. Their unfiltered brainpower can offer so much for our own world."

The screen behind her split into two slow-moving images. Concentric, vaguely yellow and black, they both resembled honeycombs, or the inside of some elaborate computer mechanism.

"On my left here," Haskins said, peering over her shoulder as though she could see, "is one of the housing structures a young Immerser imagined for his exotic pets. His private menagerie."

Lane looked closely and saw, in one of the holding cells, what appeared to be a bizarre cross between a macaw and snake.

"And on my right, we have the state-of-the-art electrical grid that stores and powers this very facility!"

She paused for dramatic effect. "With the effects of climate change and severe weather, Sonya recognized we couldn't rely on typical power grids. One prolonged blackout might cost thousands of innocent children's lives. Enter Angela Chen and her amazing research team, who discovered this formation in a young Immerser's mind and unlocked its potential. Thanks to them, Reborn now has the only fully functional, independent solar energy grid in America!"

Lane leaned even further back, trying to ride out this opening bombastic salvo. Haskins's made-up face, her buoyancy and pomp, had all the makings of a religious zealot at the pulpit. A budding televangelist. He half-expected a donation tray to circulate. He checked his phone to see if Serena had responded, but of course, nothing.

After five more minutes of bluster, the film thankfully ended and the lights rose. A gaggle of uniformed workers ushered the group from the screening room back to the large industrial complex that served as one of seven Reborn Cradle Centers nationwide. A woman in her late 20s drove up in an extended cart made to hold them all. It, like the theater, appeared dreadfully condensed. The driver, her brown hair long in the front and shorn in back, eyed the crowd with enthusiasm.

"Another welcome! Isn't Jeanne the best?" She held for a response that never came. "My name's Giovanna. I'll be your escort for the main attraction — the Observations. Since we're a full group, I ask that we fill our cart here all the way. Keep purses or bags in your laps. Get cozy — it's only a short ride."

Lane again found himself at the end of the line. The row he needed to join held three people unwilling to give up their occupied space. He nestled in, his arm pressed firmly against the woman next to him. The driver ignited the electric motor with a video-game style *ting* and, with a soft jolt, propelled them forward.

Once they passed the initial lobby, down a narrowing corridor, the tone of the building shifted. In its initial impression, the Cradle Center felt bland, pale, corporate. But now, as they reached the innards of this first floor, the walls morphed from generic, synthetic plasticity to something else entirely, something Lane could only describe as a cross between childhood whimsy and ghoulish nightmare — something from Wonka's surreal chocolate factory. The walls held mirrors cut at incongruent angles, their thick frames painted in primary colors. Infant mobiles were mounted to canvases like bizarre modern art. The cart turned down a hall, where a motley mural ran like under-the-bridge graffiti from floor to high ceiling. Various animals and faceless toys tumbled amidst sweeping gray lines, caught in a spiraling tornado. The visitors beside Lane watched in unnerving silence. In attempting to capture the complexity of the young mind, these artists had instead evoked the haunting vibe of a horror-movie carnival.

Giovanna must have agreed, because she chose to describe nothing along the ride. As a guide, so far she was failing absolutely.

The hall narrowed, and at an intersection, Lane expected the cart to wend down an open path with a similar mural. Instead, they made a sharp turn leftward. Lane slid into the person next to him and apologized. They stopped at large steel double-doors with a keypad into which Giovanna entered her credentials. An armed guard appeared as if from nowhere.

"Okay, folks," Giovanna said, "the part you've been waiting for. Beneath your seat, you will find a tray. Please remove your shoes, as well as any personal items you might have in your pockets. Especially phones. Marcos here will keep them safe."

Beyond the steel doors sat more guards, lines of metal detection to rival any airport. Their last checkpoint stood just before a large industrial elevator that held all of them.

"Up a few floors to Wonderland," Giovanna said.

The atmosphere on the top floor was decidedly different: cloistered, claustrophobic even, with bare, unadorned concrete walls and halogen lights. The cold air seeped into Lane's arms and neck. Toward the end of the hallway, another guard stood beside a heavy door holding a sleek black box. He greeted Giovanna with a familiar smile, intimate even, as though, if permitted, he would reach out and kiss her right in front of these fifty onlookers. Together they simultaneously entered their credentials and the door opened.

"Stay close to the outer walls," Giovanna called as she reached into the box and handed a thin plastic bag to each person entering. "Do not approach the center. This is important, as we'll have only about ten minutes. Any contact with the Dome will cause the tour to end. Don't be that person!" Then, as Lane reached the door, she said, "Welcome to the Viewing Chamber."

The room was immense and conical. The ceiling stretched upwards of forty, fifty feet, arching on itself to a point directly in the center. Canned lights speckled the black walls like distant planets. Cool, artificial air circulated. And at the room's center lay the Dome they were warned not to approach, an arching half-sphere made of semi-reflective, translucent plexiglass, as tall as Lane and three times as wide. He squinted, attempted to see inside, but could only make out vague shapes. It looked like a luminous birdcage. In a horrific flash he imagined an Immerser child inside, pressing against the walls, begging for release. His pulse quickened; he wondered, for the first time, whether coming here was good for him, whether his mind might play devious tricks on him.

Lane turned to Giovanna, pointing at the Dome. "The Immerser's not...?"

"Oh no, no," she said, handing Lane his bag. Inside were what felt and looked like designer swimming goggles. "They are safe in the Cradles, far underground. Go ahead and find a spot along the wall, sir. You'll see."

A woman and her three cohorts pushed past Lane, watching the room, the plexiglass dome, with the giddy anticipation of vacationers on retreat. They donned their spectacles, and Lane did the same, the strap matting his hair, the lenses filling his vision, but all he saw was a slightly pixelated version of the women, the room, the lights above sharpening into harsher focus.

Giovanna followed the last guest in. "Everyone find a place to stand? Good. I need full attention, because what I'm about to say is the most important part. You *must* stay where you are. Any movement beyond a small radius will automatically abort the experience for everyone. I repeat, you must stay where you are. Don't be that person either!"

Snickers followed from the crowd. The group behind Lane turned to one another, as though any one of them must keep the other in check.

Suddenly the door closed behind Giovanna, its thunderous sound echoing up the chamber. With the sound went the lights, and the ensuing silence, the darkness, sent Lane's pulse racing even faster. He clenched his jaw, his fists. He felt the vacuous space above him, as though the ground would drop from beneath his feet, or the walls would begin slowly collapsing. As though he had walked straight into his own death.

"It's time," Giovanna said. "Everyone, say hello to Bob Ignacious!"

Lights within the Dome rose, finally displaying what resided inside: a raised, reclined chair, similar to a dentist's office. In it rested a comatose, middle-aged, heavier man in a full black suit.

"Okay, so Bob can't really respond. Not yet. But remember his face and build. He is our Interventionist today."

Lane looked to Giovanna, who paced about the Dome in the exact way she instructed them not to. "Okay, time for the real deal. Put on your spectacles if you haven't yet. Without them you won't be able to see."

She made a signal to some unseen force.

"Three. Two. One."

In a brilliant flash, the world ignited.

Lane felt it immediately in his chest. All the others around him remained in the room, their heads shifting in stupefied marvel—but the Dome, and the walls surrounding them, had disappeared entirely, replaced by a vibrant, colorful, expressive forest. Tall, neon green grass flowed in a soft, unfelt breeze. Impossible dinosaur-like creatures flew vulturine about the sky. Beyond the other goggled visitors, the forest stretched horizonless. Lane looked to his feet, half expecting nothing, an empty blackness, that he stood nowhere and everywhere, all at once. But no— foot-tall grass waved, scattered impossibly around and through his ankles.

"You're now standing in the world of Reborn Immerser 39410, a young boy with advanced chronic obstructive pulmonary disease."

An older man gasped beside him. Lane expected to hear the dino-birds shriek, or to feel the wind against his skin. But as bent down to touch the grass, his hand passed straight through.

"You may recall," Giovanna said, walking among them without glasses of her own, her eyes roaming the crowd. "Youtopia in its first iteration allowed only one Observer. At Reborn, we've expanded Observation—or, as you're witnessing now, more like *existing within*— the Immerser experience. You are now all officially Observers!"

Lane rose. Around him, his bespeckled peers passed their hands through thin-trunked trees as though performing a magic act. Above, the dino-birds looped. One pointed its beak downward, directly at Lane, and dove. And though it was partly transparent, though Lane knew it wasn't real and couldn't see him, the creature approached with such peculiar aggression that Lane covered his head and closed his eyes. Nothing happened for ten seconds, more. When he finally opened them again, the dino-bird had disappeared.

Suddenly, from the distance appeared a horde of children kicking an unmarked ball, their smiles wide and infectious. One moved swifter than the rest, the ball hanging on his steps, his foot possessing a gravitational pull.

"As you may know, the original Observer experience was two-dimensional, matched with the Immerser's own vantage, akin to a first-person video game. Today, we've entered the third dimension. Or maybe the fourth?"

As the children raced toward him, Lane felt he would somehow recognize one of them, a friend from his neighborhood growing up. One of them might have been a younger version of himself. This was not real, he had to remind himself. It was not *his* world. The children's opaque faces were nondescript, symmetrical. Their shaggy brown hairstyles all matched.

"How can we do this?" a woman in the distance asked.

"Shhh!" another woman scolded.

Giovanna just laughed and said, "Don't worry. They can't hear you, but thank you for your question. Observation is actually the easy part. Recent technologies have allowed us to interlay Immerser Feeds instantaneously. Think Google Maps on your neighborhood block, all updated within nanoseconds."

As if on cue, a sprouting sapling next to Lane began an impossible growth. Unlike the rest of the trees, this one more closely resembled something from the real world, a cross between a healthy oak and an invasive buckthorn. Once it rose above their heads, the children assembled underneath, plucking at its branches and eating the leaves like candy.

Suddenly, Lane's glasses flashed white. He felt a shock of lightheadedness. He rubbed at his temples. A glitch, perhaps. But no, the light was a projection—a man, taller than Lane himself, heavy around the waist and broad-shouldered, had passed directly through Lane. The man's gaze stayed on the children. Intermittently, he spoke, but the children didn't respond.

"Yes," Lane heard Giovanna answer him. "Here he is, ladies and gentlemen. The star of our show. Wave to Bob!" A handful of people raised their hands. "Kidding. He can't see you either."

Bob stood just before Lane, blocking Lane's view of the children. Bob seemed content to stay where he was, to simply Observe himself, even though a handful of children noticed him and smiled. After the group's attention on Bob waned, Lane reached out a hand to the man's shoulder that, of course, passed straight through. Bob—at least, this version of him—was no more real than the others.

Then Bob turned toward Lane. He wore the same midnight black suit as the real Bob in the chair. Lane couldn't quite bend his mind around the enigmatic quality of it all, how Bob was both the man imprisoned in this very room, and the towering half-translucent presence imposing on him now. Bob's bright green eyes stared seemingly right at Lane. He said something that only Giovanna could hear, though it felt as though he spoke directly to Lane. That he held a secret he needed Lane to hear.

***

At the front desk, Giovanna handed each tourist a business card with a perfunctory thank you note and a survey URL. The tour was decidedly over. Giovanna turned her back to them, her cheery demeanor resuming only when someone thanked her. Lane had missed three calls since giving up his phone on the tour: to his dismay, none from Serena. Two were Henrick, with one accompanied by a long voicemail. Instead of listening to it, Lane called him back.

"Hey," Lane said. "Sorry I missed you."

"More like we've been missing you," Henrick said. "Just wanted to make sure everything's still kosher?"

"As a pickle."

"Okay," Henrick said, not carrying Lane's bad joke. Henrick, he knew, had seen too many FAR members mask their depression behind humor. But Lane needed a cover—he could never tell Henrick that he was standing in a Youtopia Reborn Cradle Center, that he was diving into the mouth of the beast. "Listen," Henrick continued, "can I be honest with you?"

"Always."

"I'm worried about you, taking off like that. Going AWOL. Using your mom as an excuse. And I normally wouldn't, but… Lane, I promise, I only did it because I care."

"Did what?" Lane asked.

"I called the Beacon. I know you're at Youtopia."

Lane went silent. Beside him, a fellow tourgoer bumped his shoulder while passing, offering only a curt apology.

"I just want you to know I'm here, Lane. I can only help you if—"

"That was wrong, Henry," Lane said, lowering his voice. "You can't spy on me."

"Well, Lane, you kind of forced my hand, didn't you? You can't live in a fantasy. Mantra Eight: *Separating lies from truth*—"

"*Breeds clarity*," Lane finished for him. "I know." He gritted his teeth. Around him, people shuffled toward the exit. The tourgoers were expected to leave. Lane wanted to continue berating Henrick, but he just didn't have the time. "Listen, Henry, I gotta jet."

"I just hope—"

Lane hung up before Henrick could get going again.

To shake the call, he immediately approached Giovanna, his one potential key to unlock higher-up access. She might get him a conversation with a programmer or midlevel manager. Maybe, if he was lucky, even Daniel Peterson himself, Sonya Young's number two.

Though his credit card wouldn't appreciate it, he would gladly take a flight to Wisconsin for access into Youtopia Towers.

But before he could reach Giovanna, another patron accosted her, a brown-haired, medium build woman dressed eerily similar to Giovanna. Lane wondered for a moment if they were sisters, but then the waylaying woman pulled her phone and held it between them.

"Care to give a statement on the disappearance of Sonya Young?"

The voice shot through Lane. He recognized it from various lecture halls, the sharpness reverberating about the room: Bethany Fawkes, a fellow Purdue grad schooler. They had been incoming first-years together, until the winter when Lane dropped out. While Lane languished in Youtopia, Bethany wrote and studied, studied and wrote. She entered competitions she always won, and graduated with highest honors. She beat out hundreds of applicants for a job at IndyStar, once Lane's dream job but, for her, only a steppingstone on her way to the New York Times.

Bethany's presence was not a surprise—of course the Times would put her on this beat—but the fact that Lane had missed her within the crowd earlier was. He somehow hadn't recognized the haughty air of her upraised chin or the indelible click of her high heels. He slid closer, keeping out of Bethany's sight line as she peppered Giovanna with questions.

"Why continue running these tours?

"Have Sonya Young's captors made any demands?

"Is it true that the Reborns have been hacked? That one of these hackers may be the kidnapper?

"Did Young leave a succession plan? A last will and testament? If she dies, will Daniel Peterson replace her? June Kowalski? Do either of them have a comment?"

Giovanna offered good-natured deflections, "I'm sorry," and, "I don't have the answer to that," and "Let me refer you to the company's official press release." Bethany took the hard tack, pressing and pressing, and Giovanna responded to none of it. After a few torturous minutes, Bethany fled in search of new fodder.

Lane watched Giovanna shed Bethany's intrusion like dead skin. She seemed unflappable. Lane admired her poise. As he approached, his plan adapted—he went entirely anti-Bethany, introducing himself softly, offering profuse thanks for the tour, adding flattery for Reborn's great work. Her enthusiasm for the company was so refreshing to watch. She must have done well to get a job at the most coveted company in

America. As he worked his angle, Giovanna smiled, though her eyes roamed beyond Lane to some distant place she hoped soon to be. He made a crack about the legroom in the cart, a self-effacing joke about his height that tended to open people up to him, to view him as non-threatening. He poured it on, waiting for her to crack.

Instead, she turned away at her first chance.

He slid quickly to intercept her. "I'm sorry. You probably don't want to answer a bunch of questions after all that's happened. It's just that..." He sighed, half for show, half because he knew the dubiousness of what he was about to do. "My brother is in there." He pointed in some nondescript direction behind Giovanna, hoping to take her attention off his lying eyes. "Well, I should say half-brother. He has this rare degenerative disease, and... Well, you don't need to know his whole story. The point is, I'm concerned. I mean, what if this kidnapper starts targeting the kids?"

Giovanna sighed as well. Lane couldn't tell if it was fatigue, or impatience, or something wearing at her that he would never know. "What's your brother's name?"

Lane hesitated. "Charlie."

Giovanna squinted. He waited for her to call his bluff. Instead, she said, "Look, you're concerned. I get it. But unfortunately, there's nothing we can do."

"Reborn isn't doing anything?"

"I don't mean the company—I mean people like you and me. It's out of our hands." She gave a blunt, futile smile.

Lane was running out of options. He needed to lob one last shot, as desperate as it was. "It's just that, I'd feel a lot better if I could hear it from, you know, the horse's mouth. From that Board of Directors lady—Kowalski, is it? Or maybe Daniel Peterson?"

"Wouldn't we all," Giovanna replied, ready to quit him. But then, as the rest of the visitors filtered out the front doors, her face softened. "Look, if you really want to bark higher, Peterson and Kowalski are not the right trees."

With her shoulders loosened, her tour guide façade dropped, she took on a far more human air. She was pretty, her dark eyes knowing. Lane tried not to recall the fact that, since Reintegrating, he hadn't been on a single date, or that Serena had occupied his mind these past days—her dimpled cheeks, her strong legs in summer shorts. He tried to stay on task.

"Then who's the right tree?"

"Saeed Free," she said without hesitation. "Head of Tech. The one who designed the Intervention system. He *loves* to hear himself talk."

"He doesn't happen to work in this building, does he?"

Giovanna shook her head. "LA. He's a Californian through and through." She squinted, an idea coming to her. "Jeanne Haskins maybe? As you saw with the video, dishing Reborn business is her job, and she *likes* her job. She's not here today — probably at the Towers."

Lane gave her an earnest nod. "Thank you. I truly appreciate it."

Giovanna turned to walk away, but then stopped herself. "I'd think twice about barking too loudly, though."

"Why's that?"

She looked Lane up and down. "The real reason they keep doing these tours?" She pointed a finger into the air and helicoptered it. "They want to know who's taking a sudden interest."

As Lane approached the door, he turned back one last time, expecting Giovanna to have followed him, to offer further reassurances for his imaginary brother. He considered asking her out for a drink, in part to see if he could get more information, but mostly because he needed the company. But she had disappeared behind some closed door, lost to him forever.

***

He booked his return flight for the next morning. Millie had assigned him a new game to cover, showing him the end of her leniency rope. But before he could go, he needed to see it fully through. He needed to try to find Serena a final time, no matter how long a shot it was.

He started with a string of bars around her apartment, only one of which he remembered from their college days. He inquired with bartenders and bouncers, pulling her Instagram profile picture on his phone. One after another shook their heads, shrugged, apologized. Dance music, smokers' circles on patios, the yeasty waft of beer spills... each stop had the cumulative effect of a night's bender, a tumble down a cavern with no bottom. He felt like a cheap cop in a B-film. He hit every bar within a half-mile radius, and came away with nothing.

Past midnight, lying in his hotel bed, his earbuds pumping jazz, Lane decided to scour the internet. This was a journalistic no-no, a crutch he knew his former professors would kick from under him just to see him stumble. And yet, sometimes, it did work. He needed to know if there could be any truth to Serena's assertion. He needed to believe she was in danger, and not just sending him on a frenetic, falsified chase. He needed to know she needed him.

Of course, no meaningful connection between Serena and Sonya Young would exist online. A Google search of "Sonya Young's Daughter" unearthed nothing but Young's strong but brief connection to her own mother. He did expect, at the very least, to discover something of Sonya Young herself, like her upbringing, college attendance, job history—the basics you could find on any celebrity, minor or Sonya-Young-sized. He expected an accurate, if gap-filled, map of her life over which he could lay Serena's: Serena's place of birth, maybe, in a city near Young's residence; a man in Young's life with Serena's dimples or dark eyes. The internet wouldn't be certain, but he didn't need the full story laid out for him. He needed what the internet so often provided: an offhand, speculative chance, the latent seedling of a conspiracy.

Instead, he found Sonya Young's past a uniquely impossible internet subject. Every article written on her came from second-hand accounts—a person heard from a person who heard from a person. Born in the Boston area to immigrant parents, she'd lost her father in high school, her mother while she attended college at MIT. An orphan like himself. She took no time off between a three-year undergraduate and her MA from Yale in Biomedical Engineering. As a student, she co-authored two articles with abstracts too esoteric for Lane. Her thesis advisor had long since passed. If she had a social life—clubs or intramurals or student organizations—they were listed nowhere.

As for her personal life, he found even less. Young predated social media and never adopted them once they arrived. Lane dug further, scrolling down innumerable pictures on Google, ones of her standing at podiums for fundraisers, cutting ribbons at the Youtopia Towers groundbreaking ceremony. At each she wore tight pantsuits, a brisk bun in her dark hair, and something just short of a smile. *Harsh* was the word that came to Lane's mind, like those same adroit professors he could never quite charm. Like Bethany Fawkes. He rabbit-holed downward, looking for personal photos, for anything not staged or paparazzied, but if those photos existed, they'd been scrubbed from basic online searches. Young had curated her online existence, whitewashed it into the head of Youtopia Reborn and nothing else. If he wanted more on her, particularly the side of her that might have birthed and then given away a child, he wouldn't find it here.

With Sonya Young herself a dead end, he U-turned and made toward the *Reborn for All* movement itself, hoping someone in their circle might cross paths with his and Serena's world. A woman named Nini Gunderson from Ohio seemingly started the movement on social media, coining the phrase and pushing mentions out only two weeks after Reborn's inception. For a disrupter, however, Gunderson's profiles were amazingly bland: a singular photo across all platforms, a few incendiary comments, but mostly reposts and likes and forwards and mentions. Though it was getting late, near midnight, Lane dialed Quinn.

He picked up on the first ring. Behind his voice, Lane could hear the groans and gun blasts of a first-person shooter game. Lane asked him what he might be able to unearth about Gunderson.

"Give me a sec," Quinn said. A loud squelching noise issued behind him. "Yeah, that's what I thought! Okay, *Reborn for All* you say." He went silent for a minute. Then he huffed. "Well, I can tell you right off the bat—this is a bullshit profile."

"You mean Gunderson isn't real?"

"Bingo was his name-o. A middle-aged mom from Ohio? Please. I'm surprised they didn't just go ahead and name her Karen."

"So who really started this thing?"

"Could be anyone. Russia would be public enemy number one. Or China. Could even be someone at Reborn. *The call is coming from inside the house!* Remember that movie? I think it was a movie."

"In other words, I'm tracking a ghost."

"Hate to say it, man, but yeah."

They disconnected. Taking a different tactic—and though he expected to find nothing there either—he searched Bethany Fawkes. After all, she had struck out at the Cradles, same as him. But immediately the breaking news headlines bombarded him—social media links, all the major players picking up and running her newest story. Just below resided her AP photo, a headshot from some years ago, her hair about her shoulders, head tilted. Her smile carried an affable cheeriness that grated at Lane. He felt sheer envy, he knew, feckless and trite, but it still bit. In Lane's Youtopia, Bethany had never made an appearance, a fact for which he was grateful. Whatever his unconscious mind would have cooked up between them, he didn't want to know.

He clicked on the Times link, and found an entire section labeled *Sonya Young's Abduction*, filled mainly with Bethany's articles. This newest one, under the subheading *The Latest*, read, in proud bold lettering:

YOUTOPIA REBORN'S FATE IN JEOPARDY

In the byline beneath:

Potential will of founder Sonya Young may shake up succession plan.

So, Young did have a will, one that would change the company's trajectory going forward. More importantly — as always — Bethany Fawkes had beaten Lane to the story.

***

The crowd tittered with enthusiasm as the lights cut. Into the darkness, a handful of red and yellow spotlights flailed. Contemporary pop-rap flooded the gym. Only in Indiana, Lane thought, were high school basketball stars treated like A-list celebrities.

An upbeat announcer gave the starting lineup of the Indiana Ice away team, and then started in with the home Indiana Elite five. But even with the ramped-up music, those around Lane and Millie clapped mildly, patiently. They waited. As the announcer reached the final starter, number 33, a sophomore, six-foot-seven and looking every inch when he stood, the crowd finally let out its jubilant boom. The sophomore soaked in the reverie, playing to their cheers with a cool enthusiasm.

"The next Larry Bird," someone shouted behind them, a sentiment Lane had heard at least half a dozen times since entering the gym, and at least a hundred more since the sophomore started threatening the Indiana AAU scoring record in only his second season. It was the same sentiment everyone raced to whenever a sizable white kid could knock down threes — the sentiment he had once heard about himself, before his knee injury sent him to the eternal purgatory of the what-could-have-beens.

On the court, before tipoff, the sophomore laced his sneakers in a mechanical pre-game ritual. The crowd ate it up. They had watched him since his debut last season, followed him to sundry gyms across Indiana, all leading up to him breaking this scoring record. For them, tonight was the night. His last game, he put up thirty; before that, a cool forty-seven. Even Lane had to admit, the kid was impressive.

Lane and Millie had arrived at the Indianapolis gym to represent the Weekly Beacon, but a dozen other journalists sat in the bleachers as well: Val from the Columbia City Dispatch, Andrews from South Bend. IndyStar sent one of their heavier hands, which, more than anything, told Lane this was happening tonight.

As they tipped off, the sophomore easily controlling, the crowd finally sat. Almost immediately they were up again, however, when the sophomore drove through a double-team and dropped a layup so softly over the front of the rim it felt predestined.

Beside Lane, Millie fanned herself with her program. Lane looked up to the thin-bladed industrial ceiling fans contending against the heat of hundreds of bodies.

"This state," Millie said. "No movie in history more detrimental to a collective psyche than Hoosiers."

"Jaws?" Lane offered. "The Exorcist?"

"Not even close."

Lane nodded his head at the sophomore. "Hope he enjoys it while it lasts."

"Ever still wish you were out there?"

"No." Lane looked to Millie. "Not now, anyway. I guess, in Youtopia..." He stopped, ducked low, as though he was telling Millie some deep secret: the shame FAR drilled into him. He decided to push through it. "It was different in there. I wasn't some high school phenom turned pro star or anything, but at least I got to see it through. Got to end it on my own terms."

"You had some great moments here in the real world," Millie said. "That triple-double against Belmont was a work of art."

"Didn't peg you as the basketball type."

"Yeah, well, my dad is." She nodded across the court to the upper echelon of seats, where a white-haired male with Millie's exact facial features took in the sophomore's every move. "If I wanted to spend time with him, it was in a gym."

Millie and Lane watched her father as the sophomore alley-ooped the ball to himself off the backboard and drove home a spectacular dunk. The crowd exploded.

"Anyway," Millie shouted into the din, "my point is, we should be proud of what we *have* accomplished, not be fixated on what we haven't."

The game wore predictably on. A face-painted section of students held a large handmade countdown that they flipped nearer to zero every time the sophomore scored. The Elite trailed by seven, a fact that felt oddly tangential. The record had become the main function of the game. The Elite coach, a buzz-cut, paunchy man, harped on his team with frustration, wanting the spectacle to be the sideshow. His opinion didn't matter.

When the halftime buzzer sounded, Lane looked to Millie. "What do you make of the latest in the Sonya Young case?" he chanced. "The will?"

Millie shook her head. "Bad journalism, that's what."

"You think the will isn't real?"

"I don't know whether it is or not," Millie said. "But you can see it, right? *Potential* will? *May* shake up succession plan? If Fawkes knows something, she should just say it. If not, don't write clickbait just to keep the spotlight shining on you."

"She must have a reliable source. It's the Times."

"Yeah, well, even they play the game." She reached a hand to his. "Everything okay with you, Lane?"

"I think so. Do I look that bad?"

She squeezed his hand, shutting down his sarcasm with her eyes. "Frankly, I've never seen you like this before."

"Like what?"

"Jittery. Restless. Almost... I don't know... manic. And at the worst possible time for your career."

Millie's honesty stung him. He felt an immediate impulse to excuse himself to the bathroom, flee the gym, drain his bank account, and rummage the entire Huntington area for any real trace of Immis. Quinn might know a real dealer with a real helmet, ready to take him away. Why did Young shut him out, shut them all out? He wanted to run to the imagined dream with an accessible beach, an accessible woman. He wanted to crush opponents on the court to atmospheric praise like this sophomore. He wanted anything but his current life and this current moment.

But Millie held onto his retreating hand. She looked exactly unlike Bethany Fawkes, Sonya Young, even Giovanna. Her eyes held true concern. And because she cared for him, because he never before withheld pursuits from her—he felt foolish doing so now, skulking to wild leads like some private investigator—he decided to open up and tell her everything.

Serena's message. His dogged pursuit with Quinn. His past with Serena, or at least the parts he knew were real, including her own haphazard relationship with the truth. His real reason for his Minneapolis trip. His airball when it came to finding her, to seeing anyone useful at the Cradles. His call to Saeed Free's people in California, which was immediately met with, "Read the Times tomorrow"—Bethany Fawkes striking yet again. She seemed to possess Lane's own playbook and the uncanny ability to execute it just before he could. The free-floating feeling he had now, sitting at this game, like the Elite coach or the other nine players on the court, all of whom existed as a sideshow to some other wondrous phenomenon Lane himself couldn't become.

When he finally finished, the second half began. Millie turned to him and said, "Can I ask a personal question?"

"Of course."

"How deep was your relationship with this Serena?"

Lane thought for a moment. The sophomore scored an opening hook shot and the points ticker dropped to five. "We were close for a year. As serious a relationship as I've had, I guess."

"Okay. And you say she's a liar? Attention seeker?"

"Of a type, yes."

"Then you have to consider that she's just using this story to get your attention."

"We hadn't spoken for years. Not since I Immersed."

The sophomore hovered at the three-point line, calling for the ball. With a defender in his face, he knocked down a deep ball that barely moved the net. Two points left. Even though the home team still trailed, the crowd noise rose to deafening levels.

"You think I should give it up," Lane shouted. He leaned closer. "I know I should. But there's something, I don't know... *sticky* about it all. I've followed every angle and still can't get to Serena. What if she really is in danger?"

Millie nodded but did not answer. She watched the spectacle on the court, the home team barely playing defense, just wanting to get the ball back in the sophomore's hands.

"You've gone silent," Lane said. "You're one hundred percent against an idea when you go silent."

"No, not that." Millie turned to him. "You really believe she might be in danger?"

"Yes," Lane said. "Jesus, I don't know. You're asking me if this feels real, and for me, that's a tough question."

Millie pursed her lips, an understanding washing over her. "I'd never considered that before—the games your mind must play. What if someone gaslights you? What if Serena's doing it now? Lane, I'm so sorry."

The crowd erupted to their feet. The sophomore was on a fast break, a clear path to a dunk that would tie him for the record, but at the last second a defender surged in, barreling into him. The ball floated out of the sophomore's hands and somehow, miraculously, circled into the basket. The crowd screamed, fighting between indignation at the dirty foul and euphoria that the sophomore was now tied for the record, and only a free throw away from breaking it.

"All right," Millie said as the sophomore rose and the crowd went stone silent. "I don't think you should give up. I'm even close to saying screw it and just cutting you loose."

"You're about to say, *But...*"

"But you have a performance review next week. And this is *the* Bermuda — the biggest story this year. You're swimming in the ocean, but you're acting like it's some local pond."

The sophomore's dribbles echoed through the gym. "You don't think I can do it."

"I do. It's just that your sheer will — as charming as it can be — isn't enough. You need higher access. Bethany Fawkes, NY Times-style access. A cop on the scene. Someone in Reborn who likes you."

She turned to him one last time as the ball glided gracefully off the sophomore's hand, fated for the bottom of the net.

"In truth," Millie said, "you probably need an FBI agent."

We Don't All Play Nice

Saeed Free and the Exclusory Practices of Youtopia Reborn
Bethany Fawkes, NY Times Correspondent

***

Imagine a world where nobody knows your name until suddenly, they do. You haven't done anything—instead, your boss, the ever-present Sonya Young, has been famously taken hostage. In various circles she is dubbed the Angel of Light, in others the Devil Incarnate. Your personal views, social media posts, even your troubled upbringing, become scrutinized under the public microscope. Past interviews, X posts, even the op-ed you wrote in your college newspaper, suddenly become fodder for investigations by both the authorities and the public at large.

Saeed Free doesn't have to imagine. This is his life.

I meet Mr. Free in his Los Angeles home, three days after Sonya Young's mysterious disappearance came to light. His personal assistant Margot, tanned and surfer-blonde and chipper, greets me at an outer gate. She is pleasantly exuberant. Once admitted, our van winds down a narrow driveway until it abruptly cuts off, and we reach the undeniable, defining feature of the house. In a space I'm about to find filled with juvenile toys, this is the granddaddy of them all: a medieval-style moat.

This is exactly as it sounds. Manmade, dug and designed with the estate's formation, the moat has a four-hundred-horsepower motor that creates a never-ending circular current. The water is a crystal, Caribbean blue. A drawbridge straight out of Monty Python must be lowered from the far side. The drive across feels uncertain, as though we might at any moment fall down into the moat's shallow depths.

At the house, Free eagerly admits me, shirtless and chest hair puffed, his sunrise-patterned bathing suit a size too small. He serves me cold-press coffee and scones flown in from Scotland. A classical concerto plays through invisible speakers buried in the walls. His stark black hair disheveled, his cheeks speckled with afternoon stubble, Mr. Free explicates his home as though presenting art at some Manhattan gallery. Hanging on his walls are pictures of his parents, both biological and adoptive, alongside countless Platinum records from the 1970s: Abba's *Arrival*, Marvin Gaye's *What's Going On*. He prides himself on his self-deprecating humor, up to and including the current moment.

Even with my driver and security guard, which my employer has required, Free remains acutely jovial. He reminds us, with a blend of crass and knowing reticence, that he has nothing to do with Sonya Young's disappearance, that he cares for all innocent lives, big and small. He boasts that our security guard is one of fifty authority figures that have graced his home in the past three days. He points to his house, his grounds, to leaves atop his decorative maples and the birds that adorn them, to the room in which we now stand. He is awfully, painfully aware of his tenuous situation.

Daniel Peterson, acting CFO, is watching. The world is skeptical. My first journalistic instinct is only to ask him how he's feeling, how he remains so calm relative to the circumstances he and his company face. It seems as good a beginning as any.

"What do I have to be worked up about? Unless you know something I don't. I didn't steal my boss. We at Reborn have some differences in opinion, sure, but I'm not <*expletive deleted*> crazy."

A man enters with two towels and a one-piece swimsuit exactly my size. Apparently, we are to continue our discussion outside, floating in the moat. What I assumed was a protective measure turns out to be recreational, a manmade lazy river. Our interview will become a joyride.

"I pump more money into that thing than you can imagine. Have to use it while I can."

Despite my reticence, I agree, not wanting to lose what feels like Free's ever-fleeting attention. I retreat to his marble bathroom to change.

***

Free's upbringing can only be described as tragic. His parents immigrate from the UAE with the wholehearted belief in the American notion of a better life accessible to everyone. His father drives a taxi, and his mother turns over rooms in various hotel chains.

"They were <*expletive deleted*> warriors," Free recalls.

Young Saeed attends Memorial Faith Prep, a highly Christian and competitive private school where he is ridiculed by all the other children and lauded by his teachers for his academics. He captains his math club to a New York state semifinal in sixth grade, a championship in seventh. Eventually, he will be recruited by multiple local high schools looking to build their academic prestige.

Until he turns twelve, when both of his parents meet fatal ends, unrelated and yet nearly simultaneous. For his father, a sudden paroxysm reveals a tumorous cancer growth just above his left eye. He dies within the year. For his mother, an intracerebral hemorrhage strikes just three months later. A young Saeed finds her in the kitchen that afternoon.

"Huge part of me died too," he says, eyes misty with the loss.

Free has no living relatives in the US. His UAE relatives know him only in name. Stunned Child Protective Service agents call him a liar.

"They say, 'You don't even know your aunts and uncles and grandparents?' Of <*expletive deleted*> course, I didn't!"

Free, a natural born citizen, cannot be deported. His parents' only contacts, other immigrants, mostly coworkers, have no room for him. One week later, Free enters the foster system.

In those houses, however, he finds a home. The Frees— Anthony and Alice—rescue him. Adoption at fifteen. A mutual choice to change his legal name at seventeen. The

Frees' finances, as well as their Ivy League connections, allow Free to continue the path his parents paved with his early education. He graduates *summa cum laude* in Computer Sciences at Brown. He earns a wealthy endowment and lucrative job offers. He arrives at Youtopia Reborn at just the right moment, as Sonya Young seeks a prodigy to help her design her company's reboot.

***

I ask him if he believes his tumultuous upbringing led him to Youtopia Reborn.

"Of course! Every single person in the company has kids, or has struggled with family security, or did social work before coming here. Everyone except—and I'm just coming to this realization now—Sonya and Danny *(acting CFO Daniel Peterson)*."

His mention of those two names turns the conversation somber. We have entered the moat through the sole retractable ladder—not without some difficulty on my part. In one hand I hold my recording device—my phone—in a hardshell, waterproof case through which Free assures me our voices will come clear. He turns out to be correct: when I listen back, it sounds as though we are sitting on some desolate table, leaning into a microphone. Even the soft waves of the churning tide sound pleasant.

I recently toured the Youtopia Cradles in Minneapolis, getting a front seat to the Intervention program Free helped create. I ask him if, by molding the parameters around which these young minds are shaped, he feels like a parent to these Immersed children.

"A parent? I suppose. But mostly in the sense that I'm guided by one question: what's best for the child?"

He waves a hand, as though he's just elucidated some great philosophy. It is easy to admire his self-confidence, his gusto for all things himself.

"I take that question with me in everything I do. I *was* that child. This whole transparency project was supposed to keep them safe. Do they seem *<expletive deleted>* safe? Ask Sonya how that's worked out."

Above us, my small crew, my pitiable security, paces ridiculously around the moat's edge. I wave them away, turning instead to ask Free why Sonya decided to create Reborn as a child-only enterprise. In excluding the majority of the population, hadn't Sonya incensed the very people who had likely kidnapped her?

This agitates him. He squirms in his raft. "That's a *<expletive deleted>* line of questioning, and you know it."

I ask him to elaborate.

"The victim-blaming, man. And anyway, just think about it: city parks. Day care. The public school system. Cartoons, man. You need more? Our society has any number of systems designed only for kids. So don't start throwing around this equality BS argument at me. If you're jealous because you can't have what a kid with debilitating progeria has, then you're *<expletive deleted>* to begin with."

We drift a short while along the river as it narrows, an overgrown valley oak pressing itself over the top of us like an offset umbrella. I ask what he knows, if anything, about Sonya Young's purported will.

"Oh, there's a will all right. Sonya leaving things to chance? Please. Lady was *thorough*. Had a contingency plan for her contingency plans. So why not her own death? She's not stupid."

We circle back toward the front of the house. Free's tube bumps against the dense earth wall, but he hardly notices. I offer that Sonya Young is not yet dead — that she may still be found alive.

"Incapacitated. Whatever. The point is, if a will surfaces, whatever it says, there's sure to be a fight. Danny boy. The Board. We don't all play nice."

And does he, Saeed Free, hope to be named the successor?

"Nice try. Not even I will touch *that* question."

We reach a slight downturn that brings us back to the entrance, where Margo holds our towels in her professionally-crooked arm. It seems our circular path has come to an end.

"Look, before I say something I regret — maybe I already did, I don't know — but... I consider myself a simple man. I collect rare records. When I want to feel healthy, I eat kale. When not, Reese's and red wine. I don't have kids — probably never will. But the Reborns, they're like my kids, yeah? I've visited their worlds, helped shape them, and I'm not gonna stop just because some psycho abducted my boss. <*Expletive deleted*> you. Come at me. I'm not afraid."

Free offers no more.

Chapter 3

The moment he passed through Customs, Lane recognized his mistake. At Indianapolis International, waiting on standby, he'd scored a one-way ticket to Puerto Plata for under two hundred dollars, direct flight, a steal compared to the online listings. The plane was full of tourists destined for cruise ships leaving the Dominican port. Authentically American, short sleeves and smelling of sunscreen, this group provided Lane a false refuge as they sailed over the Atlantic. He felt light in his chest, as though he breathed from the oxygen masks. He nodded to the Billie Holiday dancing from his earbuds, smiled at strangers, even snapped photos and took a short travelogue video as imagined social media companion pieces, his vocal tone and facial expressions full of wry seriousness. Observe the Herculean lengths Lane Samson traversed to uncover the truth! On his laptop, he had written five hundred starry-eyed words on his commencement: he embarked on a *hasty yet focused pilgrimage* on which he was *destined to find the one person who was herself destined for the case.*

Secure, surefooted, arrogant... the ridiculousness of this bravado dropped now into his stomach, settling there like bad food.

He walked the glossy airport aisle in Puerto Plata with hesitation. If Henrick could see him now, following whims like a Youtopia junkie. He had three shots at finding her: a cellphone number, a rental address that might not be current, and a potential place of employment. Three shots.

His first, easiest, and probably best shot — the phone number — completely missed. Ringing upon endless ringing. As it was Saturday, his second shot would be the apartment. If that missed as well, he would likely have to ride it out until Monday to try the third. He'd made no hotel reservations, no plans for meals or transport. He turned back to his plane cohorts, but they were already towing their luggage to prearranged transports. Lane realized, for the first time, how alone he was.

Mantra Ten, he told himself, trying to regain some of the optimism he'd had on the plane. *Remember to breathe.*

He walked to the taxis. A recent rain hung dense in the air. The first driver of an all-white minivan fleet, clad in all white himself from pants to shirt to hat, spoke no English. Lane's meager recall of his first-semester Spanish failed him. The language barrier—another rudimentary step he'd overlooked. The next driver was much the same. As Lane cursed himself for his appalling preparation, a man with similar hat and pants but a stark black shirt approached, presumably the boss. His stiff English hummed heartening rhythms in Lane's ears.

"Ride? You need ride?"

"Yes. I'm going… Well, I'm looking for someone."

"See waterfalls? Dune buggies? You must try dune buggies. One hundred fifty dollars. Bring you to your resort after."

The man pulled a laminated bifold of tourist attractions, many with a price tag above the cost of his flight. The third driver, a rail-thin man with silver hair in a tight bun, watched eagerly. "See?" The boss pointed at the buggies, at a photo of a masked person splashing through a muddy puddle. "One fifty. Good deal."

"No, I'm sorry. I don't want any of that."

The boss squinted, but ultimately nodded. "Where you stay?"

"I don't—" Lane stopped himself, not wanting to admit he hadn't yet booked a hotel. "I need to go here." He pulled out the notebook on which he'd written the apartment address.

The boss squinted at it, then looked back to the driver, whose expectant eyes sunk with the confusion.

"You don't want there," the boss said.

"Yes, I do."

"Food. You want food? Coffee?"

Lane looked between the boss and the driver. He needed to shake this timidity; he was here, and needed to follow through.

"After." He pointed at the address again. "First, I need to go here."

The boss stared for a moment longer. "I must talk with your driver. Okay? Then you go."

Their Spanish bandied back and forth, far too fast for Lane to catch. But then their eyes settled on him, this lonesome stranger, this tourist with his unnatural request.

"Okay," the boss said with hesitation. "Miakel will take bag, yes? He's very good. Take good care."

For twenty dollars, Miakel took Lane along the coast on Highway 5 into Puerto Plata. They passed the cruise ship quay, its two hulking offshore boats looming like prodigious empires. Lane imagined his compatriots in an enthusiastic line, foretelling their hedonistic days to come.

As they approached town, traffic thickening, Miakel lifted to the edge of his seat. His head immediately alerted to the road surrounding them. One turn off the edge of the ocean and Lane discovered why, as the bustling city engulfed them.

Like feral canines, motorbikes and mopeds with drivers of all ages pounced as if from some unseen bush. Among the riders were a toothless elderly man, a woman in a hot pink tanktop, and a couple with a baby slung on the mother's back. In response to the hectic new scene, Lane's driver generously issued his horn, without warning or cause, their minivan a wayward mongrel attempting to assert its presence in the pack. They buried farther inland, past countless tire stores and lottery dispensaries. To break the silence, Lane rolled down the window, but the smog smell seeped in immediately, as did the sound of the motorbikes, the hum of a hundred small but potent motors.

Eventually, they reached the town square, a concrete park with myriad leftover Easter decorations and a Catholic church. Miakel circled the square, found a parking spot just behind a nondescript concrete building, and ushered Lane out.

Lane inhaled, the air feeling thick in his nose and mouth, as though he must swallow it down. He paced along the narrow street, down the lines of cars parked with bumpers nearly kissing one another.

"No," Lane heard from behind him, the tone stark. He turned to see Miakel shuffling toward him. For the first time, Lane noticed a marked limp. Miakel took Lane with a surprisingly strong grip by the arm. He pointed to a building across the street. "This."

They crossed with Miakel still holding Lane's arm. Lane felt monstrous next to him, and so he ducked down, the effect making the two look like thieves stealing into the building's slim shadows. The square apartment building was limestone-colored, full of hairline cracks and small, cloistered windows covered by metal bars. The front door had a large grate as well.

Miakel pointed. "This," he repeated.

Lane looked the place up and down. He expected a buzzer system, or some other way to call the apartment. He recalled stealing into Serena's building, his stupid expectation that he could slither all the way inside her apartment. With the fortified building before them, there was no way in.

Miakel expected Lane to know what to do, that someone would be awaiting them. Lane's only options now — to bang on the door or wait — both seemed foolish, dangerous even. He tried the cell number again, but his phone's spotty data couldn't make a connection, causing him to admit that his second shot was also an airball.

He turned to Miakel, trying to keep the dejection from his face. "One more stop. Then my hotel." A small bit of Spanish returned to him as he said, "*Trabajo. Su trabajo.*" He removed his notebook, pointing to the final address.

Miakel squinted at it. "*La fábrica.*"

"Yes! Yes. Factory."

"*Está cerrado.*" Miakel's eyes pleaded with Lane to understand. He held his hands out as if to accept an offering, then clapped them shut.

"Ah, right! I know, closed. It's Saturday... *Sábado.* But still..." He pointed again to the address. "This first. *Primero, la fábrica.* Then hotel."

Miakel shrugged, then turned back toward his van.

Lane's phone read 5:33 p.m. He watched the surrounding cars and motorbikes weave in dissonant unity. They passed the entrance to some local attraction at which an open-air bus stopped. Lane foolishly found himself scanning the faces on the bus, hoping to see her among the tourists, though she had lived here now — at least as far as he could find — for over a year.

Finally, Miakel circled a three-building warehouse complex that Lane could only compare to a low-security prison: barbed wire fencing, armed security at the gate. Miakel needed to park two blocks away, and so they walked again together, step in step, down the sidewalk toward the building.

Miakel stopped them just across the street. A handful of older sedans dotted the parking lot. Lane wanted to approach the guard, but knew his broken Spanish would get him nowhere, and Miakel seemed unwilling to step any closer. Lane watched as one worker surfaced from the building, a man in stained white coveralls — a maintenance worker, perhaps fixing a pipe leak or errant wiring. Not, anyway, an assembly line worker, the group she must've belonged to, and the group least likely to work on a weekend.

The sun descended into the horizon. It felt odd, as though this hot, humid place should remain in perpetual daylit summer. His stomach contracted — his last food was a small pack of peanuts on the plane. He would ask Miakel to take him for food — *comida*, he remembered that one — since this final shot, like the others, had inevitably missed.

But when he turned, Miakel was no longer by his side.

A sudden surge of panic seized Lane at his driver's hasty flight. He had no hotel, no ride back to the airport. Nobody, even Millie, knew exactly where he was or how he got here. He stood on this street, at a precipice that FAR warned him never to cross. *Don't assume zealous bets will pay out,* he heard in Henrick's voice. Mantra Four: *Things will not always go your way, especially spontaneous whims.*

He whipped around in alarm. Suddenly, he could feel his pulse in his swollen lip. Shadows of the triplets flashed before his eyes, buckling his knees. His body instinctively froze, as though some unseen assailant crouched behind him, ready to attack. His legs wouldn't obey. He needed Miakel, his thin, long-haired safeguard, to reappear. He needed to run. These foolish, reckless situations he kept putting himself in—what was wrong with him? Did he have some self-destructive yearning to live out? Was this his way of expressing his regret for Reintegration, for Immersing in the first place? Did he feel he deserved punishment?

Lane was so lost in his desperation that he almost missed the female worker exiting the building.

She had dark hair, like the rest, but lighter skin. Her height and build. Lane squinted. As she passed the cars, walked through the gate, and turned on the sidewalk away from Lane, he felt almost certain.

His gambit had paid off. It had to be her.

This wasn't Youtopia. It wasn't some cheap Immi knockoff from a dealer like Rickie. There she walked, across the Dominican sidewalk, right before him.

Again driven by instinct, his body charged toward her. His legs moved in such anticipation that he forgot to slow, forgot that she was not expecting him, that they had never met, that, objectively, he seemed threatening, a prowler set to pounce.

She watched him from the corner of her eye as he slowed at the curb. In her hand, she wielded a can of pepper spray. The strap of a gun holster peeked from beneath her blazer. She was, after all, a former FBI Special Agent, one of reputable fame in her time. This woman knew Youtopia's secrets, had connections that might get Lane closer to his story. Closer to Serena.

He needed to slow his heart, to breathe. He needed to introduce himself to Anabel Downer, but didn't know where to begin.

***

Ana showered. Her day had gone crooked, bent in irreversible ways by this American kid, Lane, who'd appeared before her factory as though from thin air. Now, while she dressed in her bathroom, he waited expectantly on the couch of her studio apartment, where he could take in her paltry living situation on full display — small stove and unmade bed and singular garment rack of asexual, functional clothes. When he had approached her, Ana's first instinct was to run. His face was frantic, his mannerisms that of a fitful teen. He explained himself in such a manic rush that she had to coax him to slow down. His height didn't help — despite herself she felt cowered by his arching body, his elongated shadow in the sinking sunlight.

But once he ran himself out of words, when the weight of his travels and travails seeped through, Ana's investigatory instincts kicked in. She started to see a real Lane Samson: scared, naïve, desperate. A man in need of real help.

Somewhere deep inside her, Ana always expected someone from America to arrive one day. This person would entreat her to return to Chicago, to the world she'd left behind. It wouldn't be her ex-husband Paul or her ex-best friend Lonnie, no, but someone professional perhaps: her former boss Bruce Klose, or her tech agent Sergio Morales, or one of the countless fresh-faced, fledgling agents for whom she'd surveyed video footage in her final, dying half-year for the Fed. Though the Youtopia ignominy had shattered her reputation as a Special Agent, it hadn't excluded her from being a top-notch assistant for new recruits with the same aspirations she herself once held.

That, she supposed, summed up Lane: a twenty-something hopeful looking to build the phoenix of his career from the dying ashes of Ana's own. That her American messenger hailed from a small-town newspaper in Indiana was both extraordinary and fitting.

She dried her hair, put on a white blouse and her sole pair of slacks. Gazing into her small vanity mirror, she applied scant eyeliner and cheek rouge. She prolonged her routine with a hope that Lane was simply a conniving thief here for her measly possessions, and that when she emerged from her room, he would be gone.

But when she opened the door, he stood exactly where she'd left him, holding one of her few possessions from America in both hands: a snow globe, gifted from her late mother one Christmas. She didn't know why, with everything from her former apartment, the globe had made the trip. For her it carried no specific memory, no emotional attachment. It felt like any other American trinket one might find, abandoned and marked down, on a thrift store shelf.

"Reminds me of Indiana," Lane said as he rotated it, the crystals swirling. "Not in a good way."

"I've considered your proposal," Ana said.

"Proposal? I mean, we did just meet. I admit you are attractive, especially for your age."

Ana squinted at him.

"That was supposed to be a joke. And a compliment, I think." He gave a soft smile.

His modest, folksy manner felt both genuine and designed to open people up to him. As a woman of smaller stature, Ana never found this tactic useful. Instead, she needed to press, to show strength.

"Bad jokes aside," she said, "I don't believe us working together on this would be wise."

Lane carefully replaced the globe. "You know, I was pretty sure I'd never find you. Today was rough. But something inside pushed me to try."

Ana went to her table and swiped aside a cardigan, an older pair of shoes, and her gun case with her Glock 19 safely locked inside. Then she went to her undersized refrigerator, removed and handed Lane a canned mango juice that he finished in two swift drinks.

"I don't have much," she said, "but would you like something to eat?"

"Please. That'd be great."

As Ana threw together what she had, a mix of long grain rice and black beans, Lane divulged details of his life as though they were on a first date. His childhood aspirations to write crime fiction led him to an unhealthy but predictable obsession with true crime podcasts. His parents' death came in his twenties, an event he passed over so quickly, it must've been tragic. He had a resultant, complicated relationship with jazz music. He tossed wispy hairs from his forehead as he talked.

Ana could tell that Lane wanted to ask the obvious questions about her: what really happened with Youtopia? Why did you flee to the Dominican? Why vacate your entire life?

"Thanks," he said as she served him. He took a first spoonful of the steaming mixture, letting it stand to cool. "So, I guess the first thing I'd like to know is your professional opinion."

"Regarding what part?"

"Do you think Serena could truly be Young's daughter? Is she in danger? Or am I on a wild goose chase here?"

Ana replaced the pot on the stove. "Have you looked into Serena's birth records? Any potential overlap with Sonya Young's life?"

"Yes," he said with reluctance. "But that was a different time. Young is powerful enough to doctor records, to bury her secrets."

Bury her secrets. Ana wouldn't lie to him, and yet couldn't possibly tell him the truth about Sonya Young as she knew it. Where would she begin? With her slide into Paul's Youtopia, causing her removal from the case? With her amateurish mistake to pursue Sonya Young alone, her easily erased emails as her only safety net? With her failure to see Sonya Young for who she truly was: a calculated murderer of hundreds of her own clients in the name of the grotesque higher ideal that only children deserved her creation?

And now Lane asked Ana to gauge the plausibility of his wild theory. Could Sonya Young have concealed a daughter's birth in her early twenties? Of course. But would that daughter, this Serena Yarborough, have reached out in peril to Lane Samson—an ex from college with whom she had kept no previous contact? Was the disappearance of an otherwise flighty person proof of a deeper conspiracy?

The truth was, Lane held evidence cloaked in desperate, improbable connections, in an innate, flawed wish to be at the center of something bigger than oneself. When mixed together, ego and conspiracy made a potent cocktail.

"I can't decide that for you," she finally answered. "I can tell you there's a big difference between building a case and chasing a lead. With a case, you see all the facts, all the angles. Most importantly, you recognize your own."

"Journalists don't have an angle."

"Are you here for the story, or because you want to reconnect with Serena?"

Lane shifted. "Both."

Ana stepped before him. He stood at least a foot above her, yet she needed him to meet her eyes, to let the gravity of what she was about to say pull him downward.

"When I got tangled up in Youtopia, I was blind to my own weaknesses. I thought I could stay neutral, but I couldn't. You need to be honest with yourself from the start."

Lane nodded. His eyes roamed about her apartment as though searching for clues. He folded his hands together, clenching and unclenching his fingers. "I used to be something of a basketball phenom," he said, the commencement of a circuitous story: a blown-out knee derailing his prospects, his shifting focus to journalism, his speedy undergraduate work, exemplary marks, the start of graduate school. Until...

His voice caught.

Ana recognized the downcast eyes, the errant formation of words failing to reach his lips. He had come upon his tragedy, the thing that truly sent his life afloat, the thing from which he would never fully recover. For Ana, this was Charlotte. For him, the loss of both of his parents.

But then he went a step further and revealed the part of him that made Ana quiver. The part Ana should have recognized from the start.

"It wasn't the only reason I Immersed," he said. "But it was the main one."

Ana sucked in a breath. Her body seized as though threatened. She immediately thought of Paul, of watching his Feed. The manga version of herself, cowering beneath Paul's abusive hands, flashed in her mind.

"I suppose," Lane continued, "I'm scared for Serena, yes. But I've also always wondered: why kids? Why put only the most vulnerable population into a powder keg? And now the fuse is lit. They're in danger. If uncovering the story can help those kids in any way, it'll be worth it."

Ana stifled a deep sigh inside of her, a melancholic disappointment. Lane's hangdog eyes, his stooped shoulders... Of course he was an Immerser. Of course he was Reintegrating. She almost asked to see his foot, to recognize the tattooed number permanently marking him.

"I can't," she said suddenly. "My answer is no."

He tilted his head, clearly expecting his Youtopia admission to gain sympathy, not lose it.

"No?"

"No."

Lane stared at her and waited, as though brief, simple time would change her mind. When it didn't, he said, "Can I get a reason why?"

"I don't believe I owe you one."

"Owing is one thing. Common courtesy is another."

Ana held his stare. Their eyes locked for an unnaturally long time, and so she focused instead on the smoothness of his forehead, the specks of facial hair on his chin and cheeks. As it always did, Youtopia had made Lane appear both younger and older than his age.

"You asked my professional opinion before," she said. "Let me give you my personal one. This story isn't about Sonya Young's abduction, or your former girlfriend. It's a potential relapse. Instead of chasing it, you should be focusing on making meaningful connections with those you left behind."

Lane's face went ashen.

"So go home," she continued. "Forget about Youtopia. Live a real life."

Lane's stare smoldered. Ana clenched her fist, in case he attempted something stupid. But then his shoulders slackened and he let out a curt, genuine laugh.

"You sound like Henry. My FAR sponsor." He shook his head. "I just hope you're talking to me and not someone else."

Ana tensed. She hoped Lane would go no farther.

But then he added, "I mean, everybody knows what happened with your husband."

Ana stepped forward. "You need to leave now."

Lane held his hands in the air. "Look, I didn't come here to—"

"It doesn't matter what you intended to do. Leave my apartment. Now."

Lane nodded. He placed a hand across his chest. "My pleasure meeting you. I hope you find what you're looking for down here." He looked around her scant apartment one last time. "Whatever the hell that might be."

***

The next morning, tepid air flushed in through his open window as Miakel returned Lane to the airport. He felt calm in his driver's presence, as though they'd known each other far longer than a day. At the terminal, Miakel handed Lane his bag with an oversized smile, and Lane tipped him more than he could afford. He had spent too much money here, too much time. Maybe Downer was right: maybe he needed to surrender to better judgment. Maybe his best move was to return home, forget Serena's phone call, and just live.

The cheapest ticket connected him through O'Hare, departing in four hours. Lane bought two bottled waters and a muffin, and found a seat near his gate that overlooked the ocean. He ignored missed calls from Millie and instead connected to the airport wifi. Earbuds in, he planned hours of old-fashioned bebop, Mary Lou Williams or Fats Navarro, something pure to wash away his failures. Millie would only want to know what he was doing, or to remind him of his upcoming performance review. For neither did he have anything to report. If only Downer had agreed to join him. If only he had that carrot to dangle.

Anabel Downer had been, paradoxically, both better and worse than he'd expected. Better in the sense that, for a woman in her forties, American in a foreign land, she seemed adjusted and comfortable. She was strong in ways Lane was not: pointedly spoken, calculated. Her life, her speech, even her looks — straight dark hair simply done up, minimal makeup — portrayed an economy, a paring down to the essentials. If Lane's height caused him to pass for ten years older, Downer certainly could pass for ten younger. As an investigative team, they could even be peers.

And yet, she held some deep-seeded animosity, one she'd deflected onto Lane. It wasn't his fault her husband Immersed, or that she'd made the grave mistake of Observing his Feeds. Adultery, rape, pedophilia — for all Lane knew, Downer's husband might've even murdered her in his Youtopia. How could you come back from something like that? How could you ever share a bed, an apartment, a life?

They were never meant to come back, was the answer. Lane wasn't supposed to be here, or in Indiana, or anywhere but in his own mind.

The desk attendant raised her microphone, so Lane cut his bebop. She announced in Spanish and then English that their flight would board momentarily. He used the restroom a final time. When he returned, he found his seat occupied by a woman dressed in all black. Her rolling suitcase rested against her leg.

"You are going to kill me," Downer said. "I hope you know this."

Lane smiled. He must've looked idiotic, standing above her with a puerile grin, but he couldn't help it. After all, he had succeeded. Downer here with him, on a flight back to Chicago: it felt like the affirmative end to a grand conquest. It felt Youtopian. It felt better than he had in a long, long time.

"Or," Lane said, "I could bring you back to life."

95.9 FM Morning Show

July 19, 2026
8:34 AM CST
<Begin Transcript>

ROCKIN FOX: That was Kiesza's 'Hideaway' on your station for the best of yesterday and today, WKUL Kool 96. Thanks as always for joining the Sunday Morning Stroll. I'm Rockin Matt Fox, here as always with my partner in crime, the Devil Jan Devoux. Devil, you loving this heat or what?

DEVIL: It's the humidity that kills, Fox.

ROCKIN FOX: Speaking of hot, for your hottest daily takes, I present the Anchor, Placido Ankridge.

ANCHOR: Bucks in Six will rise again. Just sayin.

ROCKIN FOX: Okay, so as our regular listeners will know, we don't usually get into the weeds here on the Morning Stroll.

DEVIL: Ha.

ROCKIN FOX: But we must talk about this video...

DEVIL: Ewwww... no no no.

ROCKIN FOX: I know, I know. But at this point, hasn't everyone seen it?

DEVIL: I haven't.

ROCKIN FOX: Not once? For about thirty minutes there, it *was* the internet.

DEVIL: Until they rightfully pulled it.

ANCHOR: I saw it. I have thoughts.

ROCKIN FOX: Naturally. Well, for our listeners out there who may have missed it, let me explain.

DEVIL: Please don't.

ROCKIN FOX: Last night a video leaked from — was it Buzzfeed? The leaker has already been canned, but the damage? Done, my friends. Spread all over the web. The video depicts a... detained woman. That's all I'll say. Internet believes it's Sonya Young. Authorities have neither confirmed nor denied.

DEVIL: You watch it, Fox?

ROCKIN FOX: I did.

DEVIL: And you think it should be out there, for everyone to see?

ROCKIN FOX: Whether it should or not feels beside the point at this juncture.

DEVIL: Well, I personally find this video—and frankly, America's fascination with the whole situation—grotesque. And us right now? We're boosting it, amplifying the sicko's message. We shouldn't even be giving it airtime.

<radio silence>

ROCKIN FOX: Hot take!

ANCHOR: That's *my* turf, Devil.

DEVIL: Well shit, Plass, when we have—

ADVERTISER: Tired of energy drinks that leave you hunched over your textbooks? Ones that can't even get you through homeroom? Try OneStar Energy, the pure solution that lasts all day. Through lunch, through after-school practice, even through those late-night cramming sessions. Try all our amazing flavors like S'mores, Ice Cream Sandwich, and Bubble Gum Blast. Find your favorite burst with OneStar Energy.

ROCKIN FOX: And we're back. We're talking about the video—you know the one. And since everyone's talking about it, we have to, right Devil?

DEVIL: Whatever.

ANCHOR: I'd like to interject here.

ROCKIN FOX: Rage away, my friend.

ANCHOR: Disagreements aside, I think we can agree that someone needs to study this thing, no?

DEVIL: We could also agree that's what the FBI is for.

ANCHOR: Because they did such a bang-up job with Youtopia the last time!

ROCKIN FOX: Let's get to your point, Anchor. You're saying we can learn from the video.

ANCHOR: Of course! Can't just ignore it because it's disturbing.

DEVIL: Or a deepfake.

ANCHOR: Sure, deepfakes, whatever. Study the thing. They can detect if it's been altered. Buzzfeed would've snuffed it right away if it was.

DEVIL: Would they?

ROCKIN FOX: So you've obviously watched the video, Anchor. You learn anything from it?

ANCHOR: Look, I'm no expert.

DEVIL: Understatement of the year.

ANCHOR: What I'm saying is, if you actually *watch* the video, you see the woman for, like, half of it. Too dark. Pixelated nonsense. Then click, a light bulb, and we see her. Surrounded by gray brick, gray concrete. Slight woman, dark black hair. Hunched over until the last second, the one where she wails out —

DEVIL: Must we describe it in such detail?

ANCHOR: My *point* is... the woman's face lifts, like, a tiny degree. We get chin, maybe a dimpled cheek. Lips covered by the gag. It's no clear shot. No chance at facial rec.

ROCKIN FOX: So you're saying...

ANCHOR: I'm saying, how can we possibly know it's Sonya Young?

ROCKIN FOX: Hmmm. As always, Anchor, you've dropped a heavy one into the sea.

ANCHOR: No. No.

ROCKIN FOX: No what?

ANCHOR: No "dropped into the sea" bullshit. No cutting me short.

DEVIL: Oh, hell...

ROCKIN FOX: Listen, let's try to keep the language family-friendly, yes? And, Anchor buddy, I get it. I hear you clucking big chicken. But for me—I just don't buy the argument.

ANCHOR: Then you're as blind as the rest. This is some asshole trying to make it rich.

DEVIL: What did Fox *just* say —

ANCHOR: Some warped teens in their parents' basement. Any of the million influencer wannabes out there. Because if I really did abduct Sonya Young and sent a ransom video? I make damn sure they know it's her.

<radio silence>

DEVIL: Matthew?

ROCKIN FOX: The Fox is always here.

DEVIL: This is *your* show. Care to comment on our colleague speculating on how *he* would make a ransom video?

ANCHOR: Damn it, Jan, spare me your psychobabble —

ADVERTISER: Bikini season dragging you down? Ready to believe in yourself again? Then say hello to the new GotMax 12 camera! With advanced blemish, sunshine, weight, and even age filters, you'll be back to showing off your natural, best self with each new click. So say yes, and put your best face forward on all your socials with the GotMax 12 camera today! Available online and at all major retailers.

ROCKIN FOX: A scorcher of a discussion! My thanks as always to the Devil and Anchor. And I can think of no better way to cool it down than to let the late, great Eddie Money take us home tonight, here on the greatest hits of yesterday and today, Kool 96.

Chapter 4

Dr. Daniel Peterson stood priggish, his perfect posture bordering on overcorrective, as he ushered Ana and Lane into the seats before his desk. His eyes lingered on Ana for a moment too long. Lane he avoided altogether. Peterson undoubtedly researched him before their arrival, though he didn't inquire about Lane's credentials, or their affiliation. Instead, he acted as though Lane didn't exist.

Ana recalled meeting Sonya Young for the first time in the racquetball courts of these very Youtopia Towers—she had been all grace and subservience one minute, imperious force the next. Equal parts charming and commanding. Compared to Sonya, Peterson was stilted, awkward. He adjusted his thick-rimmed glasses with a single finger. He unnecessarily tidied his desk. If Sonya was the teacher armed with a plan for every situation, Peterson represented the affable yet inexperienced pupil.

"It is a pleasure to see you again, Miss Downer," he said. Then he nodded at Ana's holster, hanging beneath her suitcoat. "Though you would've saved me some trouble if you had agreed to leave your firearm."

"Nothing personal," she said, though she didn't mean it. Being in the Towers again, seeing Peterson: it swept her up in ways that made her feel vulnerable. Never again would she encounter Youtopia unarmed.

"I am glad you're here," Peterson said. "I want you to know that, right off."

Ana looked to Lane, then back to Peterson. "You say that as though you shouldn't be."

"I don't mean to imply..." Peterson shuffled his hands. "It's just that we're in a very precarious situation."

"That's why I'm here. To help."

"I believe you," Peterson said. "But not everyone sees it that way."

***

On the five-hour flight, caffeinated and surprisingly calm, separated from her new partner by the aisle, Ana had opened her laptop with purpose. She felt something close to the jolts she experienced when uncovering the Villalobos murderer, when shaking down Tramel for her biggest Youtopia scoop—she felt once again like Special Agent Downer, like a more complete version of herself. After navigating the plane's unstable internet connection, she researched Youtopia Reborn with her former tenacious workmanship. She went all the way back to 2024, prepared for a flight-long crash course on the very topic she spent the past year trying to forget.

Not a year after Youtopia's demise, Sonya Young planted the seeds for Youtopia Reborn. A dozen other companies had put multimillion-dollar offers on the vacant Youtopia Towers, hoping to adopt its grandeur for their own, but Sonya never sold. What, the world speculated, could she possibly be cooking up? By her own admission, wasn't the last company too dangerous?

Sonya's first step was to relieve security fears with a solution as implausible as it was simple: transparency. Access. With Reborn, researchers and law enforcement would provide necessary quality control. No more single Observers for each Immerser. No secrets. The location of the Nests, for example—renamed Cradles—would not only be apparent, but would be open to public tours—thousands of eyes, including increased security, every day. Before laying a single brick, before inviting a single child into Immersion, Sonya had spent countless hours convincing the right people that Reborn would not suffer Youtopia's fate.

It was ironic, Ana thought, or at least ironic-adjacent. Sonya Young had spent so much time convincing the world that children in Reborn would be safe, only to become a victim herself.

Once formally established, Reborn Immersed its first children. Takers were slow to start, as even desperate parents expressed concerns. The scars from the first Youtopian wound remained too visible.

But then, once again, Sonya proved masterful at public manipulation. She diverted attention from the scar. Ana immediately thought of the Senator, the nefarious means by which Sonya manipulated her first company's precipitous rise, but this time, Ana could find little that suggested foul play. Here, Sonya's methods appeared simply, effectively persuasive.

Following the trail, Ana found the sentiments popularized by *Reborn for All* had existed from the outset. *Why only children?* people asked. *All ages get terminal diseases.* General justifications fell flat: the exclusivity of daycares, tax breaks for children, and other youth-only systems that provided no real equivalent. When pressed as to why Reborn limited its clientele, Sonya could never provide a truly justifiable reason.

Because a child's Youtopia is beautiful, Ana imagined Sonya saying, *and an adult's is hideous.*

Of course, she could never say that publicly, so Sonya struck elsewhere. In truth, Youtopia had always presented the struggle of humanism against idealism, of the imperfect against the perfect. It posed questions of what it meant to truly live, to pursue a supposed *best life.* And in this, Sonya found the perfect context within which to frame her argument: reproductive rights.

Ana followed this argument, started by Sonya herself in a rare interview: "We are a haven for unwanted children," Sonya said, touching a nerve on both sides of the political aisle. "Finally, all children can fully live." Secondhand articles from Reborn representatives and allies took up this call. They recited increasing abortion restrictions throughout the nation, leading to more impoverished births, to exceptions and week limits, to questions on the true meaning of the term pro-life. Into this fraught argument, Sonya inserted Youtopia Reborn, claiming that any child could be born and cared for. They presented Immersion as an overwhelmingly improved life.

This was how Sonya won: she tapped into a nation's yearning to help not one another, not the poor or sick or needy — America had long since lost such solidarity — but the symbol of the child.

With that, Ana moved to the initial abduction, and the bloodred message, REBoRN FoR ALL oR REBoRN FoR NoNE, painted across Sonya's bedroom wall. As for potential suspects, Sonya's abductor seemed to have a clear motive — someone with a child who wasn't quite sick enough to make Reborn's cut, perhaps. Requisitioning a list of Reborn's rejected cases was a starting point, and a narrower one than simply looking for enemies of Reborn in total. She'd made that mistake in the last case with Terrance Martin, the faux-religious zealot whose animosity toward Youtopia had almost everything to do with the celebrity it afforded him. Nonetheless, just to be thorough, she checked up on Terrance. His church, ReaLife, had since closed, but Ana wondered if he still fed off anti-Youtopian vitriol. It seemed he'd gained weight, entered and exited rehab facilities, if the tabloids were to be believed. His only remark on Sonya Young's abduction was a terse social media post: *HEHEHEHEHEHE.*

No, Terrance was not a suspect, nor anyone like him looking only to make their name. This time, Ana needed to be more calculated.

This brought her to the Russian nesting dolls. The strangeness of such a calling card — of leaving one altogether — stuck out. Many criminals took perverted pride in the strange connections their minds made: in this case, the dolls could represent stolen youth, or the protection of one person cradled within another. The doll was handmade, meticulous, so searching websites like eBay and Etsy for sellers of such dolls could provide important intel. There may exist a community of dollmakers, a group that could point her in the right direction.

A steward collected trash, offered Ana a final coffee or water. She looked at him, all pomade and toothy smile, her eyesight blurry from staring into the halogen glow of her laptop. She accepted the weak coffee, ready to confront the newest information: the abduction video. The news had broken just that morning, and though she and Lane read secondhand accounts, Ana needed to see the video for herself. Film was her specialty, after all, and the main reason Bruce assigned her the initial Youtopia case.

On first search, she found that Fox and CNN and all other news outlets had pulled the footage. Youtube, too, had redacted the original and its myriad copies. Probably a good thing, and though Ana the Special Agent could have easily accessed it, Ana the civilian had a much harder time. Videos with titles like *Sonya Young Abduction!* played short ads and then unrelated clips. Dailymotion, Flikr, Vevo, Tik Tok: none produced the actual video. On Veoh, one user claiming to have the *REALLLLL VID!!!!* tastelessly recreated a spoof with their Sonya wearing a Pennywise mask.

Then on Twitch, one of her last stops, Ana discovered a twenty-second video uploaded only minutes before. It had the pulsating, hall-of-mirrors quality of a camera filming a screen, of bad horror movie found footage. The woman's hunched body quivered, bound in a dark room.

Black hair. Middle aged. Her shoulders heaved with heavy breathing.

Just a second before the video cut, the woman turned her head partway to the camera and unleashed a garbled scream.

Ana watched it again, her eyes affixed to the woman, the contours of her spine, the straight hair, the strands pasted to her face with sweat or blood. She focused on the timbre and pitch of her scream, the aquiline curve of her nose, the prominent chin.

It was Sonya.

Or her kin.

Or neither.

She had to admit that, from this video, she couldn't truly tell.

Instead, she focused on the room surrounding the woman. The concrete walls behind housed rusted, protruding snap-ties and an Alaska-shaped water stain. The dampness of the woman's clothes suggested humid air. Ana placed herself in the room, caught every detail she could, so if—when—she stood in it herself, she would recognize it immediately. She would know.

The plane's bell sounded. The captain detailed their descent, Ana's return to America. Out the window, wispy clouds thinned as the Chicago suburbs welcomed her. They passed developments new and old, ponds natural and manmade, cars and highway systems that played like the establishing shots of a favorite movie. She hadn't realized, until the moment the cityscape came into distant view in the east, how much she missed this.

Lane leaned to her as they touched down. "Where do we go from here?"

Ana straightened her back and squared her shoulders. "We start right at the top."

***

Arranging a meeting with Daniel Peterson proved easier than Lane could have imagined. So easy, in fact, that Lane had to mentally pinch himself. On the phone for mere minutes, his new partner had coaxed and cavorted Reborn customer service reps, climbing an intricate bureaucratic ladder all the way until the high rung of Peterson's personal assistant. The woman seemed to recognize Downer's voice. She would alert Dr. Peterson as soon as possible, though she could make no guarantees. Downer changed the subject, inquired on the assistant's own life within the hectic company, until, after five minutes of banal chatter, Downer circled back and pressed again. The assistant demurred. She would see what she could do.

Within the half hour, the meeting was set in the prestigious Youtopia Towers.

Lane marveled at Downer's natural intuition, her sway even after all that had happened. She could adopt both hardline and gentler personas, and recognized when each was called for. She instantly vindicated his Dominican trip, the benefits already outweighing the costs.

They had arrived.

More challenging, however, were the logistics. They needed a hotel with two rooms, and a rental car. Lane didn't know whether to discuss splitting costs—he'd made the asinine assumption that Downer would be independently wealthy, or that the investigation could happen close to Huntington, or something else, he didn't know. He foolishly hadn't taken the itinerary this far.

Thankfully, at the rental car service desk, Downer signed and paid, and didn't ask him to chip in. He repaid this kindness by finding them a hotel, two rooms just outside of Kenosha, that turned out to be nothing like its online pictures—one story, stained entry doors along a cracked pavement path. The green siding was sun-faded and wind-worn. Downer said nothing, just grabbed her slim bag and gave him a starting time in the morning—six sharp—before retreating to her room, which must have been the same as his: an aged desk chair and thin, faded comforter and a musky smell that reminded him far too much of his 2000s childhood.

Before turning in, he needed to update Millie, from whom he had four missed calls and a slew of texts. At least now that conversation would start in a good place.

"Where the hell have you been?" she asked before Lane could even speak.

Instead of responding, Lane filled her in with the highlights of his story.

"That's great, Lane," she cut in without her usual enthusiasm. "But since you clearly haven't read what I sent you, I need you to listen now."

"All right."

"The board moved up your review."

"Moved up? When?"

"Tuesday."

He rubbed at his forehead. "Tuesday," he repeated. "As in the day after tomorrow."

"Unless you know of some other Tuesday."

"I can't make that. Didn't you just hear what I said? We have *Daniel Peterson*—"

"I hear you, Lane. This would have been useful information sooner."

"We didn't have him sooner. Can you just put them off for me? I'm on assignment, after all."

"Lane," she repeated. She never said his name this often. "This moving up could be a good thing. They might want to offer you something, but only if you're *here*."

"I'm on assignment."

Millie shot a sigh through the phone. "You keep saying that. First it was Minneapolis. Then the Dominican Republic? Now Wisconsin."

"Meaning?"

"Meaning we're the *Huntington* Beacon. Meaning the board won't accept this deep chase as an explanation."

"Deep chases are what make me good at what I do."

"There's a line. You know there's a line."

"A line? Mill, I haven't used any company money. And honestly, what paper doesn't want this story? It'll be picked up by IndyStar, The Times, Fox News. Tell them I'm about to blow Bethany Fawkes out of the water."

Silence. A long enough pause where Lane questioned whether Millie held the line.

"Mill?"

"I need you to shoot straight on this. Give me practical Lane, just for a day. Then you can go back on the hunt."

"This is what I need," Lane said. "The hunt."

"And you'll be back at it before you know it. After you walk out of here Tuesday morning."

"There's no—"

"Lane," Millie had interrupted one last time. "No excuses. See you then, bright and early."

***

Peterson smiled, eyeing Ana like a long-lost friend. His mustache was dyed black, but gray seeped through his temples and neckline. His thick-rimmed glasses reminded her of the first time they spoke in Central Control, where her descent began.

"So your colleagues don't want you talking to us?" Ana said.

"Some. I invited you here, but as the interim CFO, I also have certain... obligations."

"What about your obligation to Sonya?"

This unseated him. He paced to the all-windowed wall. Ana hadn't meant to come on so harshly, and yet, hearing Peterson's voice, something of the past resurfaced. She transported back to 2024, to the constant need to remind Peterson and other male figures of her authority. That switch, apparently, liked to flip itself.

So she continued to press. "I assume by now you've seen the abduction video."

Peterson's body visibly shuddered, as though shaking itself dry. "Abhorrent. That the video exists is one thing, but to put it out into the world like that... It's degrading. Sonya is so far above..." He stopped and shook his head.

"You believe it's Sonya," Ana said.

"Who else would it be?"

"A doppelganger perhaps, meant to disrupt the investigation." Then she added with a feigned ignorance, "Or a family member who looks like Sonya—a sister, or daughter."

Peterson reacted to this as she expected: his heavy brow creased in confusion. Sonya Young's lack of family was public knowledge, certainly known by the FBI Special Agent in charge of the first Youtopia case.

Instead of responding, he squared his body on Ana. "The security breaches of Youtopia have haunted me these two years, Miss Downer. I am still uncertain how they happened. Naturally, that made me fear for Youtopia Reborn. But Sonya's greatest gift is her resolve, her inherent belief in the *goodness* of what we can accomplish."

He seemed sincere, though Ana knew people in high positions like Peterson as the most polished, practiced liars. Did he know the truth about the Youtopia murders? Did he know about Ana's lie to cover them up? Was he simply putting on a show for Lane? Ana leaned forward to press, to glean what she could.

"It did seem odd," she said, "that after so many deaths, Sonya was willing to jump right back in. Unless she knew something the rest of us didn't."

"Risk cannot be eliminated completely, only managed—a simple cost-benefit ratio. Our contribution to the world was far greater than the risk of another perpetrator."

"By what measure?" Lane asked.

"We lost two hundred and two people in Youtopia," Peterson replied, though he continued to look at Ana. "Reborn has saved over seventy thousand. Simple math proves the measure."

"So until Sonya is found," Ana asked, "you plan to keep business as usual?"

Peterson's thick brow descended. "As to business as usual, I have a question myself. You are no longer FBI, Miss Downer. You've lived abroad. Your presence here, now, seems far from *business as usual*."

"What exactly is your question?"

"Why are *you* here?"

Lane turned to her as Peterson resumed his unrelenting stare. He had asked the obvious, and yet, they didn't have an obvious answer, not without revealing the peculiar, fantastic circumstances that led to their arrival.

"Lane is on assignment for his paper," she said. "I owe him a favor."

She looked over to Lane, who curled his lip and nodded in reply.

"That is a sizeable favor," Peterson said.

Lane shuffled in his seat. With his height, his discomfort played out like a siren, blaring and obvious.

Ana needed to steer the conversation back to the case. "Lane wants what everyone else wants: to know why someone might abduct Sonya Young."

"I apologize, but the why seems obvious."

"Unless it isn't," Lane said.

"Youtopia was created for anyone. Reborn was not." Peterson folded his hands. "Whoever this psychopath is, he believes we have excluded him."

"But there are missing pieces," Ana said. "If that's truly his motive, we would have ransom demands, ultimatums for Sonya's return. The perpetrator might just want someone else in charge—someone like you."

At this, Peterson turned his stare beyond Ana, out his window. Ana thought she'd finally hit him with something damning, but then he held a finger to his ear, to a miniscule earbud, pitch black and hidden there. His eyes drifted to the door.

"Yes," he said to someone beyond—someone who had likely overheard their whole conversation. Ana reminded herself that she was home now, in America, the land of ubiquitous cellphones and virtual assistants and earbuds, all recording their every conversation. She needed to be careful. "Yes, thank you." He turned back to them. "They're ready for us."

"They?"

"The Board of Directors. They've called an emergency meeting, in the third Tower."

Peterson approached the door, ready to cut short their conversation and move them, as though he was just one stop on some Youtopia Towers tour.

"Hold on a minute," Ana said. "This Board of Directors... Who are they?"

"Part of Sonya's transparency project. They provide key oversight, appease various stakeholders. Basically, they free up Sonya's time for more important matters."

Lane rose, but Ana stayed firmly in her seat. They hadn't gotten much, if anything, from Peterson regarding Sonya, his relationship with her these past months, his ambitions now that he sat atop the Reborn throne. His position made him the likeliest subject. They couldn't just lose him now.

"Peterson," she said, her voice dropping into a motherly tone she hadn't used in years. "Cut the corporate jargon. The Sonya I remember would never divide her own power. So why this Board? Did someone force her hand?"

"The idea was not hers," Peterson said. "But eventually she saw the wisdom in it."

"It was your idea."

"Yes," Peterson admitted with reluctance.

Lane watched this exchange like a tennis spectator, his eyes darting back and forth between them. Ana wondered what all transpired in his inexperienced mind — how an outsider's view of this insider conversation appeared. Was he putting together the pieces like Ana? This Board of Directors, a group influenced, if not assigned, by Peterson himself, with the power now to control the company, called this opportune emergency meeting, including a request to meet Ana and Lane. It all felt like a culprit wanting to see, and likely intimidate, an investigator — to look the enemy in the eye. The old Ana would've relished such a bold challenge.

"All right," she said, finally rising. "Let's go."

Peterson took one more step before turning to Lane, finally acknowledging him. "My apologies, young man. They've requested only Miss Downer."

Lane's face turned incredulous. His shoulders immediately slouched. At his height, any body language felt exaggerated, like an overgrown child in the squirming, opening throes of a tantrum. How difficult it must've been to hide with his stature. How open, how vulnerable, one must've felt to the world.

That same motherly side of Ana felt for him. He didn't deserve this exclusion, but if they were to truly partner, they couldn't let egos and petty mistreatments derail them. They needed to move forward in whatever way possible. After all, this was why he came to her. It was, in a skewed way, exactly what he wanted.

She attempted to relay all this with a look, but with his sunken shoulders and sulking lip, Lane did nothing to hide his emotions.

"I'll fill you in after," Ana said.

"Don't worry about me," he said without enthusiasm. "I've got my own board meeting to worry about."

Ana didn't know what he meant, so she simply said, "Trust me. I'll ask the right questions."

Chapter 5

It had all gone wrong, starting with the interview, where Peterson treated Lane like an unnecessary piece of furniture. Next, they abandoned him here in the hallway outside the conference room like some child awaiting his mother. Any giddiness he had over his prospects, including seeing and stepping foot in the hulking Towers for the first time, disappeared with this petty kid-table treatment. *He* was the one Serena reached out to. *He* brought Downer here. He would've left in protest, if he hadn't come this far already. He would've pressed his ear to the door and listened in, if the entire place weren't completely soundproof.

Back against the wall, one leg up, he stood doing the only thing he could think to do: scroll through news sites on his phone. He searched Bethany Fawkes, taking vindictive comfort in her own lack of breaking news. The abduction video's omnipresence usurped her grip on the story, far overshadowing her interview with Saeed Free, opening a window for something else — for some*one* else — to enter. Someone like Lane Samson. If only they had allowed him in that room. Downer had promised to fill him in, and he would see to it that she kept her word.

He closed his browser. Though he had no text notifications, he opened his thread with Serena in the faint hopes that he had missed something. He called her — an act that bordered on obsessive habit — and it rang and rang, never giving way to voicemail, leaving Lane to hope that somewhere on the other end, she might recognize him and respond.

Instead, an incoming call interrupted the ringing: Henrick again. It had been one week since Lane attended the Midnighter, since he saw Henrick in person, and days since their snippy phone conversation. Lane had some mending to do there — he needed to remember all the times Henrick helped him cope with Youtopia withdrawals. He needed to remember that Henrick caring for him was admirable, and not a nuisance.

"Henry," Lane said. "What's the good word?"

"You know the word, buddy," Henrick said. "Or have you forgotten?"

"All good, man. I'm on a new assignment, actually. That's why I haven't been in. But I'll try to swing by tomorrow."

"Good. It'll be real good if you do."

A long silence. Lane expected Henrick to ask the intimate questions one never asks except in FAR rehab: *How much pain are you in? Have you fantasized about hurting others? How many times have you contemplated suicide?* Instead, the silence continued.

"You good, Henry?" Lane finally asked. "Everything okay on your end?"

"Yeah, definitely." More silence. "Okay, maybe not really. I've been having these dreams—not relapses, mind you, but actual *dreams*. You know, at night. I can't seem to shake them."

From the far end of the hallway resounded the ding of the elevator. A woman in high heels clacked out, an oversized purse at her side and her face in a tablet. She was mid-fifties, a pompadour of bleached blonde hair bobbing above her, face fully made up. Lane recognized her immediately from the video on his Reborn tour: Jeanne Haskins, the PR face of the company.

Henrick started describing his dreams—some nonsense about a chimera and flaming swords and naked women—as Haskins approached. Her timing was fortuitous and fortunate, but Lane knew he now needed to hang up on Henrick, once again.

"I'm sorry to hear that, Henry. I really am."

"It just sucks that—"

"I know man, I know. But I really can't talk right now. I'll call you later and we'll chat, okay? I promise."

Lane abruptly cut the line without waiting for an answer, the small twinge of guilt he felt quickly erased as Haskins sidled down the hall. She nearly passed Lane before noticing him.

"Excuse me," he said. "You're Jeanne Haskins."

His recognition immediately warmed her. She smiled, revealing the age lines beneath her layers of concealer.

"Saw you just recently," Lane continued. "On the big screen, I mean. I toured the Minneapolis Cradles."

"Oh, yes," Haskins said with the mock-humility of a performer. "If you're on tour now, I'm afraid you're a bit lost."

"No, no. My name's Lane Samson. I'm with the Huntington Weekly Beacon."

"Lane Samson," she repeated. "And how did a representative of the Huntington Weekly Beacon end up in this hallway?"

"Waiting for my partner." He nodded to the conference room door.

"You're partners with Anabel Downer?"

Lane paused at this. Downer's return, their presence here: it had felt covert, undercover. But now the Board meeting, this Haskins woman... it seemed news spread rapidly at Youtopia Reborn.

"I am." He looked at the door. "For the moment, at least."

"Consider yourself lucky. She's the best."

"So they say."

A pause ensued, in which Lane expected Haskins to shuffle away to an office, but she stared at Lane with concerned eyes.

"You're a Reintegrator," she said suddenly.

Taken aback, Lane instinctively looked to the floor.

Then Haskins added, "Like me."

He looked up, and immediately knew she spoke without judgment, without the presumptive feeling that being a Reintegrator meant being a coward, a depressive, a failure. "How did you know?"

"We just know," she said. "We're not so big a community. Not anymore." She slid the tablet to her side. "I used to run a Reintegrator recovery facility of sorts. Nothing too organized, but I like to think it helped people like us."

"A place like FAR."

Haskins shook her head. "I find their methods... unsatisfactory. Youtopia wasn't an addiction—it was *us*." She reached a hand to her neck, toying with a gawdy ruby pendant dangling on a gold chain. "As best I could, I tailored my methods for each pupil. In return, they would give me gifts. This one was from Billie Barnett. It belonged to his grandmother."

"Why did you stop?"

"As you can imagine, the work was taxing. For every person I saved, another..." Her eyes lowered. "The heart can only handle so much."

In the middle of the hallway, her head now hanging down, Haskins seemed even smaller than her short frame.

"Early on," Lane said, "one of my closest confidantes in FAR was Mike Penrose. Older guy, all grit and gristle. But no nonsense. Someone who'd tell it straight."

"I can guess where this story goes."

"It threw me. I mean, he left this *awful* note. He cursed everyone, especially us. All I could think was, what's the point?" He shrugged. "I'm better now."

"I'm glad to hear that," Haskins said. "What other Reintegrators do is not our fault. Society would have us wear their actions like a stain, our own large, red *A* stitched to our chests." She smirked. "My apologies. It's a reference."

"*The Scarlet Letter*. I aced high school English."

"Me too." She looked toward the conference door. "The main thing is never to let *them* decide who you are. Youtopia was only part of our past. It certainly shouldn't dictate our future."

Lane nodded. He was finally making something of this debacle of a day—an unexpected connection that could unlock doors for him, doors like the one Downer and Peterson had just slammed in his face.

"You know," she said, "Anabel and I have something in common. We both lost a child." When she softly shook her head, her hair stayed immutably in place. "Do you have any yourself?"

"No."

"The highest blessing. It's why we need Reborn. Why we need Sonya." Her eyes went skyward, as though in prayer.

"About Sonya—"

"Ultimately, we Reintegrators need to find *purpose*," Haskins continued. Her mind was on its own track now, and Lane could only follow. "A reason to get out of bed and face this difficult world of ours. No matter what I taught my pupils, it always centered on that one simple fact."

"It seems you found yours."

Without hesitation, Haskins nodded. "Giving children what my Oscar needed. Making sure nothing like what happened to him *ever* happens again."

"You believe Reborn can save every child?"

"Yes," she said unequivocally. After a moment, she added, "That is, every child whose parents cannot."

Lane recognized the gilded optimism in her look. This woman not only sold Youtopia Reborn, she lived it. And yet, he knew grief all too well, knew the temptation of finding a glossy cover for that deeper, darker pain inside, the one she would rather not confront. He'd never lost a son as she did, but he'd lost his parents, and so he knew the incomplete feeling, the small portion of one's true self gone. Like constant blood loss, over time it sapped a person.

"What was yours like?" Haskins asked. She didn't clarify, and yet he knew exactly what she meant.

"We're not supposed to talk about it. Even think about it."

"Mantra Eleven," Haskins said. *"The you in Youtopia was not the real you."* She stepped closer to Lane. "I know what they sell, but it was our *lives.* They're our *memories.* They happened, even if the world won't admit it."

Lane's mind instinctively flashed to his lustrous Youtopian past: pick-up basketball games with former Indiana legends on his painless, reconstructed knees; sun-filled coastal beaches with, among other women, Serena Yarborough; jazz festivals with his resurrected father.

Quickly following, however, were the deviant moments, the extremes his mind pushed on him. At times, he behaved pettily, even abusively, toward those same women. He also felt a dastardly rush when injuring up-and-coming high schoolers on the court. In Youtopia, he became the dirty player he never was in real life, throwing elbows, cutting at knees. In one of his final Youtopia memories, during an alumni game in front of a crowd of thousands, his hyper-aggressive block on a former crosstown rival sent the guy sprawling and bloodied to the ground. As the EMTs carted him off on a stretcher, neck-braced and unconscious, Lane hovered above with a devious smile.

"It was exactly like they say," he said. "The best, most perfect, most narcissistic place my mind could imagine."

The resultant pause between them hung like fog. His journalistic instincts pushed him to ask more, to get as much information from Haskins as possible, but before he could turn the tide of the conversation back to Sonya Young, she stepped away.

"You'll be okay," she said as a farewell. "Find your purpose. That's as perfect as we can get."

***

"Miss Downer," June Kowalski, the towering chairwoman heading the long conference table, said. Then, through a voice thick with brazen condescension, "A pleasure to meet you."

The room, like all rooms in Youtopia's third Tower, was lavish and grandiose. Teak paneled walls with a deep mahogany finish ran floor-to-ceiling. The chairs, though wheeled and modern, had fleur-de-lis backs and matching cushioned seats. The table itself had curved edges, the legs hand-carved and claw-footed. It seemed like the dining room of some long-ago English royalty, and Kowalski the estate's empowered Duchess.

Peterson hovered behind Ana. No one had offered her a seat. Eight other board members flanked the table, four to each side of Kowalski, appraising Ana as though she'd walked into a job interview, and had so far made a poor first impression. Kowalski glared with particular disapproval.

"The pleasure is mine," Ana said, trying to gain footing. She scanned each board member, noting small details: the fidgeting fingers of the curly-haired woman to her left, the evading eyes of the bald man to her right. The baby of the bunch, a guy even younger than Lane, eyed his phone on the table with visible yearning. Ana noted to investigate each immediately afterward, to dive into the pool of their backstories.

"Pleasantries aside," Kowalski said, "we do find ourselves in trying times. It is important for us, as a Board, and for all Youtopia Reborn employees—" She shot Peterson a daggered glare. "—to exercise discretion."

Ana nodded, as if to agree with Kowalski. She waited. One of her first lessons as a profiling FBI Agent—the habit that bled into her personal life and interactions—was to never unnecessarily fill silences. In turn, Kowalski bristled. She clearly intended a fight Ana wouldn't easily give her.

"To put it bluntly," Kowalski said, "we cannot speak with any Tom or Sally who simply waltzes in our doors."

Ana half-smiled. "So you invited me here to say you can't speak to me?"

"We need to know *why* you're here," the bald man interjected.

As Kowalski silently chastised the man with a look, Ana considered his prompt. Why was she here? Would even the full truth of the answer satisfy them? What half-truth would they accept?

"I asked to see Mr. Peterson," Ana said. "He agreed."

"But surely there's more to it than that," Kowalski said. "A disgraced former FBI Agent, chased from her job because of her... *situation* with Youtopia, returning now at the first sign of trouble for Reborn. You must recognize why the Board is interested in your motives."

"Same for me and yours."

This brought Kowalski to her feet. She struck an imposing figure, nearly as tall as Lane, her shoulders square and jaw set firm. "We have given our full cooperation to the authorities, including your former employer. They are, I remind you, the *real* investigators on this case. Your presence here is asinine. It can only cause trouble." Kowalski raised her eyebrows, a direct challenge.

Ana resisted the temptation to smile broadly. Under the watch of the FBI, she would've proceeded carefully, would've considered protocol.

Now, unmoored from the bureaucracy, she was actually enjoying this exchange, as though watching it from the safety of a relaxing movie theater seat. She admired this Kowalski, even if she didn't much like her.

"You," Ana said, "and I mean *every one of you*, might stand to gain from Sonya's disappearance." She turned back to Peterson, whose body remained stiff. "You can hide in conference rooms all you want, but to the public, silence implies guilt."

This struck the Board. They turned to one another with scowls. Ana could almost see the retaliations dangling on their chastened lips. None of these people, standing atop Youtopia Reborn like the gods of Olympus with an absent Zeus, felt that a lowly mortal like Ana should question them.

"Stewart," Kowalski said, turning to the bald man, "please call security and have Miss Downer escorted from the building."

"I don't think that's necessary," Peterson said, stepping before Ana. "I imagine, June, you have much more important matters to address. I will see Miss Downer out."

Kowalski stood still for a moment. She clearly wanted the show of force, the display of her unique power. Finally, with a flick of her wrist, she simply dismissed them.

Peterson extended his arm, leading Ana through the thick doors out into the hallway.

"Quite the ray of sunshine," Ana said once the doors closed behind them.

"June is a decent person," Peterson replied. "It's hard to act calmly under such direct accusation."

"Hard? Sure. But that comes with the territory."

Halfway to the elevator, Lane sat slumped on the ground, nodding to loud, trumpeting music pumping through his earbuds. Ana stopped Peterson before they reached him.

"How closely have you worked with Kowalski?" Ana asked. "With the Board itself?"

"Not very. The control they wield is mostly ceremonial."

"You sure about that?"

Peterson slid in front of Ana, severing Lane from her view. His face adopted a secretive look. "Before we rejoin your cohort there, I wanted to inquire on your husband Paul. How is he doing?"

The question jarred Ana. What did Paul have to do with anything?

"I don't mean to pry," Peterson continued. "I can see I've upset you."

"I'm not upset."

"Good. It's only... I keep a keen eye on the Reintegration project. As you can imagine, I feel a personal responsibility to them. In those first months, I begged Sonya to reopen Youtopia."

"Paul would have leapt at the chance then." Ana swallowed down hard, her mouth suddenly dry. "But he's okay now."

"I'm so glad to hear that. I take inspiration from those like Paul, rediscovering life. I admire him."

"That's a good way to look at it."

They continued down the hall. When Lane saw them, he stood and removed his earbuds. He looked immediately to Ana, but she softly shook her head, telling him with her eyes to wait, to be patient. He would get his information, but not under the glaring eye of the Youtopia Tower cameras.

Easy listening music escorted them down the otherwise silent elevator ride, the two men flanking Ana and staring at their own warped reflection in the stainless steel. Their silence weighed on her—they both wanted to speak to her but not to one another. This was why she always worked alone, why, even now, things needed to change if they were to move forward.

Just outside the elevator, Peterson's assistant intercepted them and escorted them through the open space of the first floor, past tables and an eatery and front desks all occupied by silent, somber employees. Near the doors, Peterson thanked the assistant and turned to Ana and Lane.

"Miss Downer," he said. "It has been the most pleasant of surprises seeing you again."

"One last thing," Ana said. "I'd like to ask you about our last case— how that ended, how it might tie to Sonya's purported will."

Peterson cast a quick, furtive look to Lane. "I don't feel comfortable discussing that right now."

Ana turned to Lane as his former sulkiness turned to resentment. He stood upright, his figure imposing when he wanted it to be. "I'd like a word with Miss Downer myself," he said.

Ana looked between the two. She needed to talk to Peterson, but Lane's demeanor screamed that he simply wouldn't wait.

"Just a moment with my partner," Ana said.

"Of course."

As Peterson stepped out into the open corridor, Lane ducked down. Even with a whisper, his voice carried in the wide space.

"Enough of the boxing me out bullshit," Lane said. "You need to tell him I'm part of this too."

"Peterson knows something he's not telling us. I can get it from him." Ana stared straight into his eyes. "You need to trust me."

"What happened in that meeting?"

Ana cast glances at the vaulted ceilings, willing Lane to understand. "Peterson was right. This is not the place for that conversation."

Lane straightened again. "You're here because of me."

"I'm here because you can't handle this on your own."

"What's that supposed to mean?"

Ana breathed in. "Honestly, Lane, it means I don't know if I can trust your judgment yet. The way you're acting right now, for example, impeding the investigation for the sake of your fragile ego. I don't know if you're stable enough to—"

"Stable enough?" Lane didn't mask his anger now. "You know, for all the Reintegrator bullshit I put up with, I thought at least *you* might come up with something original."

Ana stepped forward. She had faced down men far more imposing than Lane Samson. "You can keep up this getting-in-my-way nonsense," she whispered through clenched teeth, "or you can let me do what you brought me here to do."

Lane abruptly turned and stomped away, passing Peterson with a vindictive glare as he went.

When Peterson returned, Ana felt the need to apologize for Lane, to further explain his presence. But Peterson seemed unfazed by it all, and Ana felt grateful for his utter disinterest.

"When I said a pleasant surprise," Peterson said, "I truly meant it. I needed a reason to smile."

"Daniel," Ana said, calling him by his first name for perhaps the first time. "I want to find Sonya too, but I can't help if you don't let me."

"We should speak on this in a different setting."

"Name it."

Peterson touched the interface on his massive watch. "I have to take care of..." He scrolled, his unfinished words replaced by a strange snarl. "Tomorrow. Lunch. On me, of course."

"Every minute matters, Daniel. Every minute is one she's still in their grasp."

"I know, Miss Downer. I've felt each one like a boulder on my chest." He folded his hands across his body. "Lunch. My assistant will contact you."

Ana didn't want to wait a day, had nowhere to go but a hotel by herself. She wished she could press him, but without the weight of her

FBI badge, she had little leverage. And Peterson's eyes drifted now to his watch, to his myriad obligations other than her. To push would risk losing him entirely.

"Tomorrow then."

***

The Greyhound driver scanned Lane's virtual ticket with a grunt that resonated all the way into Lane's chest. They were departing Milwaukee at 1:00 p.m. but wouldn't arrive in Fort Wayne until after 11:00. After days of whirlwind success, he was now begrudgingly homebound to his yearly review, and farther away from Serena and the Sonya Young story than ever.

He sat up front, the engine rumbling beneath his cramped seat, facing many hours and few stops with only his phone to entertain him. He swiped it to life, wiping at the smudged fingerprints that marked his unlock pattern: a glossed streak that oddly resembled a heart. He could check the news again, could see if Bethany Fawkes had uncovered anything related to the abduction video. He calculated how many jazz albums he could listen to along the ride, how long his battery would hold while siphoning data.

But instead of pulling up anything, he opened his recent call history and, again, on the thinnest of whims, dialed Serena.

He waited out the ring, which went on and on. He hung up and, like a repeat caller trying to win a radio giveaway, hit send again with no real hope of hearing a voice on the other end.

So when the line did pick up—when her voice softly hummed through—Lane's throat caught.

"Yeah?" she repeated. "Anybody there?" A rumbling noise for a moment. "Laney?"

"Yes," he finally said. "Serena, it's me."

According to his phone, he had dialed her thirty-five times since the voicemail night, yet he foolishly found himself with no plan of what to say.

"It's me," he repeated, trying to shake his head free of its fog. "How are you, Rene?" The nickname came back to him instinctually, as though the time between their relationship and now had folded, accordion-like, back onto itself. As though they were still lovers.

"Life, right? It's... you know. *Shhh, shhh, shhh.*" These last sounds were not to him, but to someone on her end, a rambunctious friend perhaps, or another lover. Though if that was the case, why did she answer now?

"Serena, on that message," he said, playing straight to the point. Then he heard a wail, a piercing shriek, taking him off-balance. "Are you okay? Everything all right?"

She laughed. "Just peachy keen, Laney."

"Serena, I have to ask you. The other night, you called me..."

"I did."

"You said something to me, something about your mother. About you being in trouble."

The line went silent. Lane feared he'd lost her.

"Serena?" he said. "I'm here. For whatever. I want to help."

When her voice returned, it was somber, sober. "Best way to help is forget I ever said anything."

"That's..." he said. "That's kind of hard for me to do right now."

"I was just talking shit, Laney. You know me."

He shook his head as the bus lurched forward. She was right: he did know her. At least, he used to. And the Serena he knew back then would never have confessed to a lie, would never have claimed to be *talking shit*. That Serena would have doubled down, would have pushed the lie further, or at least turned it into a joke. Either Serena had changed, fundamentally and deeply, or something was wrong.

"Rene, I want to see you."

The line was already dead. Lane stared blankly into his phone, but it only confirmed that she was gone.

JOSEPH REIN

Chapter 6

Ana plodded forward as the unremitting sun began its descent. Jogging outside in this, the dead of the heat, was foolish, yes, but she needed to clear her head—needed some release. She sweated her way through the crowded, eclectic intersections of Bay View until she reached more open land, roads without sidewalks or shoulders. The thick air carried the scent of cut grass and cow manure.

Even after returning to her hotel and taking a cold shower, her body continued to sweat. A local restaurant delivered her two vegan dishes, decently priced and presented. Peterson's promise of lunch was still half a day away, so she ate alone in her room, with time to kill and few weapons to wield against it.

She could investigate Serena Yarborough herself—Lane needed an olive branch—but the daunting thought of the wide-open, commercial internet kept Ana away. For years, field agents had scoured the web on her behalf, young Michaels and Jades who knew how to distinguish the useful from the useless. They knew under which digital rocks to dig. Surely, Lane had already found any information on Serena that Ana might unearth herself. It would be a waste of time.

More fruitful would be the Board members. At their helm, Kowalski loomed as a domineering figure, the alpha female. But treating her as the puppetmaster, with the other eight attached to her invisible strings, would be a mistake, a move of rookies and recruits. Each Board member played a part, maybe one of them more outsized than at first glance.

Their names and email addresses were easy to find, Reborn's transparency mantra borne out across their illustrious website. Finding cell numbers proved slightly more difficult, yet still manageable. She dialed Stewart Newborne, the middle-aged bald man and the only one to speak other than Kowalski. His phone rang and rang. His voicemail system was automated, perfunctory. Ana left a brief message. On down the line, she called numbers with area codes across the country: Dallas and Maine and Idaho. Some had personalized message systems, some had none. Nobody answered. She thought to text them all, to offer herself up and seek a response that way, when suddenly her phone rang.

It was Newborne, his voice full of adolescent impudence. "Stop calling us."

Ana smiled to herself. "Just want to ask a few questions. Did you have any previous knowledge of Sonya Young's will?"

"You bitch."

Ana let that sit between them. "Are you truly angry with me? Or did June Kowalski instruct you to be?"

Newborne huffed. "I'm angry because some FBI dropout is harassing us. Leave. Us. *Alone*."

"If you don't know anything, Mr. Newborne, you could just say that. Your anger has implications."

"Yeah, well, I don't give a flying fuck about your implications. Stop calling us." He cut the line.

Ana immediately retried the other Board members, the men and women who saw her call and must've immediately reached out to Newborne in fear. One of them might have something to tell her — might, if nudged correctly, slip and falter. She called, texted, called again, and was met with only silence. It seemed a dead end until one of the text threads enlivened with the three pulsating dots of a potential response. The person on the other line was writing back. Ana waited. But then the dots disappeared and nothing replaced them.

She looked at the number — it belonged to Rob Reddy, the kid, twenty-four and fresh out of graduate school at Columbia. From his online profiles, Ana pegged Reddy as equal parts wunderkind and anti-socialite. She called him, texted again, but whatever impulse Reddy had experienced was gone. She needed him in a room, eye-to-eye. She needed the weight of an FBI subpoena. She needed her former self.

Restless, with nothing to do but attempt sleep that wouldn't come, she looked up a local liquor store that delivered her a bottle of red wine, overpriced but good. Old habits. In the Dominican, after long, labor-intensive days, her bed had often beckoned her into a mindless, drifting sleep she would never find here in Wisconsin. The wine would help.

Glass in hand, she returned to her phone, recognizing that she was about to indulge another old habit. She knew she should stop, but Lonnie's Instagram profile was easy to find, as public as Lonnie herself wanted to be. Ana needed to toss her phone, finish the wine, and go to bed. It had been years. She was about to discover things she didn't need to know.

Immediately, the visuals bombarded her: Lonnie and Paul's faces, pressed close together in Lonnie's profile picture, then her most-liked photo of the two kissing on their moonlight beach wedding in some all-inclusive destination. Lonnie shared small life accolades like a teenager: *My hubby's first quiche! And it was edible!* below her oven-mitted hands sporting the brown-edged ceramic baking dish. Next came, *It's official – first downtown gallery!* under snapshots of Paul's black-and-white charcoal drawings. Ana examined his art closer. The sketches had improved, had gained a certain vibrancy since his early post-Youtopia days. Paul himself, however, posted nothing on Instagram or other social media aside from occasional prints for sale on his professional Facebook page. His last personal post predated his entry into Youtopia. In that, he remained the same as always. It made Ana happy, in this small way, to know he hadn't completely changed.

She should've been happy overall, for him and Lonnie. When Paul had finally checked out of Abundant Life Reintegration Center, Ana recognized a ruddiness in his cheeks, a clarity in his eyes, that hadn't been there before. She allowed herself to hope, to imagine a future.

Two days later, he suddenly announced he was moving out, to a small studio apartment in Cicero, to the fresh start everyone, including Ana, had told him he needed. He hadn't even unpacked his suitcase. Ana watched him pass remnants of their former life that she'd revived just for his return—a picture frame from their wedding, his favorite mystery novels—without grabbing any of them. He marched to her like a traveling husband going away for a brief weekend, not for the rest of his life. He said drily, "I'll need an Uber."

Ana breathed deep. She tried not to feel wounded. This was, after all, a scenario she'd fantasized about in her lonely hours: life without Paul, without the guilt of him. And yet, looking at him then, the stubble shaved from his face, his hair dyed shimmering black, a youthful freshness in his eyes, she felt only emptiness.

"What will you do for money?" she asked, part out of concern, part petulance. "You don't have a job."

"I'll find something. You don't need to worry about me, Anabel."

He left to wait on the street. Ana couldn't remember the last time he'd used her full name. Pre-Youtopia, certainly. Pre-Charlotte, perhaps. And just like that, they were over.

The immediate loss of Paul was not, however, what sent her to the Dominican for her own fresh start. No, Paul left, and in truth Ana felt lighter, energized, as though shedding heavy winter gear for a pending spring. She called Bruce and begged for a bigger assignment. She rejoined her gym, started again her abandoned vegetarianism, her tenacious daily schedule and regimen. At odd moments she felt the knifepoint-sting of her loss, of Charlotte—always Charlotte, but also Paul, the life they could have regained—but she allowed herself these painful moments, felt it healthy to indulge them, until they tired themselves out. Like children, her thoughts eventually got bored of the same story, and would turn to the future. She would return to the Bureau, lead large-scale cases again. She would track the nefarious and demented. She would save others, and thus save herself.

Even when Paul contacted her about a divorce, his voice oddly professional, she felt confident they were on the right path. He engaged a lawyer—with what money, Ana wondered, but not too deeply—and emailed the papers to sign. It all seemed boilerplate: Paul wanted so little. He hated her apartment. They had no living children for custody issues. He acknowledged that his time spent in Youtopia disqualified him from any legal right to the assets Ana had accumulated while he was gone, which had been a sticking point in other Youtopia-related divorces. Ana felt ready to apply her digital signature, to release Paul into the wilds of whatever life he hoped to lead, when she scrolled to the top and noticed Paul's address: 1576 Sycamore Avenue.

At first, she thought it was a mistake. It wasn't the address of some apartment in Cicero—it was Lonnie's house.

She worked through the plausible explanations: Paul couldn't afford his own place, and so Lonnie took him in, helping him to get on his feet; or worse, Paul was homeless and needed to use Lonnie's address for legitimacy.

But, of course, neither was true. The simplest and most obvious answer came clear in the color in Paul's face, the light in his eyes: he and Lonnie were a couple.

The truth of this hurt, but only briefly. A revitalized Ana recognized that, ignoring her own emotions, this was probably the best thing for both Paul and Lonnie. It may, in truth, have been where they belonged from the start.

Ana phoned Lonnie, who didn't answer. Paul either. She texted for Lonnie to call her back, but after hearing nothing, she went to her computer and composed an email. It took twenty minutes of typing and deleting, wrong wordings and rehashings. The draft peaked at ten paragraphs that she ultimately whittled down to two. She wanted them to know that she was okay, that she was, indeed, happy for them. She wouldn't stand in their way. In fact, she wanted to help them if possible. She wanted them all to be okay.

For two days, Ana received no reply. The divorce papers lingered in her inbox. On the third day, as Ana hit mile five on the gym treadmill, electric music pulsing from her earbuds, her phone finally rang.

She stopped the treadmill and stood with feet splayed on the side tracks. "Hey, Lonnie," she shouted to overcome the gym noise. "Can I call you right back? I just need to step out."

Lonnie's pithy voice shot through the phone. "Just sign the papers."

Ana stood startled. Ten seconds, more, of silence followed.

"Look, Lonnie, I'm glad you called. I really think—"

"Just sign them, Ana. And don't call us anymore."

She hung up. Ana never heard from either of them again.

Looking at Lonnie's socials now, Ana recognized the intentional absence of Paul's pre-Youtopia life, of his post-Youtopia time in Abundant Life. That some therapist may have advised Lonnie and Paul to wipe his life clean didn't help. No past meant no Ana, period. She felt like the contaminated variable in some experiment gone awry, like the person whom everyone important in her life needed to forget.

But in Lonnie's profile, Ana also saw that, by escaping to the Dominican, she had perfectly enacted Paul and Lonnie's plan. They did this to her, but she also did it to herself. They wanted to expunge her, and she obliged. That was not, *could* not, be Anabel Downer—not who she was, nor who she would be from here on out.

She opened a DM and typed a simple message, knowing that Lonnie wouldn't respond, but that the happy couple would have to see it, discuss it, and discard it—knowing that they might choose to erase Ana, but that Ana would no longer erase herself.

Wanted you to hear it from me. I'm back.

***

Though finally back in his own bed, Lane slept in unsteady fits. His stoplight-red alarm clock read 2:12, 2:27, 3:17, 3:40. His dreams flittered between flashes of Downer scolding him for petty mistakes, and an inebriated Serena showering her perspiring body on his. His stomach felt both expanded and empty. He wished he could vacate his body, could float away into the emptiness of deep sleep. He tried not to think of Youtopia. He tried not to think of his parents.

At 4:58 he surrendered to coffee and pushups and ab crunches. He stretched and balanced in tree poses until his limbs turned gelatinous. He risked a few weighted squats and his knee held up. More coffee. Then to his kitchen table, where he spent an hour at his laptop prepping for his performance review.

Proving his past worth would be an easy sell. His stories were well-researched, in-depth—far beyond what an overachieving undergraduate from Purdue could produce. Firing him for someone new would create a cumbersome and costly process. But was that really the argument he wanted to present? That he was entrenched and little more? Instead, he focused on his future potential. He had a monumental lead in the Sonya Young story, exclusive to him. No, not just a lead, something that could change the landscape of the investigation, of Youtopia Reborn itself—could change the world, even.

No, no, he couldn't go that far—Youtopian hyperbole wouldn't save him. He was who he was: better at his job than anyone else at the Beacon. Useful. Valuable.

He entered the office, cleanly shaven and hair slicked back, donned in his only suit, classic black, off the rack but tailored for his long arms and broad shoulders. He wore his father's favorite tie, stripes with a subtle music note pattern. The office felt subdued, quiet for a Tuesday. Millie, also wearing a black suit, met Lane with a smile, but even she seemed understated. She offered a mute hello. She led him to the back room, the place where they hashed out leads and pitches in their weekly meetings, where Millie goaded and cheerled and assigned with her effective charm.

He turned in the doorway, expecting three or more board members aligned on one side of their long, rectangular table. Instead, he only found one, an older woman whose stature and thick glasses vaguely resembled Ruth Bader Ginsberg.

"Mister Samson," she said in a sopranic voice, "please have a seat."

"Can do." He shuffled into a chair. He breathed too loudly; his hands, in his lap, were shaking. "In truth, I was expecting more of you."

"That won't be necessary," the woman said.

From behind him, Lane heard the soft click of Millie closing the door. She hadn't entered, hadn't sat beside him. He was alone.

"Mr. Samson," the woman continued, her eyes over a sleek gray laptop. "Your writing this past year has been good. At times, exceptional."

"I like to think so."

"Your expose on Reintegrator prescription drugs was fine journalism. Local and national appeal. A real eye for detail."

"Yeah. People ate that one up."

"Can you tell me what your future plans are?"

"Well, one day I'd like to settle down, buy a house..."

The woman stared. His joke flopped. Much as he could try to charm her, she would not have it.

"Let's try your next story."

A lump caught in his throat. He inadvertently coughed, instigating something inside him, pitching him into a spell. The woman offered him water from a pitcher, and he took a long drink. With the lump still lingering, in a raspy voice, he began with his past week: where he'd been, the leads he'd pursued. He detailed his imagined stories on Reborn, maybe a series of exposes. He threw out Downer's name like a prize catch. The entire time, the woman, pragmatic down to her single-stud earrings, looked him dead in the eye. She reacted to nothing he said. Lane willed himself not to break eye contact, but their locked stare felt invasive, penetrating. He started to wonder if she was even listening.

He finished, feeling out of breath, as though he'd just finished wind sprints.

"Millicent speaks very highly of you," she said. "It seems you are a good worker."

In the ensuing pause, Lane felt a *however* coming, followed by a doomed proclamation that, unfortunately, came true. For the next five minutes, she couched his layoff in gentle praises: he had great writing, but it was too nuanced; it lacked local flavor; subscriptions were low, and the faithful readers they maintained wanted Huntington fare. Lane alternated from looking at her and closing his eyes, an acute pressure thrumming against the peak of his forehead. Her dark-lined eyes never wavered from him. She was impressively impersonable, implacable at her callous job.

Indignation rose in him, residual from his failed weekend. Serena evading him. Downer and Peterson pushing him aside. Now this: Millie and the Beacon had recalled him here simply to, once again, cast him out.

She finally finished. Lane waited a moment, then said, "You could have told me all this over the phone."

The woman's eyes narrowed. "This is your career, Mr. Samson. We do this as a professional courtesy."

"*Was* my career, you mean."

The woman did nothing in reply.

Lane wanted to stand, to hover over the table. How could his work on the Sonya Young case mean nothing? He had a contact nobody even knew about! He brought Anabel Downer back from obscurity! He felt pressed, boxed in, like he was sixteen again battling under the boards with guys twice his weight. It took everything inside him not to slam his balled fists against the table.

Then the woman slid a piece of paper before him, forcing him to consider what he might lose if he blew up. Mantra Four: *Things will not always go your way. Your negative reactions have consequences.* The woman said *severance package* as if delivering Christmas gifts: three months' pay and benefits, and the promise of a solid, workable recommendation from Millie. She wished him all the best with a handshake he expected to be cold, hard, but it was the opposite. Her eyes finally softened.

Lane's anger melted to an insipid resignation. After all, she simply performed her duty. As much as he would like, this woman was not the villain. Fighting her would do nothing to save him.

***

Peterson greeted Ana outside the Capital Grille restaurant. For all her time in Chicago, Ana had never driven into downtown Milwaukee, into the rough industrialism of the city. Built on steel and cream-colored brick, famously home to a German beer-and-sausage heritage, Milwaukee's inner workings churned like that of a mill itself: methodical, smoke-filled, sweat-stained. The whole city felt like a noir film come to life, all shadows and edges. Ana recognized the scene, felt comfortable in it, though such places could always be deceptive, dangerous if you didn't look close enough.

They passed through the ostentatious outer door into a similar interior with old-fashioned, dim décor, all maroons and golds. Pinnacled chandeliers hovered over thick tables. Pineapple chunks swam in a vast aquarium of vodka. Before Ana and Peterson even reached the hostess table, three separate people recognized him and shook his hand.

"Come here often, do you?" Ana said.

Peterson smiled. "From time to time."

"Doesn't seem the place to discuss sensitive information."

"Sometimes, Miss Downer, it's best to hide in plain sight."

The hostess led them through the dining room, past scores of tables framed by taxidermic animal heads with soft white and brown fur. There were many bucks — a nod to Milwaukee's NBA team — but the most impressive was a ram, its neck thick, its curved horns aglow in soft underlighting. At the back of the restaurant, beside the swinging doors leading to the kitchen, the hostess walked them through an unlabeled, windowless door into a private dining room.

The table was large but set for two. With its crimson walls, silk chairs, and bronze sconces, the room felt like a throwback to old supper clubs, or the back room of some seedy speakeasy.

"Thank you, Sinead," Peterson said to the hostess, who left them with menus and a nod. "See? Even the most public of spaces can still afford privacy."

As the door clicked shut behind them, Ana pressed a forearm to her Glock at her hip. Though it was unlikely that Peterson himself was involved in the abduction, Ana couldn't dismiss it. She needed to be careful. Into such back rooms needed to be the farthest she was willing to go alone.

"All right," she said as Peterson approached his chair. "Tell me what you know."

***

Lane's phone glowed in the bar, dark even though it was hardly past noon. Late 90s boy-band pop played from the candy-colored digital jukebox. The bartender, a woman he vaguely remembered from high school, poured him his second whiskey. The first hit him harder than he expected, the pour deeper and his stomach emptier. The smart move would've been to refuse another, return to his apartment, and sleep. Instead, he sat here in the Tarnation Tavern watching the bartender's second pour reach three fingers. After all, he'd had a terrible 24 hours. He raised the glass to his nearly-healed lip, letting its cold edge rest there. Let the pain cool. Let the sorrows drown.

Whiskey in hand, he stood and walked through the empty bowels of the bar. The jukebox welcomed his touch. He scrolled past the Top 40, the Country and 80s and Frequent Favorites, digging deep into the search engines to find what he was looking for: Tuba Fats Lacen. They only had one track, "Mardi Gras in New Orleans," so, though he'd just lost his job and source of income, though he'd been blowing through what little cash he had, Lane paid the extra ten dollars to download the entirety of *The Legendary Tuba Fats* album, then another five to play it straight through.

As the deep throes of the tuba resounded into the bar, the bartender shot the jukebox, and then Lane, an enquiring look.

"My dad loved jazz," Lane said, returning to his barstool.

"Fine by me." She rearranged bottles of gin, for no apparent reason other than to have something to do. "You look familiar. You play basketball here?"

Lane nodded. "Go Vikes."

"Thought so. I remember my dad saying you were the next—"

"The next Larry Bird. Yeah. Go that a lot, back then."

The bartender took a long look at him. "You mind if I ask... what happened?"

"What didn't?"

The bartender nodded. Then she pushed Lane's wad of bills back to him. "Yeah, well, to hell with 'em. That one's on me." She left him to his drink.

When the drums and trumpet entered, the bartender nodded her head to the beat, though Lane hadn't played it to win her approval—in truth, he chose the record because it recalled for him the only real vacation they'd had as a family, to New Orleans. He was seven, or eight, somewhere in that age of just-remembering. He recalled little of the city itself, snatches of old pillared buildings and salty seafood and damp air. But the sound... he remembered the sound, and his father's fascination with it. The one night his parents had taken Lane out past dark, buskers lined the streets with blaring flutes and trumpets and snare drums and saxophones. Above them, dark clouds amassed. His father guided him and his mother to one of the seemingly hundreds of jazz clubs, this one with large open-air windows covered by aluminum awnings. Inside, a hostess ushered them to a table right before the stage. The band was between sets. His mother ordered a cosmopolitan, the pinkish liquid refracting the low stage light. The band started up again just as, outside, a soft rain tinkled the awnings.

Tuba Fats, by then already a legend, arrived on stage with a heavy swagger. Lane's father became transfixed. For an hour, longer—for Lane, the memory was etched so deep it could have been all night—they listened to Tuba's band and the outside rain flow, jive, play off one another. His father had never given anything that level of attention—his work, their house, Lane's budding basketball obsession. He didn't know his father had such devotion in him. From that night on, his father played constant jazz records in the house, the sound becoming the background music of Lane's life.

Then, suddenly, his parents were gone. In a fit of rage, through free-flowing tears, Lane smashed his father's record collection. But when he entered Youtopia, the jazz inexplicably followed. From grocery store speakers, in dance clubs with Serena or other women, on the basketball court, the breezy melody of trumpets and pianos and hi-hats filled his life. His mind resurrected his father — but not his mother, for reasons Lane was afraid to contemplate, would *never* contemplate, not his mother — and together they flew to jazz festivals across the country. The music became a comfort, something he could never leave behind. His FAR cohorts reported similar things — chain-smoking or surfing or stuffed animal collecting — that, of course, Henrick would inevitably discourage in their Reintegration. Mantra Fourteen: *Youtopian comforts are harmful backslides.* They were roads leading to the one destination to which they could never return.

And yet, sitting in Tarnation, the tuba blaring, Lane felt the exact opposite. Instead of sinking him backward, toward Youtopia or depression or worse, Tuba Fats dragged him from the dredges. He was jobless, yes, and hemorrhaging money, but Serena called *him*, and had answered his recent call. *He* brought Downer back to the Sonya Young case. If he could find Serena, he could still get the story. He could still help her. Nothing had fundamentally changed about his plan, his path forward. He'd never abandoned a story. He was still the same Lane Samson. He was still here.

As the record switched tracks, he pulled his phone and texted Quinn.

Need your help again. Meet me at Q&C?

Lane waited only a few moments. Quinn, like most tech-savvy people, reliably replied.

This about voicemail girl?

Yes.

Meet you in twenty.

Fifteen minutes later, he met Quinn inside the hectic front office area of Q&C. Quinn wore a fat pair of sunglasses that Lane assumed he would take off, but he never did. Tech magazines draped tables and the floor like ocean flotsam; metal parts and cables huddled in sloppy corner piles; a row of Apple monitors stood in military-like display. The space was more packed than before, resembling some teenage hacker's basement.

"You should fire your cleaning crew," Lane said.

"We're moving. Or maybe downsizing. People don't window shop anymore. Online or bust, man."

Lane nodded down the hall. "Hauling all the backroom stuff too?"

"One of these days." Quinn tossed his keys on the reception desk. He sipped from a gas station coffee. "That's how you can repay me. Help me lug all this to my apartment."

"I can do that. Whatever you need."

Quinn's shoulders dropped. "That was *way* too easy. You're going to ask me to do something illegal."

"I need to find her, Quinn."

Quinn sucked air through his teeth. "Sheesh, man. I don't know. Phone tapping is serious business. Even if you can get past their defenses, the phone companies are keyed-up. You gotta bounce madcap—like *around the world* crazy—or they might pick you off. That's *felony* charges we're talking."

"And yet I need you to try."

"Damn it." Quinn took a distracted drink, then nearly gagged. His face shivered as he swallowed. "Great. You made me burn my throat to boot. You've tried her friends? Mutual contacts?"

"I tried breaking into her apartment."

"Yowza." Quinn tapped his fingers in a patterned rhythm, right to left and left to right, across the desk. He finally took off his sunglasses. "Gotta ask man: does she want you to find her?"

"Yes." Lane said it instinctually, not knowing if it was true.

"Because, my friend, this kinda sounds like high-level stalker shit."

Lane sighed. His first impulse was to cajole, to bargain, to find Quinn's buttons and press with a firm thumb. Quinn, for all his grandstanding, had lived no saintly life. He had likely done the same thing Lane now asked of him, or worse. Lane recalled a high school rumor—unsubstantiated but plausible—that Quinn hacked the grading software and had, for upwards of six months, altered test scores for himself and anyone willing to pay. When administration finally caught wind, they searched and interrogated, but since all Quinn's clientele were as culpable as he was—subject to receiving the terrible grades they actually earned along with punishment—they all remained impressively mum. They bonded together in a mob-like code of dishonor. With no paper trail, no informants, and no real computer savvy, the administration couldn't reliably retract grades without facing backlash, or even lawsuits. In the end, Quinn and the rest got away with it. And though he couldn't advertise it, Quinn's reputation as an underhanded technological mastermind was born.

But Lane was also tired—tired of persuading, of lying, of feeling underhanded himself. What he asked of Quinn appeared nefarious—*high-level stalker shit*—and yet his intentions were pure. He didn't want to doctor test scores, or to harass Serena. He wanted to help her.

He wanted the truth of it all. So, standing in Quinn's pandemonic shop, watching his friend sip scalding coffee, he once again divulged his story.

With Quinn, he gave almost everything: his journey to the Dominican, Downer and Peterson at Youtopia Towers, Millie and his job. Put together, the story sounded fantastical and yet all too real, like a strange mix of dream and memory. It was Youtopia without the luster and gloss of inevitable success.

Quinn absorbed it without saying a word. His brow raised and wrinkled in equal measure. When Lane finally finished, Quinn set down his coffee and rubbed at his eyes as though he had emerged from a dark movie theater to the light of day.

"Dude," he said. "Dominican Republic? FBI agents?" Then he laughed, deep and bellowing. "I love it! It's crazytown, man."

"Glad you find my life amusing."

"Sorry, man, it's just... I've been dealing with all this BS." He floated his arms about him. "I needed something with a little *umph*, you know?"

"So you'll help me find her."

Quinn's face turned serious. "Last time, my friend. If she bails again, you gotta wake up and smell the truck stop coffee."

***

A tall waiter brought their orders: a pepper-crusted steak for Peterson, a quinoa and beet salad for Ana. As the waiter left, Peterson asked Ana for permission to eat the steak in her presence.

"I should have asked about your dietary restrictions," he said.

"Don't let me stop you."

Peterson nodded and cut into the steak delicately, inspecting it like a surgeon. Ana picked around her salad. She wanted to adopt Peterson's methodical pace, wanted to let him gradually reveal what he knew, but at this rate, she might never get it from him.

She decided to push. "What do you know about Sonya's will?"

Peterson set down his fork and knife. "Unfortunately, as much as you do. That one may exist."

"You've never seen it?"

He shook his head. "I've never been one to focus on the unknown. I prefer a clearer path."

"Which is?"

"I'm afraid I can't say."

"Then why am I here?" She placed her palms up. "If this is going to work, you need to let me in, Daniel."

"I don't disagree with you. You recognize I was rather quick to accept your meeting request."

"The Board is the problem, then."

"Unfortunately, after our... *unsuccessful* meeting yesterday, the discussion focused almost solely on the fact that you were unable to conclude the last case. The vote was nearly unanimous."

"Nearly? Someone voted yes?"

"One abstention."

"Who?"

"I'm afraid I don't know."

Ana plied at her napkin, folding and refolding. The Board had roadblocked any straight attempts at investigation, which meant Ana needed to try other routes. "So we don't tell them. We pursue Sonya on our own. You're savvy enough to hide our fingerprints."

"What you suggest would get me fired."

"The alternative may cost Sonya her life."

Peterson removed his glasses and rubbed at his eyes with the meat of his palms. His eyebrows puffed and mussed. "I shouldn't be telling you this." His surreptitious face took on the air of a spouse about to reveal an illicit affair. "We have a lead."

Ana sat back in genuine surprise. "That's good. Who do the Feds have on it?"

"They know nothing. As you can understand, I don't put much trust in outside institutions."

Ana took a bite of her salad. The old FBI version of her would tell Peterson to alert the Fed and local PD immediately, that he was being reckless, irrational. But this new version understood that FBI intervention would lose her both the case and Peterson's trust. "What type of lead?"

"A hacker, though not in the same sense as before." He shifted his glasses. "One of the main differences in Youtopia and Youtopia Reborn is how we oversee the Immerser experience. When you investigated the initial murders, you Observed from Central Control—large screens, akin to video surveillance. Now, we do far more than that. We Intervene."

"Intervene? Meaning... you enter Youtopias?"

"Correct. To guide when necessary." Peterson sat back now, in the familiar territory of explaining his company's inner workings. "From the start, Sonya was against it. As you know, she has always been a purist. She believed inserting ourselves into one's Youtopia amounted to tampering. Corruption of the young Immerser's mind. A cardinal sin."

"But you thought otherwise."

"I have a broader view. Adults, and even adolescents, who entered the first Youtopia had previously established formations of the world. For them, the mind could navigate itself because of preconceived barriers and boundaries. They had passed, for example, the mirror stage. They'd imprinted on other humans, and recognized their own existence."

"Intervention is a teaching tool."

"We quickly discovered that putting a child into Reborn too early severs necessary connections. Like building a house before pouring the foundations, so to speak — they were left on shaky ground."

Ana sensed an opening, a way to see how much Peterson really knew about the past. "Sonya also believed that Youtopia tended toward certain... illicit desires. I know it plagued her to see her creation reduced to a sadistic slaughterhouse. Do you see this in Reborns too?"

Peterson's eyes moved upward, a potential indicator of lying. But then, Ana never put much stock in facial expressions. His eyes tended to wander, to not look at her own, even when telling the truth.

"That feels reductive," he finally said. "If Sonya believed that, Reborn would not be here."

"Still, I assume children aren't exempt. Some of these Immersers must lead disturbing lives."

"Far less, I would say, and muted. Adults tend to enjoy... *bending* the rules. Manipulation, subversion. Egotism, one might say."

"And kids don't?"

"Reborn Immersers are young enough to *create* the reality they desire. Subversion of the rules becomes unnecessary. As such, many of the Reborns build their realities around positive attributes: acceptance, perseverance. Love."

She smiled. "Sounds too good to be true."

Peterson took a final bite of steak, chewing it down before speaking. "When it's not, we have Interventions. If an Immerser presses too hard on those *illicit desires* you speak of — "

"You punish them," Ana interrupted.

"No. We simply offer another path."

The waiter arrived to remove their plates. Peterson thanked him with a nod. After he left, Ana said, "So this lead... I'm guessing someone Intervened where they don't belong."

"We didn't think it possible. But then, we didn't with Youtopia either."

But it was Sonya then, Ana wanted to say. *Nobody hacked Youtopia except your boss and her bodyguard.*

Instead, she said, "Tell me about this Intervener."

"Just over a year ago—mere months after Reborn launched—we detected the hack." He said this with a visible wince. "Likely a Trojan Horse, dropped into one of the closed servers at the Cradle Centers. We flushed the servers, chased him out, but the premise was set: someone could find a way in. It was all but certain he would return."

"What has he accessed?"

"He floats through various Reborns. Until now, he has had no malicious intent. He's there just to—well, just to *live*."

"He lives in Immersers' Reborns?"

"Yes."

"Doesn't that affect the Immerser?" Ana asked. "Having an intruder in their mind?"

"Certainly. If he ever interacted directly with the Immerser... well, we don't really know what might happen. But he has proven adept at hovering beyond the Immerser's immediate radar."

"How is that possible?"

"The human mind is vast, and adheres to object permanence, so when Immersers vacate an area in their Reborn, those spaces don't disappear. Instead, they enter a mental stasis, awaiting the return of the conscious mind."

"Like empty rooms," Ana said.

"An individual Immerser can host hundreds. For the most creative, thousands or more."

"And the hacker lives in these static places."

Peterson nodded. "In those spaces, he feels no pain, no fear of danger. Youtopia Reborn still offers all these things, even if stolen."

Ana immediately recognized the obvious: this intruder would want *Reborn for All.* Peterson's hacker had a clear motive.

"Do you have records of the people who entered the Cradle Centers?"

"Yes. But with the tours, with employees and oversight, that number is quite large."

"I'll still look at them."

"Until recently," Peterson said, "we believed he'd moved somewhere overseas: Romania, Czechia maybe. But the abduction has turned our thinking domestic."

"You've never tried to track him?"

"Tracing a server is, unfortunately, a fool's errand." His face turned grave. "I believe the best way to find him is to catch him in the act."

"You mean, hunt him down in Reborn?"

"He has his favorites. And the kidnapping has emboldened him. If we can accost him, we should be able to make a positive ID."

"You can't see him on the Feeds?"

"Unfortunately, there are no *Feeds*, as you conceive of them, not of those thousands of unconscious spaces."

"So you Intervene in an Immerser's world and, what... *feel* him out?"

Peterson nodded. "We believe this presents our best opportunity to find him."

"Who is *we*?"

Peterson didn't reply.

"You're telling me all this, so you must want my help." Ana sensed something in his eyes. "Do you want *me* to Intervene?"

He shook his head. "I'm sorry. The Board—"

"Despises me. I know. Do they know everything you've just told me?"

"I'd rather not say."

Ana sighed. She didn't want to show visible frustration, but Peterson's droll delivery of this information—of a potential suspect— crawled under her skin. After this conversation, he seemed less like a suspect, and more like a fragile man without the fortitude to wield his newfound power. He needed to be stronger. She risked a hand across the table, onto Peterson's wrist adorned with his large-faced watch. He responded as she hoped, with a softening of his shoulders.

"Daniel," she said, "you don't trust the people you work with, so trust me. I can help you find this guy. Together, we can save Sonya."

His eyes considered for a moment. Then the waiter interjected himself again, pressing a dessert menu before each of them. Peterson seemed to recall where he was, who he was with, and what was at stake for him if such a collaborative gambit with Ana failed.

His shoulders squared. "I will press the Board," he said. "Without their approval, having you Intervene will only make matters worse."

"Worse than Sonya dying?"

"Don't," Peterson said. His voice, for the first time, sounded markedly pained. "Don't make me make that choice."

***

- 103 -

Lane landed at MSP well into the evening, with the July sun casting its last crimson glow in the west. The airport was pristine, packed. He passed table upon table with gleaming pads offering games and entertainment. An artificial lilac fragrance misted from the bathroom stalls. As he rinsed his hands, looking at himself in the mirror, he could only think of his insane previous eight days. In that time, he had been to the Twin Cities, the Dominican, Chicago and Wisconsin, home, and now back to the Twin Cities. He had traveled far. Hopefully, he would find his end here.

He stopped at the airport's sole open restaurant, a beachy Americana joint decorated in crossing surfboards with shark bites on each end, and ordered a coffee. The bartender put on a new pot just for him and asked him where he was off to, assuming he would travel on a redeye out of the city, not deeper in.

"To hell and back," Lane said, which he expected to earn a laugh. The bartender only smiled politely. She didn't charge him for the coffee and wished him safe travels.

In his Uber up 35W, into the heart of Minneapolis, he watched the blur of vast suburbia pass to the sound of Coltrane's *A Love Supreme*. The address — 1786 Fremont — revealed an older, two-story L-shaped building that lined the intersection. He thanked his driver, tipped as generously as he could afford, which was little. She sped off like an animal uncaged.

Across the street, a drunk couple fumbled their way down the sidewalk, the man in a vintage zoot suit, the woman in a sequined dress and faux fur shawl. Lane thought the woman might be Serena, but the couple walked on, never once turning toward him and the apartment, acknowledging nothing in the world but each other.

He pulled out his phone and texted Quinn.

She still there?

Quinn quickly replied.

Still there. Cutting the cord. God speed man.

Lane approached the intercom system. Apartment 231 was listed under the name Mack Flanders, a person Lane had never met but whom, according to old Instagram posts, Serena had befriended a year ago. Lane pressed lightly, expecting some sort of mechanical buzz to interrupt the relative quiet, but it was soundless on his end. He counted to thirty, then tried again. Still nothing. He took out his phone to call her, the thought of spanning six hundred miles only to rely again on a phone call weighing on him.

Then, behind the glass door, an elderly man with a reluctant shorthair cat on a leash shuffled down the interior stairs. His eyes glossy from cataracts, his hands arthritic around the leash, the man ushered out the cat and said nothing when Lane held the door ajar behind him. The night outside was fully dark. Lane slipped through the door.

Inside, the decrepitude of the building revealed itself immediately in the stains on the wall, in the musty smell of body odor, like an unwashed jersey stuck in the back of some forgotten locker. Lane took the skinny stairwell to the second floor. At door 231, the final number hung crooked from a missing nail. Flanders's door had no peephole, no knocker. Years of hands had worn away the knob's brass finish. He almost put his ear to the door, but feared how it would look if someone, the cataracted man or otherwise, returned to the hallway. He recalled skulking in Serena's apartment building, the skeptical neighbor. If someone called the police on him, he would have no defense.

Then he heard the metallic shing of a deadbolt slide, so quick his body froze. The dry door hinges creaked. A woman's soft, throaty voice let out a shush of air as the door swung inward.

And out backed Serena, her shoulders slouched, her hair bedraggled, arms full of something.

Lane stood close to the opening, too close. Serena stumbled into him, tripping him backward with surprising force.

"What the hell?" she said, her voice gone brash. Her eyes immediately registered disbelief. "Laney?"

She turned her body to him, and Lane saw that she carried not something in her arms, but someone: a young boy with straight, pitch-black hair and dimpled cheeks. A boy who clung to Serena as only a child would cling to his mother.

A boy who resembled nothing more than a youthful Sonya Young herself.

JOSEPH REIN

Interlude: West of Omaha

The outer door of the Fat Toad at midnight. Note the drunken revelers, the patient Lyft drivers, the homeless couple with backpacks at their feet. Note the relative calm.

Time: Bar close.

At rise: The Graduate flees with intent. His driver waits in a compact Toyota. A smaller woman in an unseasonable scarf, hands diligently on the wheel, eyes ever forward, she speaks little and smiles less. Her personality comes through only in the samba music that rattles her speakers.

Observe the Graduate fidgeting, leg jumping. An undeserved ire rises.

Escape the blazing light-pollution glare of downtown. The darkness of the countryside feels comprehensive. Rural roads and lolling land abound.

The driver tightens her grip on the wheel. The roads wend and slink serpentine as her headlights cast slithering beams before them.

At a lonely gas station perched on a clandestine corner, the Graduate stops her. He steals from the car. Inside the station, he hunts down two shrink-wrapped sandwiches, browning bananas, a bag of vinegar chips. He pays in silence.

Back on the road, the Graduate does not eat his wares. At an unmarked, nondescript intersection, he stops her a final time. Nothing in sight, not a farmhouse or silo or even another car. He pays with his phone and silently exits.

The Toyota sighs dust as it flees. His driver will return to the city, the soft shiver in her spine dissipating with each mile she places between herself and this desolate man, this desolate nowhere. By the time she picks up her next fare, she will have shaken the Graduate. By tomorrow, he will fade beyond memory.

In distant fields, nocturnal animals observe the Graduate as he walks the dark road, plastic bag swaying at his side. Half a mile he traverses until he reaches his small coupe. Its engine rumbles to life. The dry, fetid scents of the heartland waft in through his windows as he passes fields of endless corn and soy. Farther down the road we go: beyond these farms, we reach untended land plagued by the July drought, the ground arid and dust-filled, pocked with sandbur and patchy grass too stubborn to die.

Note, however, the Graduate's body releasing its pinched tension. Note how he feels, finally, at home.

Gravel crunches under his feet as he approaches his door. The stoop has shifted in the summer heat, the cast-iron rail leaning like a tired old man. One key for the knob, another for the deadbolt. Diligently, his German Shepherd Roscoe surges behind the door and lets loose her grisly growl. The Graduate savors her bark.

When he does enter, he relishes her murderous eyes in the second before they recognize him. Roscoe leaps, tail flapping and haunches shaking. Nine years old, graying around her eyes, and still she pounces like a pup. She noses the plastic bag. The Graduate scratches and nuzzles Roscoe like kin, asking her questions to which she can only frenetically snip in reply.

With her paws clawing at his back, the Graduate moves through the living room to the kitchen, passing the tables where used brushes with dried tips and half-used paint jars rest spattered between the half-finished Russian nesting dolls he will soon bring to life. He walks beyond them to the pantry, where a can of wet food awaits his good girl. Roscoe attacks the metal bowl he places before her. Within seconds it is gone.

He makes for his small hallway, fusty with dust and age. A noise like a washing machine churns from the room at the hall's end. He passes one door, closed and padlocked on his end, then another, his smaller bedroom.

The final door stands open to a nearly pitch-black, larger bedroom. Even so, we can immediately see it...

Behold the haunting outlines of his creation: a strange mechanical Apparatus that appears alive, extending with appendages from a thrumming central hub. The machine whirrs and thrums in arrhythmic synchronicity with the heartbeat of the old man – Arthur – connected to its tentacled arms.

The Graduate speaks, though Arthur does not, cannot, respond. Arthur's mind resides elsewhere. This the Graduate knows.

The Graduate navigates the thick wires entangling Arthur's seated body like a spider prowling his successful web, checking each line, running a finger along the suction-cup contact points with Arthur's forehead and forearms and torso. One has dried out; he circles its edges with petroleum jelly, feeling the faint pulse beneath. He gently, approvingly squeezes a half-filled IV bag labeled KALI.

Then, suddenly, he stops. Panic in his eyes.

Something is wrong.

The Graduate focuses on Arthur's hand, on the heartbeat so fast we can almost feel it. Imagine it rising like the Tell-Tale Heart from the floorboards of the body's chest, reverberating over the drum of the Apparatus. The old man's lips twitch. His eyes flutter as though ready to open.

The Graduate rushes down the hall. On his kitchen table, he shoves his beloved nesting dolls to the floor like common refuse. Then the couch, the end table... The Graduate needs something, and badly.

He pauses briefly at the cellar door, his panic spiking. It can't be, his eyes seem to say. It can't be.

He darts to his small bedroom and tosses his disheveled bedsheets. He's in such a hurry he nearly throws his missing treasure – his laptop – to the ground with them.

He stops. We expect relief as he picks up the laptop. Instead, with his other hand, he slaps his head, hard. The smack echoes. Then again, and again, he flagellates himself with dictatorial intensity. He draws blood; he could knock himself out. In his eyes blossom self-inflicted tears. Even in the dim light, we can see the bloodshot-red burn.

Just as quick, the Graduate runs back to Arthur. He plugs into the Apparatus and opens a screen resembling a security video. Fractions of seconds race on a meter. All appears dark, yet slight rainbow outlines of light pulse, as though he watches the back of someone's eyelids.

Then, in a blink, the screen enlivens.

The Graduate smiles. He recognizes this stunning place with horizons of neon, its buildings in perplexing geographic shapes. A fantasy. A Youtopia.

But then – an Outsider aggressively steps into view. Upright, with thick glasses and heavy brow, this man is far too old to be the Immerser.

The Graduate seizes.

GRADUATE: Get the hell out, Arthur! (Hammers a finger on the laptop, upping the audio feed)

OUTSIDER: (to Arthur, though with the screen it feels as though speaks to the Graduate, to us all) Tell me your name.

GRADUATE: *(Darts immediately to the Apparatus)*

OUTSIDER: I said, who are —

GRADUATE: No no no. *(Cuts the feed. Rushes to pluck the suctioning tubes as the old man moans and writhes, his frail body pulsating with each pull. Wipes at Arthur's perspiring forehead)* I'm here, Arthur. I'm here.

ARTHUR: *(Sucks a torturous gulp of barren air, the blue sinewy tendons of his hand bulging like crossroads across the desolate desert of his feathered skin. Writhes in pain — nothing but pain)*

GRADUATE: No. *(Reaches beneath Arthur's neck, his waist, hoisting him from the chair with all the care he can muster. Carries him down to his bed, a full-sized mattress without a frame, his tortured other place, as his convulsing body begs for relief)* No. *(Indecision crests in waves on his face)* No. *(Raises a fist, as if to again self-flagellate)*

GRADUATE: No. *(Breathes deep, exhales into the dry night. Pounds his chest with a fist, willing confidence into himself)* No. *(Gathers the container of petroleum jelly. Removes his shirt, the slim contours of his body and face reflecting through the crystalline laptop screen)*

GRADUATE: You want me, asshole? Come and get me.

Chapter 7

Someone was calling out to him, the voice a familiar, deep baritone. *Lane. Lane, I'm here.* His father? He stepped to the voice. His bedroom walls surrounded him, oddly concave and bare. Dark. He was standing in his bedroom, but also in the Viewing Chamber at the Youtopia Reborn Cradles, amidst a child's somnolent dream. He reached up to feel the goggles, to peel them off and return to what was real, but he couldn't feel his own fingers on his face.

Not his bedroom: a motel room, brought clear by the ugly beige walls, the chalky air. He sat up on a hard queen-sized bed, floral bedspread and runner below him. Bad art dappled the walls. The sun burned fiery outlines around two curtained windows that couldn't contain it. A motel, yes. On the adjacent bed, Serena and her son curled against one another, their foreheads and knees forming a twisted heart.

He looked to his phone to remind himself: July 22, 9:38 a.m., Wednesday morning. They occupied a small motel in the middle of nowhere, Minnesota. Last night, they'd been only a few miles down the road from Flanders's apartment, driving at a feverish clip in Serena's small Nissan, dodging dangerously between highway cars and eighteen-wheelers, when Serena rolled down her window and abruptly threw out her cellphone, condemning it to immediate roadkill.

"What are you doing?" Lane asked.

She reached out her hand. "Yours next."

"What? Rene, I don't know who you think is following—"

"*You* found me, didn't you?" She turned her stark stare to him. "You telling me it wasn't because of my phone?"

Lane stayed silent. She had him. Her face brimmed with a frenzied energy, and yet her eyes were focused, lucid. She seemed in control, more than Lane himself.

"Okay, I'll ditch it. Just let me get some numbers down first."

She directed him to the glove box, to a sole pen and stack of napkins. He pulled his contacts, looking for people he might need: Quinn, of course. Millie, Downer. In his haste, he almost forgot Henrick.

That was it. His phone contained far more music than people. He held, on a feathery napkin, the scant list of those he might need, who might need him.

Once he'd banished his phone to the asphalt, he turned to Serena. "Where exactly are we going?" He looked back to Serena's son, who watched them with intent eyes. He lowered his voice. "On the voicemail that night—"

"Laney," Serena said. "I will explain everything. But let's put some real estate between us and Minneapolis first, all right?"

Lane said nothing as they continued on. At intervals, he looked back to her son, a replica of Sonya Young, even down to the long, stark black hair ponytailed behind his head. On his shoulders rested red, donut-sized headphones attached to an old iPod in his lap. Lane expected him to put on the headphones, or to drift to sleep, but he simply stared out the window, watching the world pass.

After a particularly long stare, Serena said, "You can talk to him, Laney. He's human too, just a smaller one."

Lane nodded. "What's your name, little guy?"

The boy's eyes migrated upward. "Andrew."

"Well," Lane said, extending his hand awkwardly over his seat, "I'm Lane. Nice to meet you, Andy."

"Andrew," the boy repeated.

"It's a whole thing," Serena said, then looked at Andrew in the rearview. "A boy should be called what he wants, right, Andrew?"

Andrew nodded his head, offering a soft smile in which Lane could clearly see the resounding ripples of their relationship.

"Not a single nickname," Serena said. "You want a death stare? Try *Scout* or *Champ*. I'm surprised he let you get away with *little guy*."

Lane turned his gaze out the windshield. "I know it's not my business, but can I ask—"

"Don't worry," Serena cut in, beating him, as she always used to, to his own punch. "He isn't yours."

"Didn't think he was."

"I mean, are you kidding? Andrew here's my little munchkin. Shit. You didn't hear that, Andrew." She appraised Lane with her eyes. "You're Bigfoot."

"And you're charming as ever," Lane said.

Serena flashed her close-lipped smile, tilting her head in that adolescent *Who, me?* way that Lane couldn't resist, then or now.

"Besides," she said, "Andrew here's a language whiz. Piano prodigy too. You should see those little fingers wail. His father was a musician, naturally."

"Naturally."

They drove well past midnight, until even Serena admitted she needed to stop. Lane felt a healthy fatigue, one bred of a long, impossible day. He had found Serena. They were checking into a motel room in Rothsay, Minnesota together. Things were finally going his way. As he drifted to a much-needed sleep, he had felt oddly at home.

Sitting up in the motel bed, he needed to recapture that feeling now. It was still there. He needed only to find it again.

He turned to Serena, lying on her side, her arm covering half her face. Her dark hair draped down, her deep, open-mouthed breathing, reminded Lane of a forgotten memory: he and Serena occupying a beach on the eastern Mexico shoreline. The sun rose resplendent over the ocean. Lane had dragged Serena from their bed to witness it, to soak in at least one before their vacation ended. After mere moments, she fell back asleep in her reclined chair. Lane wanted to softly shake her awake, but instead of watching the sunrise, the bleeding, horizon reds simmering into a cascade of oranges and yellows against the morning clouds, Lane instead watched Serena. Her eyes fluttered behind her beautiful, resting eyelids. The sunbeams settled on her tanned skin like a flattering spotlight. Like they were made only for her.

But no, it wasn't a memory — it was Youtopia. That beach, that trip, never happened. It wasn't real.

He was slipping. Was this Youtopia too? Was he sitting on some begrimed couch in an apartment like Rickie's, drugged and dreaming? He couldn't be with Serena again. Her lithe body, her lupine breaths... This wasn't real.

In Henrick's voice, he heard Mantra Three: *Separate the real from the unreal.*

He was getting mixed up. They'd stolen away in the night like thieves. Had he really thrown away his phone? How could he know what was real? Pinch himself — but Youtopia had pain too, just none that lingered. No headaches like the one now playing its symphony through his skull. No anxiety, no paranoia either — nothing like the paralyzing doubts he felt now.

He looked upward, staring at the stained motel ceiling as his heart pounded thunderous drums in his chest. Mexico wasn't real, but this was.

This was real. This was real.

***

In her room, Ana indulged in a mediocre breakfast while calling Peterson at set fifteen-minute intervals. After two hours, she gave up hope that he would answer. She listened again to Peterson's generic voicemail message: *You have reached the personal line of Dr. Daniel Peterson. If you need immediate assistance, please dial...*

She would return to Youtopia Towers, to demand his attention. She'd aggravate the guards if need be. In her years as an FBI Agent, access was granted. With the heat of the badge shining on them, few could say no. She needed to impress that same urgency upon Peterson, even if she no longer held the authority behind it. She needed that part of her old self, even if only a shadow.

As if cued, her phone buzzed a familiar number. She was surprised it had taken him this long. Still, a part of her instinctively bristled, her body raising its guard. She'd forgotten that feeling, the strange mix of pit-of-the-stomach dread and adrenalized exhilaration accompanying every call from her former boss and head of the FBI Violent Crimes Division, Bruce Klose.

"About time," Ana said.

"Shoot me straight." Bruce, as always, cut to the point. "What'd you think you'd accomplish in the goddamn Dominican?"

"It wasn't about accomplishing anything. Life isn't always measured in cases solved."

"For us it is."

A pause followed. Ana imagined Bruce nodding to himself for his wisdom.

"If it wasn't," he continued, "you wouldn't be poking around Youtopia Reborn."

"Bruce, you haven't been tailing me, have you?"

"Let's cut the shit," Bruce said, his tone taking on its paternal, caustic bite. "You need to step away."

She laughed. Though he would never admit it, Bruce always admired strength, even — or especially — in women inferiors. He wanted pushback, a fighter. So Ana would fight.

"Not happening, Bruce."

He let out a huff. "Good to see the Dominican hasn't changed you."

"I'm serious. Peterson took two meetings with me, one in private. I know I can help."

"I'm not talking from their end. With what happened last time... Ana, your face is the last thing we need associated with this."

She bristled. In her temples, she felt faint pulses, like the lingering vibrations of a strong migraine. After just months in the Dominican, her migraines had lessened, both in frequency and intensity. She hadn't had a serious one in half a year. Something of Bruce's voice, of the stresses of her former job, awakened the suggestion in her body.

"There is no *we* anymore, Bruce," she said. "I don't care about the press. You didn't used to either. I can catch this guy — that's what matters."

"With what intel? Who's your cyber?"

"Cyber isn't the only—"

"Ana," Bruce interjected. "You chose to get out. So stay out."

She felt the phone, hot in her hand, and fought the impulse to throw it across her room.

Bruce continued. "I'm just trying to—"

"I know what you're trying to do. I tolerated this save-me-from-myself bullshit when you were my boss, but you're not anymore." She stood, her legs light, her body dizzy from fast-flowing blood and fury. "Do me a favor. When I solve this case, don't ask me to come back. The answer is no."

***

Andrew showered. Serena still slept prostrate on her bed, her hair snaking in a strewn mess across the pillow. Lane pulled a peek of curtain to permit the high sun across their room.

He believed Serena about Sonya Young, about being in danger. He did. But he needed more from her. He needed to gain some footing.

He moved to wake her, sitting gently on the bed. In the sliver of sunlight, she looked peaceful. Her skin sheened. He imagined her in some dream-like paradise, her mind's own Youtopia, though he had no idea what that would be for her. Perhaps such haphazard dramas — secrecies, nights in seedy motels, life on the lam — were exactly what made a person like Serena thrive. Perhaps, deep inside her, dragging her only child along some high-stakes, life-or-death road was perfection.

Her eyes opened suddenly but softly, without the intuitive fear of waking unaware. Her lips curved upward in a smile. She took Lane's hand in hers, pulled it to her sweat-sparkled face, and nestled into it like an animal seeking comfort.

"Listen, Serena. We—"

She moved his fingers to her lips. His body flushed with heat, with something he hadn't felt for a long time, not with Serena or any woman. Her warm breath ran along his fingertips, into his palm. She reached with her other hand and pulled him down.

The shower water from the bathroom ran, and Lane thought for a brief second of Andrew returning to this, to them. But then Serena brushed her mouth to his neck, gently kissing the stubble that had grown there. Then up to his ear, her tongue sliding around its curves. Her hair redolent of tea tree oil, her hands gripping at his shoulder blades, all pulled him back through the years since they'd last been together. Serena simply, sensually slid out of her clothes. Her dark nipples perked to his touch. She unbuttoned his pants, worked his underwear down to his ankles and slid immediately atop him. Her weight pressed down on him, welcome and warm. When he entered her, he no longer felt any anxiety in his chest, in his mind. He felt the moment. He felt only Serena.

After, she nestled into him as though they had always been lovers. He buried his head into her hair, the sharp scent transporting him back to her college bedroom — her adolescent pink bedspread, the Norah Jones and Vampire Weekend posters on her wall, a thrift store armchair she never used in the corner. This, Lane remembered, was the magnetic force of Serena that kept him coming back. She was mercurial, yes — like riding an addictive roller coaster both exhilarating and nauseating: you wanted more and needed less — and yet she had this side as well, a side you only saw if she let you close enough. That side slowed down and gave herself to you, fully, attention and mind and body. That side needed you. In these moments, he felt exclusive, singled out. Maybe even loved. Lane had never felt that with anybody, not even his parents, until Serena. He certainly hadn't felt it since.

The shower in the bathroom stopped. Serena loosened in Lane's arms but didn't rise. She looked at him with her intense brown eyes. "Still got it, you dog."

He laughed, genuine and deep. "Not because I'm practiced, I can promise you."

"But leaving the socks on?" She pointed to his feet. "That's new."

"Swept up in the moment, I guess," he lied.

Serena spun to her back, her hands behind her head, her breasts flattening on her chest. Her lack of self-consciousness, her utter comfort in her body, had always impressed him. "Lane Samson... My oh my. Life's happy accidents." She eyed the stained ceiling with wonder, as though looking at the stars.

"It wasn't exactly an accident," he said, sensing an opening. He didn't want to sour the mood, but he also couldn't wait. "The call, your voicemail... Do you really think you're in danger?"

Instead of answering, she stood. She searched for her underwear entangled in the sheets. Methodically, with a placid calm, she put on her shorts and tank top.

"I'm just trying to understand, Rene. How long have you known? How did you find—"

She held up a hand to silence him. He turned to the bathroom, expecting Andrew standing there, but she simply wanted him to stop talking. She grabbed her leather backpack-style purse and pulled from it a worn, accordion-style brown envelope.

"Here," she said, handing it to him.

Inside, standard mail envelopes in various stages of disrepair clumped together like roadside debris. Many were yellowed, fraying. The smell of old paper wafted into the air, as though he'd unearthed the archives of a forgotten library.

"Once a year, exactly on my birthday."

She picked one for Lane. No return address, though its postmark stamp placed the sender near Boston. From inside, he pulled a generic Hallmark birthday card with an Emperor penguin hovering over a fluffy gray child. The inside of the card, in a feminine handwritten script, simply read: *Watching over you always.*

"Creepy," Lane said.

"Has to be her, right? See, check this one. She wasn't exactly hiding it."

She handed him an oversized envelope with Peruvian postage and international ink stamps across the front. Inside, a similarly generic card held the same salutation.

"Why didn't she write anything else?" he asked.

"Your guess is as good as mine." She touched the inside of the card. "I'm sure part of her wants to pretend I never existed. I'm the one mistake she needs to forget. But the controlling part—that alpha-female—takes over. A *mistake*? Sonya Young doesn't make mistakes! Type-A Mama Bear needs to keep her tabs."

She took his hand again. "I know I sound crazy sometimes. When we were together before—all the lies I told—I know now that it was my way of protecting myself. If nobody took me seriously, then I didn't have to hide all the time." She looked in his eyes. "I'm not saying it was right, just that... Shit, Laney, I'm sorry for putting you through all that. I know I'm a hard one to love."

He flipped through the envelopes. If Young had truly sent them, they represented a strange scrapbook for an even stranger relationship. Since college, since she'd known Lane, Serena had dealt with this all. He'd cared deeply for her and knew nothing of such a fundamental part of her. He had no idea who she truly was.

And yet, on the road the night before, Lane had told Serena nothing about his parents. And his socks — part of him didn't want her to know he'd been an Immerser. He held back his anxiety, his everyday struggles with Reintegrating — fundamental parts of himself that he didn't want to tell Serena, all in the name of something he no longer recognized or understood.

"I believe you, Rene," he said. "I really do. But Sonya Young kept you a secret, right? So I still don't know why *you* would be in danger."

She pulled out a final envelope. It was bulging, stark white, and newer than the rest. Her hand hesitated, as though not ready to reveal its contents.

"This just happened to come my way." She offered it to him as though handing over a bomb that might at any moment explode.

The postmark read Grand Forks, North Dakota. Serena's name and address were scribbled in a stilted hand, far different than the cards. He pulled the folded documents out — a hundred pages, at least — and saw, through the transparent back page, the dense, typed text of a legal document.

"Shit," Lane said. "Is this it?"

He flipped the stack over, revealing the thick headline of the cover page.

THE LAST WILL AND TESTAMENT OF SONYA BEATRICE YOUNG

Chapter 8

Two Youtopia Reborn guards stopped Ana at the gate. She sighed, recalling how she used to simply walk through this first barrier to the Towers, how she commanded the Feeds in Central Control. Even two days before, when Peterson passed her and Lane through, the gate felt like a minor nuisance. The female guard must have recognized Ana now, and still she radioed inside with a hushed tone and capricious eyes. Ana felt echoes of Paul and Lonnie's ghosting, their unfair and unflagging denial of her existence, so she leered right back. If she had to, she would fight to get inside.

The guard stepped forward and removed the sunglasses pinned to her face. Wisps of her blonde hair stuck to her forehead in the heat. "Miss Downer," she said through the window.

"Daniel Peterson wants to see me."

"That's not—" the guard said, but then stopped. She listened to something coming through her black earbud. "Yes," she said. "Of course. Right away." She hastily turned back to Ana. "We need you to clear the way."

"Pull to the side," her male counterpart shouted. "Now!"

His abrasiveness jolted Ana. She slid to the shoulder. Not a minute later, a cavalcade of black Cadillacs approached the gate from the inside. The male guard marched to the control shed. Freed from his antipathy, Ana stepped from her car and moved to the front hood.

Pulling through the gate, the first Cadillac approached her. When the window rolled down, she was unsurprised to see June Kowalski, dressed in her full white pantsuit, her face decidedly somber.

"You persist," Kowalski said as the guards watched from a close distance. "I thought we were clear in our previous meeting that—"

"I'm not here to speak to you."

"Daniel Peterson is not available."

"My FBI colleagues beg to differ."

The lie threw Kowalski. She squinted at Ana.

"I spoke with Bruce Klose," Ana continued, "head of Violent Crimes."

Kowalski tilted her head, as though examining a subordinate. "It is with all professional courtesy that I repeat: go away and do not come back. You were, and always will be, a stain on this company."

From the shed, the male guard let out a soft snicker.

"I only want to find Sonya," Ana said.

"You do not listen. Maybe you will hear this." Kowalski placed dark designer sunglasses over her eyes. "This morning, the Board filed a restraining order against you. If you don't willingly leave now, you'll find yourself on the wrong side of the authority you claim to wield."

***

Serena handled the will like a piece of prized art. She flipped through the thick pages until she pointed to one and said, "Here it is."

Lane traced his own finger across the lines, reading aloud, "In the case of Sonya Young's demise or incapacitation..." He mumbled through legalese, words binding words, until he reached the sentence that stopped him:

"...Youtopia Reborn will immediately cease all operations."

He sucked in the thick motel air. Then he went further, the next line sending shocks through his body:

"All Immersers will be released from their Reborns, and will formally begin Reintegration back into society."

Lane's head dizzied, as though he'd risen too quickly. His mind flashed to a place he tried to forget, a moment that FAR wanted whitewashed from memory: his own Reawakening.

In his last moments in Youtopia, the entire world had suddenly felt... *heavy.* Thicker than even the July heat. He succumbed to a deep tiredness he hadn't felt before, a gravitational pull to nothingness. For the first time since he could remember, he felt a deep, existential fear. He thought he was dying.

Instead, he woke slowly, agonizingly, back to the real world. His eyes burned from the dazzling light. His head felt swollen with sharp pain. His body instinctively tried to rise, to jump up, to free himself, but his limbs didn't answer.

In the ensuing days, through cramps and shivers, Lane heard doctors and psychiatrists all offer the same mix of condolences and optimism. The worst was over. Day by day, his body would wean off the KaliSerum. He would rebuild muscle. The debilitating pain would subside. Reintegrating to the world, they'd told him, would only get better from here.

Better. Lane would laugh now, if it were at all funny. He looked at the words on the will again—"formally begin Reintegration"—and saw only the prospect of seventy-five thousand children experiencing what he had experienced. All he could feel for them was dread.

He turned to the envelope, noticing again the North Dakota postmark. "We're trying to find where the will came from."

Serena nodded. "Someone knows about me. I need to know who."

"Doesn't that feel a bit... risky, Rene? What if the will came from the same people who took your mom? You'd be walking right into a trap."

She shook her head. "They knew where I was. If they wanted me, they would have just taken me."

The bathroom door opened. Andrew exited with a beige hotel towel around his waist. Lane suddenly felt his own bareness, sitting next to Serena in only his underwear. He covered himself with the shoddy bedding. Serena leapt to her son and took him into the bathroom to dress.

Lane dressed as well, and when the bathroom door reopened, only Andrew emerged, dressed in jeans and a plaid shirt. The room felt suddenly silent. Lane expected the shower to run, the sink water to flow. After a minute he recognized he must say something. Andrew needed to feel, if not comfortable around him, at least unafraid.

"Your mom says you like piano?"

The boy's eyes raised to Lane. He nodded, his wet hair bobbing into his eyes.

"I used to play too, probably about your age. It was the only thing I did that my father enjoyed." At the mention of his father, the boy's eyes shifted downward. "He died, a few years ago now, but if I play... I don't know. I still feel like maybe he hears me."

Still looking to the ground, Andrew said, "I know *Ave Maria.*"

"No kidding? I was never *that* good. And you're only, what, eight?"

"Six."

"Right," Lane said. He had no conception of children's ages, but felt Andrew, though small and thin, must've had a touch of Sonya Young's genius. He wished that somehow this middling motel room contained an electric keyboard, a fake baby grand, something to let the boy showcase his talents, and to continue this small connection they'd made.

Serena exited the bathroom, her face donned with eyeliner and blush, her hair in a tight bun. She smiled vaguely at Lane as she gathered her purse from the counter.

"Come on, baby," she said, taking Andrew's hand. "Need to get him something to snack on. He's prediabetic. Allergic to dairy and gluten and all the nuts. More that he can't eat than can."

"We can find a place."

"Thanks, Laney, but no. We'll just grab something and be right back."

As they approached the door, Serena stepped to Lane. She pulled him down and kissed him, long and deep. "Back in a jiff."

Lane returned to the bed, struck in silent awe for a moment. What a crazy ride. This felt like exactly what he'd been missing—some thrill, some adventure. Something to look forward to. Just weeks ago, he routinely fretted on how he might endure the lasting hours of a single day. Now, he wondered if today could contain all its infinite possibilities.

A few minutes passed and, with no phone to occupy him or music to listen to, his optimism quickly backslid into anxiety. He ripped through two sets of diamond pushups; he held warrior poses for minutes. He flipped a quarter to himself, stringing together heads and tails in varying successions, playing juvenile games in his mind: heads she loves me, tails she loves me not. Heads she's crazy, tails I am. He paced. For a minute he stood at the door, staring with puppy obedience. He waited.

At fifteen minutes, he felt a prickling in the back of his neck. It was taking too long. They left with such haste, with everything they'd brought. Her purse. Where was the will? The envelope and papers were gone. He couldn't shake the lurking sense that Serena was gone too, that she abandoned him and had again gone on the run.

He tore open the curtain, flooding the room in summer sun. For a moment, he was blinded. A body stood blocking his way, silhouetted in the light, some stranger he wanted to shout at to move, to let him see her empty parking spot, to stare down his pathetic fate.

Except the figure was Serena, with Andrew behind. They reentered the motel room, a peeled and half-eaten banana in Andrew's hand.

"Jesus H. Christmas, Lane," Serena said, "you looked like a deer in the fucking headlights."

"I thought..." he started. "I couldn't see you."

"Yeah, well, heeeeeere's Johnny." She flashed a maniacal Jack Nicholson smile. "Time to flee the Overlook."

Lane gathered up his things, which amounted to a small duffel bag, the clothes he wore, and a billfold with a depleted stack of cash. He counted a hundred and twenty dollars, even less than he thought.

"Rene," Lane said. "I didn't exactly plan for days and days on the—"

As only she could do, Serena thwarted Lane with a brisk, upraised hand. "Did I forget to mention? What do you journalists call it? Burying the lede?"

From her purse, Serena revealed a folded stack of hundred-dollar bills. "This also arrived in the big envelope."

Lane gazed as ten thousand dollars, maybe more, all flopped flippantly in her small hand.

"No more excuses, Laney," she said. "We used to be quite the duo, no? Time to rock this reunion tour."

***

Once the last of the Cadillacs raced from view ahead of Ana, she removed her phone from her pocket and stuffed it into the glove box. Then she U-turned and circled right back to Youtopia Towers.

With Kowalski and her minions vacated, and the looming threat of a restraining order, Ana knew this was her last chance. She hoped the male guard would somehow be gone too, but there he stood with his partner, though they were joined by a third person, a young, suited man with prim hair. Ana recognized him from his profile photo: Rob Reddy, the Board member who almost reached out to her via text. A potential ally.

"Okay," Ana said aloud. "Here we go."

The irascible guard approached, already glowering. Clearly Ana's reappearance cut into the smug satisfaction of her last exit. He looked ready to physically shove her car backward.

She rolled down her window. "I lost my phone."

"Why do I care?"

"I probably dropped it here."

The guard rolled his eyes. Good. He read Ana's incompetence as a nuisance, but unworthy of alerting anyone inside. She stepped out of the car, though he positioned himself between her and Reddy. Ana pointed toward the road's shoulder. "Maybe over by those bushes?"

He turned to look. When Ana moved forward, he met her step-for-step, clinging to her like an afternoon shadow, giving her no path to Reddy.

She abruptly stopped. "Can you back off? You're making me uncomfortable."

"You know what makes us uncomfortable? I've got a mind to—"

"Come on, Terry," Reddy said from behind him. "Take it easy. She just needs her phone."

Ana took the opening and slid past the guard to Reddy. He was short, features perfectly trimmed, and yet his shoulders were slouched forward, his manner timid. He seemed the kind of person Kowalski would overshadow in all things.

"Mr. Reddy, is it?" Ana extended a hand that Reddy reluctantly accepted. "I was hoping we'd have a chance to talk. Many of your colleagues have been —" She flashed a look back to the guard. " — outwardly hostile."

"It's..." Reddy's eyes shifted to the shed, the gate, anywhere but Ana's own. "It's been a week."

"I can imagine." She sidestepped, trying to fetch Reddy's gaze. "I've met with Daniel Peterson twice now, but for some reason he hasn't responded to me today."

"No, no," Reddy said. "It's not that." His eyes drifted down. A gravid pause followed, during which Ana recognized the incoming tide of bad news. "There's been an accident."

"An accident?"

Reddy nodded, then looked into Ana's eyes for the first time. "Dr. Peterson is in critical condition at Ascension Medical Hospital."

We Don't ██ Play Nice

Saeed Free

nobody knows your name
You haven't done anything
your boss   Sonya Young
                        is
        the Devil Incarnate

She

toys

with

innocent lives and

leaves
them in
awful pain

Daniel Peterson is

only

the

beginning

Unless

Reborn

will become

accessible to

everyone

all the children

will

meet

fatal ends

You

have One week

Chapter 9

Though the gauge read half-full, Serena's Nissan nearly ran out of gas as they bisected Fargo on interstate 94 and cut north toward Grand Forks. They made it to the station on fumes.

"Have to mind the mileage instead," Serena said. "I know, I know. I should get it fixed. Add it to the list."

At a truck stop more reminiscent of a minimarket, Lane fueled up and bought five sandwiches with Sonya Young's cash. He didn't realize how hungry he was until he devoured two. He ate standing near the bathroom, his eyes alert to anyone who passed. Serena and Andrew shuffled through the aisles, pointing out strange foods and hokey local decorations to one another with snickers. As Lane finished his sandwich, they approached, Serena with two prepaid phones in her hand.

"In case of emergency, break glass and buy burners," she said with a strange smirk, handing Lane his new phone.

"You've done this before?"

"Wouldn't you like to know." She shook her phone. "Gotta check in with school before they sound the sirens."

Lane booted up his phone and activated it with his seldom-used Hotmail account, thinking of whom on that short list of numbers he might call. Perhaps Millie, to let her know he was okay. Or Henrick. Lane owed him as much. He moved past a line of people at the checkout and stepped outside, the curtain of heat immediate.

Henrick always answered, even calls from unknown numbers, so when Lane's call went to voicemail, his anxiety prickled. He called again. On the third try, Henrick picked up.

"Henry?" Silence. "Hey, it's me, Lane."

"Lane train," Henrick finally said. "The good word."

"Sorry I haven't..." Lane heard strange voices through the phone. "Hey, Henry, you good?"

Henrick was slow in replying. "Right as rain, my friend. Right as rain."

The chatter intensified, whispers becoming laughter.

"Hey, man, you there? Who's with you?"

Henrick couldn't seem to hear him. The laughter roared, and Lane knew: he was too late. Henrick was back on drugs, whatever cocktail that rejected his real world and pushed him toward his Youtopian past. Lane had failed him.

"Hey," Henrick said back into the phone, his voice shooting through quick and clear. "Lane train. You ever think, yep, this is it? This right here?"

"I'm sorry, Henry. I really am. I hope you know that."

Lane didn't know whether Henrick heard him or not, but after more laughter, he couldn't take any more. He hung up.

A queasiness settled into his stomach. He wished he could have stayed home, to help Henrick through his troubles, as Henrick had for him. Too many times, Lane had called Henrick at two in the morning, his heart sucking into his chest, feeling as though it would implode — times he could barely breathe. Henrick had been patient, had talked him through as long as he needed.

Now Lane wasn't there for him. Henrick wouldn't even remember he called. Part of him wished he hadn't.

There was one more person he needed to call, one who might offer him some optimism. With a bit of digging, on the Times website he found a contact number for Bethany Fawkes. She would answer, standing as she did on the leading edge of the premier story across the country. Only three rings proved him correct.

"This is Fawkes."

Her voice chafed at him. He recalled their small graduate classroom, pale brick walls stained with putty and tape remnants from removed flyers. The dusty mist of chalk, the circadian click of a heating coil.

"Hey, Beth, long time no see. Well, actually, I saw you at Youtopia Reborn about a week ago, but I couldn't catch you."

"I'm sorry, who is this?"

"Lane. Lane Samson." An awkward pause. "With the Weekly Beacon."

Silence for a moment. "Lane. You mean formerly, right? I heard the Beacon had some pretty deep layoffs."

He gritted his teeth. Of course, Bethany already knew. She was a hawk for information, even information that seemed irrelevant to her.

"I'm working a different beat now, something up your alley. That's why I'm calling."

"You got a scoop?"

"I might, but I'm trying to verify. Any chance you can give your source on Sonya Young's will?"

"Just tell me what you've got, Lane."

He paused, thinking carefully about what he could give Bethany, and what he might expect in return. In truth, he wanted names from her, and wanted to give her nothing. He wanted from her what no seasoned reporter would ever give.

"If the will is real," he said, "someone's got it. Your source might be the person. Or they might know who is."

"That doesn't answer my question."

The silence thickened between them as he considered other angles: playing on their shared past; drumming up sympathy—if she would have any—for his lost job with the Beacon; begging. None of them seemed effective for a woman like Bethany Fawkes.

In the end, a simple drawn-out silence moved her. Bethany said, "Look, I don't owe you anything, all right? But if you must know, my source was anonymous."

Shit. Lane was afraid of that. "You verified it though?"

"I talked with enough people that we felt comfortable running it."

"You know what the will says?"

"Maybe."

"But you can't tell me who leaked it."

"No."

"What about the authorities? The FBI? Whoever knew about the will might be involved in her abduction."

"Lane," Bethany began, and then, with an exasperation he'd never heard in her voice, "I don't see how that concerns you."

He looked out into the truck stop, to the handful of people leaned against their vehicles. He'd hit the end of this road, unless he was willing to divulge Serena and his only handle on the story, something he couldn't do now, if ever.

"Thanks, Beth. You keep on keeping on."

"So you don't have anything?" Bethany asked.

"Unfortunately, no. Just a hunch. Was hoping you could shed some light on it."

"If you do get something, call me back. Otherwise, keep your hunches for the dinner table." As quickly as she'd answered, she hung up.

He returned to find Andrew sitting alone at a small booth nestled behind a T-shirt rack, headphones on his ears, dissecting a shrink-wrapped sandwich. Serena's voice came in a raised whisper, just beyond the T-shirts, as though she wanted to yell but couldn't. She slunk into the table next to Andrew, her new phone to her ear. "I understand. Sure. Yes, Martha. Yarboroughs are not *truants*. He will be back as soon as he feels better. I'll forward the doctor's note first thing."

As she hung up, she made a face of disgust at her phone. "That bitch never liked me."

Lane slid in across from them. "You'll have to be more specific."

"Ha ha." She twirled strands of Andrew's ponytail in her fingers. "I don't check in with his school? They panic. I do check in? They put me through the goddamn wringer."

"What's he like to listen to?" Lane asked, nodding at Andrew. "It isn't jazz, by chance?"

"Is Mozart jazz?"

Lane smiled. "No. But he did influence a lot of the jazz greats."

"Well, there you go then. My boy likes jazz."

An hour later, they arrived in Grand Forks. The downtown was a familiar Midwestern mix of chain restaurants and quaint, if failing, small businesses. The post office building stood across from a mall complex that, for a Thursday afternoon, seemed oddly populated. Serena parked between two pickup trucks, grabbed her purse, and made to exit the car.

"Hold on," Lane said, taking her arm and flopping her back into her seat. "Let me do it."

"What? Hells no."

"If someone in that post office knows about this, they could recognize you. It might spook them into silence."

"So what's *your* plan?"

"Feel it out, get the lay of the land. You look in from the window, see if you recognize anybody I'm talking to. I'll signal you to come in if it's right."

"Signal me? Who are you, Hercule Poirot?"

"I don't know who that is."

Serena looked dubiously at him. Then she shrugged, pulled the will out, and offered the envelope to him. "See what you can do with that, detective. The real deal stays with me."

"You don't trust me?"

"As much as I trust anyone." She opened her door, and the humid outdoor air surged into the car. "Gods above, how's it even hotter here? Just make it snappy. And if you get in trouble—as you always do—send up the Bat Signal. Andrew and I will fly right in."

"Batman can't fly."

She gave him the finger as she took Andrew along the eastern side of the post office, toward a patch of trees with middling shade. Lane turned to the building and entered.

The line was long. A dozen Grand Forks citizens held packages of various size, rocking back and forth on their feet. Outside the square windows, he saw a picnic table where Serena led Andrew. She looked briefly to Lane and gave a mock salute.

He waited for ten minutes, more. As he approached the front of the line, he looked out the glass to Serena and Andrew. They silently observed cars passing by, until they simultaneously leapt back and laughed. Andrew marked something on a small notebook. They were playing a game, one they'd clearly played before. In their camaraderie, Lane recognized that Serena, for any faults, had an indelible bond with her son. She was unquestionably a good mother. He tried to remember any games that he and his mother shared, but if they did, they were gone now.

"Sir?"

Lane turned. A male desk worker awaited him. He was short-haired, bearded, paunchy. His nametag read Kyle. Lane stepped toward him armed with the envelope. He slid it onto the counter. Kyle tilted his head as he reached out for it.

"Got a unique request," Lane said. "This was sent from this post office. I'm wondering if you could tell me who sent it."

Kyle turned the envelope over in his hands. "A return address would answer that."

"Tell me about it."

Kyle gave the envelope a shake, as though developing a polaroid photo. Then he offered it back to Lane. "Unfortunately, I can't help you."

Lane eyed Kyle, gleaning whether the quick rejection came from familiarity with the envelope, dislike of Lane himself, or just a penchant for simple protocol. Or perhaps all three.

"This must've been scanned here," Lane said. "Tracking, informed delivery. Something like that might tell us."

"We do track everything, yes, but mail gets routed to our station from counties far north and west of here. It's a wide net."

"Can we take it that far, at least?"

"No."

Next to them, a woman coworker looked to Kyle. She continued her transaction but slowly, with shifty eyes.

"We can't," Lane said, "or we won't?"

"Both."

"How about a supervisor?" Lane pointed to the woman worker. "Her?"

Kyle's eyes widened in anger. He pointed the envelope in his colleague's direction. "Mal?"

The two slid back to converse. With an eye on Lane, Kyle explained the situation to Mal. Lane hoped for a sympathetic turn, a softening of her face. But then the customer to his side issued an audible grunt; everyone in the line behind him stared with agitation. He had quickly become the enemy here. He wanted to pull Mal aside, to explain himself—in vague terms, playing up the will but leaving out Sonya Young—but instead, Mal approached the desk.

"Sir, I understand your request, but what you're asking is illegal. Unless you're a law enforcement officer?"

"No," he said. Then, risking a lie for his last shot, "Just a family member looking for some closure."

The sympathetic look from Mal came, but too late. "I'm sorry, but you'll have to find your closure elsewhere."

***

Ana arrived at the hospital parking lot in a befuddled frenzy. The rainbow aura of a migraine arrived and spread, staved off only with twice the recommended amount of painkillers. She had seen Peterson just the day before. He had confided in her, but instead of enlisting Ana's help, he decided to Intervene himself into a dangerous Reborn, without alerting anyone he was doing so.

As she stepped through the doors, she shook her head at the foolish speculation that Peterson had anything to do with the kidnapping—that he, of all people, would have nefarious motives. Peterson always had an antiquated, chivalrous air about him, the desire to protect. His loyalty was unquestionable, impenetrable. And it landed him here.

She passed the front waiting areas, rode the elevator up to the third floor, and walked down a long hallway, all before encountering law enforcement. Glad they were protecting Peterson, she still found herself irritated by their foreboding posture.

"I saw Daniel just yesterday," she told them.

The officers simply stared at her. She looked beyond them, hoping to see a doctor or administrator or some medical professional who could help her penetrate these arbitrary, necessary boundaries. Instead, from Peterson's room, Kowalski and four of her male Board cronies emerged, Newborne included, all wearing suits and scowls.

Ana stepped back from the officers as the black-suited gang huddled around their white-suited leader.

"Miss Downer," Kowalski said with her usual pomp. Ana detected a few misplaced hairs from her usual tight bun, crease marks uncovered by her usual makeup. Signs of stress, even if slight. "You are like a weed, popping up everywhere unwanted." She turned to the officers. "Please escort—"

"Daniel was my employer," Ana cut in, risking another lie—that she and Peterson had indeed made the arrangement. Then, a truth slipped out. "He was my friend."

As she said it, she realized how pathetic it truly was, a man she barely knew as one of the only people she could consider a friend. "I just want to make sure he's okay."

"Why don't you see for yourself?" a new voice called out.

From Peterson's room, Saeed Free—the architect of Youtopia Reborn's Intervention program—sauntered out, wearing prescription sunglasses and a shifty smile. Californian through and through, with a deep tan and open-toed shoes, he cozied up to Ana like an accomplice. She had expected to meet him under different circumstances, if at all. Then again, she should've known better than to have expectations while investigating Youtopia.

Kowalski shifted her weight from one leg to the other. She seemed unnerved by him. "That's not appropriate, Saeed."

"And tell me again, *June,* why your opinion on what's appropriate matters?" He stepped forward. He stood shorter than Ana herself, and yet he approached Kowalski with an undeniable force. "We have an official Board vote on this? A motion? Call to question?"

"Saeed," Kowalski said, almost a plead.

Saeed turned to Ana. "You see, with Sonya gone, nobody wanted to do *anything.* Sit on our hands and hope. But Danny..." Saeed stopped. He seemed shaken. "So we're going to put aside these petty quibbles today, aren't we, June? Miss Downer, follow me."

"Saeed," Kowalski repeated. "This will have far larger consequences than you realize."

"Consequences. Yes, I agree. Which is why Dan's friend is going to see him. Because unlike the others in my present company, maybe she can actually fucking *do something* of consequence."

Saeed paused, took a breath. His eyes glossed, fighting back genuine tears. "Dan had the guts to go after this son of a bitch. We owe him to do the same."

Inside the room, the heartbeat monitor didn't beep. The dissonant absence of sound felt invasive. The only voices came from the hallway, Kowalski and her clan huddling beside the guards. Before Ana, Peterson's comatose body rested, the feeding and breathing tubes strapped to his mouth, IVs in each arm.

"Will he come back?" Ana asked.

"Not sure." Saeed shrugged as if in defeat. "Even if he does, they have no clue what he'll remember. He seized like crazy—foam at the mouth, heart racing like a fucking Nascar engine."

Ana turned to Saeed. His bushy, stark black eyebrows, his quaff of tufted hair, stood prominent in the halogen light of the hospital room.

"I wouldn't be surprised," he said, shaking his head, "if poor Danny's stuck in La La Land forever."

***

From the outside, the Grand Forks Public Library appeared just like the post office, its old mustard brick lusterless with age. The inside, however, had been completely remodeled and renovated, with modern steel sconces and railings, geometric patterns on the carpet, glass end tables. A vast children's area rivaled an outdoor playground. Kids of Andrew's age climbed stairs to the second floor and then jetted down a covered, corkscrew tube slide back to the first. Others jostled one another at a four-poster-style table with swings as chairs. Lane expected Andrew to partake, for Serena to follow him into the fray, but instead, he beelined for the teenage area. With impressive haste, he picked an armful of books and found a beanbag.

"Always been ahead of the game," Serena said. "If you don't know what a word means, ask him."

"You aren't worried about what he'll be exposed to?"

"Sometimes," Serena said. "Mostly not. The world's more fucked-up than those books."

Lane filled out a visitor's form to gain access to the public computers. He chose one far in the corner, away from other patrons. Serena perched near the glass wall overlooking the library, keeping an eye on Andrew. "You should've let me take on the postal workers," she said. "You think you're smooth, Lane Samson, but people can see right through it."

"Thanks."

"That *is* a compliment. It's what makes you adorable — your complete lack of charm."

He pulled up a web browser. The library's homepage had an old-world allure, replete with black-and-white photos. He scrolled until he found *Directories*, and chose *Telephone*, which prompted a list of counties including Grand Forks and the surrounding areas.

Serena let out a soft chuckle. "See! You're searching the goddamn *phone book*. Somewhere in that freakishly tall body is the heart of a septuagenarian."

"We tried it your way. Now we try mine." He scrolled the list of nearby counties. "We cross-reference phone directories with lists of former Youtopia employees. The first Youtopia headquarters was an hour west of here, in a town called Devils Lake."

"You think our guy worked for her back then?"

"It makes the most sense. She can't trust Peterson or other current employees — they might want Reborn for themselves."

Lane clicked on Grand Forks, prompting a search bar with over 82,000 possible names.

"My first instinct is family," he continued, "but Young doesn't have much. Her parents are dead. No siblings or noted kin."

"Other than the hidden ones," Serena said, her tone droll. "I wouldn't think too many former employees still lived around here."

"Let's find the ones that do."

He opened another browser, this one with the list of employees made public as part of Youtopia's dissolution in 2024: over 15,000 names, far too many to cross-reference. He dug further, finding a list that included length of tenure, and narrowed it down to those who worked with Young from the beginning. Seventy-seven. Still a lot, but far more manageable.

He turned to Serena. "This might take a while."

"My little man will sit for hours. Me, on the other hand..."

As Serena wandered off, Lane dove in. He typed each employee name in the Grand Forks search bar and, when he didn't get a hit, moved on to the next. With each name — Anderson, Attlay, Barnett, Candall — he hoped for a North Dakota address. The name Henley hit, but the first names didn't match. He ended Grand Forks without a single connection.

He moved to nearby Traill, Steele, Griggs Counties, all with the same failures. In Eddy County, fifty miles west of them, he landed his first connection: a Stewart Dobbing, formerly an IT tech at Youtopia. A cursory Google search showed a picture of him: sixties, glasses and gray hair. Social media posts boasted of his pilgrimages to Alaska. Lane dialed his phone number, and predictably, it went straight to voicemail. He noted Dobbing's address and continued on.

The next three counties came up empty. His search felt timeless, though at least an hour had passed when Serena reentered and tapped him on the shoulder. Two more people had taken up computers and he hadn't even noticed.

"Andrew and me are getting some grub. You want anything?"

"I'm good. I've got one name already. If we don't find anyone else, we can start with him." As she turned, he added, "Hey, be safe out there."

"You know me."

"That's why I said it."

He searched on. An hour, more, passed. In Cavalier County he got another hit—a Nicole Veselov—and tried her phone to no avail. Same with a final match in Dickey County, a Gregory Planes. He felt comfortable he'd cast a net far enough to cover the mail that would travel through Grand Forks, with three names out of seventy-seven to show for it. If a former employee sent the will, it was likely one of these three.

Yet, they lived hours apart. He could make the drive easy, but Serena had Andrew to consider. Having something more solid would help. He tried the numbers again. Dobbing went to voicemail faster each time. Planes the same. But on his fourth try, Veselov—a woman with no social media or other internet presence Lane could find—picked up on the first ring.

"Who are you?" she demanded. Her voice carried an Eastern European accent.

"Miss Veselov? Hello—"

"Who are you?"

"I was just getting to that. My name is Lane Samson. I was wondering if I could take a minute of your time."

A long pause. Lane saw Serena through the glass, entering the library with a fast-food bag in her hand. When she saw Lane, she waved it in the air like a carnival prize.

"Do not call here again," Veselov said, then hung up on him.

***

"How much did Danny show you?" Saeed asked. "The Interventions?"

Ana shook her head. "He wouldn't let me in. Kowalski spooked him."

Saeed rocked back, his hair wafting like thickets in wind. "So he just goes himself. Damnit, Dan! You *knew* never to enter without Oversight." He stepped to Peterson's body, hovered over it with probing eyes. Then, much louder than necessary, he shouted, "You stupid bastard! If you can hear me, I want you to know that you could have just *called me!*"

"Maybe he didn't trust you."

"Oh, and *this* is much better."

Ana approached Peterson. His body looked frail, dwarfed by the inclined hospital bed, the rails, the contraptions attached to it. His heavy brow stood prominent on his face, no longer hidden behind thick glasses. He was imprisoned in his own mind, the irony of which did not escape her.

"Ahh, what's the use," Saeed said, backpedaling and slumping into the sole chair in the room. "Danny boy had a reckless streak. More than anyone gave him credit for, hiding behind Sonya all these years. No one ever asked if it was *her* reining *him* in."

"Was it?"

Saeed's eyes narrowed to her. "Does it matter? He's here. Probably forever. Unless they decide to be merciful and pull the plug. And Sonya... well, neither of them got the good end of it. Dan must've been sooooo close."

"What about the Immerser? Did they suffer any harm?"

"She. And no, not physically. But psychologically? Emotionally? You bet your ass."

"How did the hacker do this?" Ana asked. "How did he put Daniel in a coma?"

Saeed exhaled. "I don't know. I can't tell you how much it hurts me to say that, but shit... I don't know. He and Dan were connected in a way I never thought possible."

This answer, more than any, gave Ana pause: that the man who helped design the Interventions did not fully understand its capabilities, its potentially destructive power.

"And now," Saeed said, "he's threatened all our Immersers."

He pulled his phone and showed Ana a version of Bethany Fawkes's article on him covered with black, redacted text. *Unless Reborn will become accessible to everyone, all the children will meet fatal ends. You have one week.*

"Could he do it?"

Saeed slowly nodded. "I doubt it's possible from the inside. But the Cradles run on an independent power grid. We're armed to the teeth there, but theoretically, if he could shut it down... well, you see what happens when it snows in Texas."

"So seventy-some-thousand children's lives could be lost."

"Seventy-five thousand, four-hundred and twenty-four."

From his bed, Peterson's body emitted a soft shiver. Ana and Saeed turned to him, but it was no more than an involuntary twitch.

"You could save them," Ana said, "by pulling them all out. Start Reintegration."

Saeed scratched at his forehead, his eyes squinting. "Would that I could, dear. But who's even running this show now? The Board won't sign off on *that*, not after all the troubles from Youtopia proper."

"So the only thing left is to find the perpetrator. Finish what Daniel started."

He didn't immediately answer. Instead, he looked to the hallway before turning back to Ana. "There *is* one person who's probably seen him, other than Danny here."

Ana stared at him for a moment. "The Immerser."

Saeed motioned for Ana to slide closer. "When this asshole found an Immerser he liked, he set up camp, made himself at home. Immersers would feel it from first go, but he knew to avoid their direct consciousness. Hovered in the shadows."

"So the Immerser may not be able to ID him?"

"After what happened in there, my guess is she can." He tapped his fingers together. "But her seeing him is only half the battle, and not necessarily the harder half."

"What is?"

"Getting on her good side. Gaining her trust. After all she's been through? Unpacking *that* trauma?" He raised one hand and fiddled, as though doing calculations in his mind. "Might take a good dozen points of contact, just for her to trust anyone foreign."

"What if we pull her out?" Ana asked.

Saeed's face immediately cringed.

"I know, it's not ideal, but with Sonya gone, and this..." She held a hand toward Peterson. "It has to justify the means."

Saeed shook his head. "It's not just the shock. Pulling her might throw her whole memory into question."

"Why?"

"Think of it this way: you ever wake from a dream, and in those first seconds you've got it all? Images, words said to you, the *feel* of it, so vivid it's almost real? Then you stand up, take a piss or whatever, and suddenly, whoop, there it slips, like grains of sand rushing from your hand. Next thing you know, you can't remember a damn thing. If we pull her out, chances are the important stuff might not come with."

Newborne abruptly stepped into the doorframe. He seemed intent and yet lost, as though he'd entered the wrong room.

"Stew," Saeed said. "Have I told you you look *fantastic* in those skinny slacks?"

Newborne squared his shoulders and puffed out his chest. "I'm surprised they haven't canned your ass yet."

"Who's this *they*? You?" Saeed rose, came between Peterson and the door as though protecting him. "Unless you've got a reason to be wasting this particular space of earth, you mind pissing off?"

"Two more minutes."

"Who made you the warden?"

"Just finish up, Free. You've been in here long enough."

"We'll be done when we're damn well ready to be done, Stew."

Newborne extended his middle finger as he turned back to Kowalski and the group.

Saeed smirked at him, but then quickly returned his attention to Ana. "Pretty boy. He and Sonya never got on well. Can't imagine why."

She reached out to Peterson and touched his hand, careful not to disturb the mound of tape holding in his IV needles. His fingers felt surprisingly warm. An image flashed to her, of her own body stiff and pallid under the thin hospital blanket, tubes extruding from her mouth and arms, with Peterson standing above her, wracked with the same guilt she felt now, amplified a hundredfold. What would he do? Would he even hesitate?

"Just so I have this straight," she said. "Our only chance is to Intervene in the Immerser's Reborn. Gain her trust. Get a visual of the intruder. Get out."

"Bingo."

"And I'm the only one who can Intervene."

Saeed shrugged. "I need to run Oversight, to pull the plug if things go batshit. To be the safety net Danny *should* have had."

From the hallway, the gaggle of Board members boomed out inappropriate laughter.

"Probably ASAP too," Saeed continued. "The alternative is those fuckers outside. Or your FBI buddies. That place is going on lockdown in, oh..." He feigned a look at his watch. "T-minus tonight."

"So right now then."

Saeed smiled. "Can I just say, I love your enthusiasm. Brilliant. Unfortunately, there's one more catch."

"The intruder might still be in there," Ana said.

Saeed nodded. "That means..." Saeed pointed to Peterson's comatose body. "You're taking on *that* possibility."

Ana squeezed Peterson's hand, felt the faint pulse in the crook of his thumb.

"Would he be foolish enough to stick around?" she asked.

"Foolish, no. Arrogant, yes."

She released Peterson's hand. "If the intruder is still there, then all the easier to identify him."

Saeed shot a whistle through his lips. "So the papers were true about one thing: you are a bit crazy."

"Or arrogant."

Saeed's laugh matched the Board's. They turned their attention to the room one last time as Ana said, "Let's go."

***

With his burner phone's data flitting in and out, the sun descending on their long day, Lane finally got the NY Times to load and caught the latest headline:

YOUTOPIA REBORN'S DANIEL PETERSON IN CRITICAL CONDITION

"Shit," he said, too loudly, causing Andrew to eye him from the backseat. "I just saw him a few days ago." He held out the phone for Serena to see.

She took in the headline without reaction.

"Rene," he said, "if this guy can do to Peterson—"

"You're about to say he could do it to me," she cut in. "Always could, Laney. Doesn't really change anything."

"What about Andrew?"

Together they looked to him. Serena lowered her voice. "I'm afraid for him most, Laney, but we're worse off at home."

"Is there someone we could drop him off with? A friend? Distant relative?"

Serena kept her eyes on the road, but Lane saw the sting in them. He had struck a painful chord—the answer was no.

"If anything," she said, "this makes what we're doing more important. Keep moving. Find the person who sent the will. Whatever happens, I will not live in fear."

Eventually, the road to Veselov's house took them beyond the capability of his phone's GPS. He marveled that, here in 2026, places still existed off the grid. Amidst old, one-story houses buried deep in their lots, they approached an immaculate yard hidden behind a composite wooden plank fence. At the peak of the yard stood a towering two-story lit up by the setting sun, a house that bespoke the wealth of someone from corporate America—a former employee of Youtopia. They snaked up the steep driveway. Before Serena even put the car in park, the massive barn-style front door opened. Lane slid out of the car just as the woman—this Veselov—stepped outside.

She was large, muscular and lean, a dark ponytail holding her severe hair back, and yet her movements were nimble, catlike, as though she was once a gymnast or martial artist.

"I told you to stay away," Veselov said, primed and prepared to fight. Since Lane's phone call, she may have been waiting by her window for him to arrive. "I have nothing—"

Then she suddenly stopped. She stared through the car's window, directly at Serena, with a stunned recognition.

This was it. They'd found their woman.

***

The Viewing Chamber shimmered like a diamond. The floor and walls and high ceiling were constructed of the same sparkling fiberglass material, as though Saeed had transported them directly into the stars. Ana recalled entering Central Control just years ago, the dizzying rush of the Immerser Feeds flashing before her on the concave screen, the faux-Charlotte of Paul's deepest mind. She'd expected something similar, or a simple virtual reality headset, the way thieves like Tramel used to peddle stolen Feeds. But this... this she didn't expect. It was built for grandeur, for spectacle. It was extraordinary.

When she stepped into the room's center, her hip jutted into something padded. She looked down to a reclined chair, covered in black leather, with arms and extended legs and an elaborate headrest, eerily reminiscent of a dark dentist's chair.

"We usually keep the Dome down," Saeed said. "But you damn Feds... you poked around more than you needed to this morning."

"I'm not one of them anymore."

"And proving it by the minute. Heads up now."

Hanging from the ceiling, directly above the chair, the transparent, semi-circle Dome descended. Saeed controlled it with a small black baton, taking Ana back once again to the Youtopia Feeds, to the sheer power she felt wielding her own baton. As it lowered, its pulley mechanism whisper-quiet, the Dome adopted an off-white color, layered with something like fog sifting between the panes. He stopped it just above the chair.

"You remember the old way of watching Feeds? This is *nothing* like that." He reached into his pocket and pulled out a miniature earbud. "You won't see me, but you can speak to me through this. Once you're in, though, you won't feel it in your ear. It's a little... *jarring*."

"You'll just be a voice inside my head."

"I know. Spooky shit. But it's the best way."

She took the earpiece. A shiver ascended her spine, and she suppressed the need to shake it away in front of Saeed. She felt the smooth, velvet-like texture of the earpiece, knowing that, in a moment, she would not feel it at all. She would not be in this room, head back on this clinical chair, surrounded by a lucent Dome in a dark, arched room. Instead, she would be in the Immerser girl's world. She would be deeper on the case than Bruce would ever allow her to be. She would be herself again.

"Can you record it?" Ana said as she sat in the chair.

"As long as you're seeing it, I'll catch it." From beneath the armrests, Saeed pulled black leather straps to bind Ana to the chair. "Sorry. Your body won't move or anything, but with Danny... Just need to be extra cautious."

Once he strapped her down, Saeed removed a small syringe from a thick plastic case.

"Stop," Ana called, her voice echoing. Her bound hand instinctively called for her Glock. She tried not to feel like she was about to undergo invasive surgery, or some mad scientist's experiment.

Saeed looked at the syringe, then Ana. "Shit, sorry. Where *is* my bedside manner? We haven't had someone new in so long, it's like autopilot at this point." He moved the syringe closer to Ana's face.

"KaliSerum. A microdose. Just enough to acclimate your body to Youtopia. Nothing that will last."

"I don't want any drugs in me."

"Then our jig is up."

Ana weighed the possibilities. Saeed—this young, immature man she just met—could be telling the truth, and the drug would simply let her do what she needed to do. Even then, she could end up in a hospital bed next to Peterson, or worse.

On the other hand, Saeed could have brought her here under nefarious purposes, and the drug would incapacitate her, would lead to her bound somewhere in a basement, perhaps next to Sonya Young herself. Ana could become the next victim.

She looked Saeed in his intense brown eyes, trusting, as always, her instinct.

"All right," she said. "Make it quick."

Saeed pulled her sleeve up and swabbed her skin with the precision of a nurse. The needle caused little pain, but the liquid itself snaked into her bloodstream like an icy invader.

"If it gets dicey, I'll pull the plug," he said as he applied a bandage. "Oh, I almost forgot. Close your eyes, on both departure and arrival."

Ana nodded as the drug bled frigid into her torso. She decided to feign a confidence she didn't feel. "Only pull me if you absolutely need to."

"Here's to hoping it won't come to that."

Saeed's hand moved about the baton as he stepped backward, his eyes steady on her. A low whirring noise reverberated about the Dome, echoes bouncing off echoes. Before she could prepare herself, Saeed initiated a countdown: Ten, nine... five... one. She forgot to close her eyes, or perhaps willfully, subconsciously, she didn't want to. Perhaps she wanted to experience the journey, this transformation from the real world into the imaginary depths of Youtopia Reborn, like teleportation, or reincarnation. Like waking.

Immediately, she regretted it. Balloons of crystalline light exploded in her vision and her head swooned, as though all the air had been sucked from her body. Her stomach catapulted. She closed her eyes, but too late—her head already felt tossed about, chewed and spit out. She was Dorothy, victim of the violent tempest bringing her to Oz. The absence of sound, of some imaginary wind whipping about her, unsettled her. She gritted her teeth, wanting it to end.

Then it all stopped. She kept her eyes shut. Saliva leaked from the corners of her mouth. She expected to be lying on the ground in the middle of some dismantled field, the carnage of a natural disaster strewn about her.

Instead, she felt the ground firmly beneath her feet. The air felt still. The hair on her arms and neck bristled with possibility.

Her head fogged, her stomach still lurching, Ana opened her eyes.

Feed Link: 013222: 07.22.26

The world alights to...

AN EFFERVESCENT BEACH

...and ANA stands with her feet embedded deep in the sandy shore.

Brilliant, painstakingly vibrant colors surround her — school bus yellows and fire hydrant reds and Caribbean Sea blues. Tree branches wear their tufted leaves like hairdos, shining and confident.

Déjà vu — Ana has been here before. She bends to the ground, feels the foamy texture of the sand, like running her hand through a bubble bath.

And yet, all is placid around her, silent. No waves in the ocean. No birds in the cerulean sky. A latent world on pause, waiting for the Immerser's conscious eye, for Ana's invasive presence to register.

She looks to the horizon. Deep along the shore stands a large elephant with an elaborate, gravity-defying chariot strapped to its back. Stock still, it sleeps in its unnatural pose.

Ana recognizes it... but from where? How does she know this place? To the other side, yellow creatures with green stars on their stomachs rest around a fire ring.

That's it: a Zumble-Zay, the Sneetches. Past the beach sits Seussian water; past the sandy shore stand Truffula trees. She occupies a world inspired by the Immerser's favorite books.

Ana looks down to her own hands, expecting an approximation, something humanoid, but no. Dotting her fingers are the same marks and hairs: the accumulated wrinkles on her wrist, the L-shaped scar on her index finger where, in a panic, she'd pulled Paul's razorblade from a curious Charlotte's hands.

The same hands, and yet another mystery: on her left hand has mysteriously appeared her WEDDING RING.

ANA: I'm me. The real me.

Her voice carries a hollow, acoustic, fishbowl quality. Her voice boomerangs back to her.

SAEED: Yes. Important for her to perceive real humans.

His voice echoes omnipotent. She feels it in her stomach. And yet, she is not unnerved. Nothing unnerves—no jitters or fatigue, no insidious precursors of a migraine. In her own body, she feels blissfully detached from its aches, its visceral woes. Everything is in perfect order.

She has no time to marvel at this...

...for the world AWAKENS.

Waves CRASH to the shore. Chilled, brackish water braces Ana's ankles. The horizon shades a vibrant orange. Winged titans flock in unison, passing with a resounding WHOOSH.

Behind Ana, THE GIRL—the Immerser, the Architect, the Witness—suddenly appears.

She presents as tall, with dark skin. Her hair waves as though underwater. Her body is fully naked and underdeveloped. In Ana's world She would be malnourished, yet here She moves gracefully, with a sinewy elegance. Her eyes present as pure black.

SAEED: Easy now.

Ana turns fully to Her, offers her hands palms upward— a sign, she hopes, of a truce.

Instead, a thunderbolt CRASHES.

Reptile-like creatures RISE from the foamy sand. Brute and tall, with tails twice Ana's size, their crocodile snouts SNAP and HISS. More emerge from the sea, animal conglomerations on foot and hoof and wing. Above her, the titans circle like vultures. Gone are the soft Seussian curves and edges, replaced by lurid malice.

SAEED: Breathe, Ana. And remember, we expected this. She's on high alert.

The animal gangs STOMP forward.

SAEED: Gain Her trust. Say something.

Ana risks a step forward, but finds she cannot move. Again and again, her feet step but her body stays in place, the ground treadmilling below her. She looks to the Girl, marching at the head of Her GROWLING and SNARLING animal horde.

ANA: Veronica.

The Girl halts. The animals too.

ANA: Can I call You Veronica?

The horde pauses, though the Girl's quizzical face offers no reply. In it resides a deep, adolescent thoughtfulness, though She was only five years old when She Immersed. *Five years old*, Ana repeats to herself. *Charlotte's age. Five years old.*

SAEED: Good. Keep with it. Make a connection.

Her attempts at walking fruitless, Ana bends at the knees, subservient, an unworthy visitor. A friend. She kneels.

ANA: You've experienced many difficulties lately.

SAEED: Simple. Simple words.

Ana raises a hand to her heart.

ANA: You hurt. I know.

Ana again offers her hands. The Girl squints at them.

ANA: I know. I can help.

The animal horde slowly recedes, their motion now silent against the rhythm of CASCADING WAVES.

SAEED: Good. Good. Now we're getting somewhere.

The Girl approaches. The lighted sky whisks from orange to a bright red.

Ana moves to stand.

But no: the sand creeps up over her legs, binding her.

She cannot move.

The Girl smiles.

Then, in a sudden FLASH, She CLAWS Ana's left hand, CRUSHING the ring into her skin. Needles of unfamiliar pain SHOOT through Ana's arm. Down to her legs, up into her head, into her heart it SURGES—an orgasm of pain.

SAEED: No. No no no.

The Girl's voice drowns out his mutters. It issues from Her and everywhere, from the sky itself, cutting out the waves and animal calls and the world.

VERONICA: *Get. Out. Now.*

The pain centralizes in the peak of Ana's head. A pinprick of concentration. A shooting embolism.

Ana tries to pull her hand away. She thinks, *I'm here to help.* She thinks, *this is what the kidnapper did to Peterson.* She thinks, *I wish She would stop.*

SAEED: I'm pulling you out. I'm —

She thinks, *I'm going to die.*

The Girl's hand incandesces a white so pure it sparkles. *She doesn't want to do this. She's just a scared kid.*

SAEED: Shit! She won't let me —

The sky CYCLONES above and around them.

The pain mushrooms, billows into Ana's face, her shoulders.

If only You knew how much I understand. I want to help You.

SAEED: Free your hand! Ana!

Conjoined, their white-hot hands BURST into flame.

ANA: No!

In a sudden FLASH...

...the world goes silent.

***

THE BEACH

...is where we return.

Ana still kneeling.

The Girl still holding her hand.

And yet...

Everything has changed.

Pain gone. Their hands no longer aflame.

Ana slips free.

The animals have dispersed. Only a small gaggle of plain-colored geese waddle at the shore's edge, parents leading their copper offspring. The water reflects a glittering yellow sun above. On the horizon, swelling white clouds congregate.

Ana and the Girl lock eyes. They sense something, together.

SAEED: Ana? What the hell...

They turn simultaneously. On the far edge of the beach, her back to them, building a castle with multicolored beach molds, crouches a STRANGER.

A newcomer. Another little girl.

SAEED: Ana? Say something!

They can't look away. Her brunette hair, in tousled pigtails. Her simple turquoise two-piece swimsuit. She erects a typical child's castle, half of the spires missing, walls crumbling with incoming tides.

In a fantastic world, Ana knows... this is all too real.

SAEED: What was that? Ana, if you can hear me, say something. Touch your eyes. Goddamnit!

The Girl steps to the stranger. Her slow, deliberate march holds none of Her earlier menace. No army of creatures. No guard.

SAEED: What is this?

Ana's legs feel weightless. She stands. Simple, granular sand flows from her thighs to the ground.

SAEED: Ana, talk to me.

ANA: Do not pull me out.

The stranger rests on bent legs. Back upright, she appraises her makeshift masterpiece. A butterfly bow holds each pigtail. Five years old — an actual five, not an approximation, not a projection. A real five-year-old girl.

The Girl steps to her, kneels as Ana did. With Her finger, She swirls into the stranger's castle. The sand DANCES and LEAPS in scintillating flames toward the sapphire sky. Grains BURST and POP as miniature fireworks. The stranger CHEERS with delight.

SAEED: I've got no read on this. Could still be dangerous.

ANA: Just... watch.

The Girl settles crosslegged into the sand next to the stranger, like kin.

ANA: Watch.

With joy, the stranger RAVAGES her castle. She tears fistfuls of sand to offer up to the Girl, who ROCKETS them in every direction.

Then, the stranger drops the sand and extends a hand to the Girl.

Ana's heart seizes. *Don't take her hand. The pain...*

But nothing changes. No white glow. No imprisoning sand. Only calm.

Ana feels the sun's heat streak down her face.

But no, not the sun...

...her own tears, hot and full.

For when the stranger turns, Ana already knows her face. The even bangs. The small dimples. The missing lower incisors. Her Charlotte.

Small and strong, just as she was, as she will always be. Beautiful.

For the briefest moment, Charlotte turns to Ana. The look is quick, wise beyond her age. Ana feels the comforting wave of true bliss.

Of returning home.

Of being exactly where she needs to be.

Then Charlotte leans to the Girl, cups a hand to Her ear. They share the pure secret of unfamiliar children, whispering like lifelong friends. Like sisters. Their LAUGHTER carries and ripples along the breeze. When the Girl shoots a look back at Ana, Charlotte gives Her hand a reassuring squeeze.

Their intent eyes reach an understanding.

The Girl walks back to Ana, but Ana's eyes fixate on Charlotte.

ANA: Come too.

It is barely a whisper. Charlotte does not hear it. She returns to her decimated castle.

ANA: I'm here, baby. I'm here.

Charlotte commences simple renovations, returning the loose spires and porticos to their imperfect form.

The Girl's waifish body cuts Ana's view of Charlotte. The sky darkens.

How will I get by Her, Ana wonders. *How can I –*

SAEED: Look at Her, Ana.

ANA: I'm trying to.

SAEED: Up, Ana. Look Veronica in the eye!

Ana startles. She looks up. In the Girl's sympathetic face, in Her pure black eyes – Ana finally remembers why she is here.

The Girl extends a hand to Her side. The sand RISES.

Her hand commands swirls of tiny, turbulent tornados BOUNDING from hand to ground in some invisible barrier that reveals itself as...

HUMAN LEGS. A TORSO and ARMS.

A HEAD.

SAEED: No fucking way.

The grains JITTER like anxious molecules. They BOUNCE and yet FORM.

They show shrunken shoulders, a lilt in the left leg. Hair wispy, wrinkled skin weathered.

SAEED: Stay on the body. This is... I can't believe this.

The shapeless head CAVORTS and DIVOTS, like clay molded beneath a thousand hands. A sunken eye, then another. Low, sagging ears.

The Girl inhales as the final formations of a face develop. The body settles into the form of Her Intruder.

SAEED: It's him. Holy shit. We got him!

The Girl's pupils shrink now, circled with a rainbow prism of light.

Ana nods to Her.

ANA: Thank you.

The Girl's hand retracts, spilling the sand into a hilly pile. Her face turns grave.

VERONICA: *You must go now.*

Please, Ana thinks to say. *Please. You can feel her. She is here. She needs me.*

VERONICA: *Go now.*

ANA: Please...

But as Ana looks beyond the Girl, she can already sense what she will not see...

No sandcastle, no pigtails.

Charlotte is already gone.

JOSEPH REIN

Chapter 10

The four of them sat in Veselov's west-facing veranda, the setting sun bleeding through the floor-to-ceiling screens. Veselov made lemongrass tea, which Lane felt obligated to drink. Andrew grew restless; Serena told him to play his music, but he asked to be excused to roam Veselov's woods-facing backyard. Serena relented, stood to escort him, but Lane knew Veselov wouldn't open up to him. He needed Serena there.

He took her hand. "Rene, he can stay in the yard. Isn't that right, Andrew?"

Andrew's lips pursed in skepticism, but then he nodded, recognizing the opening for a freedom his mother didn't usually allow.

"All right," Serena said. "But you know the rules, Andrew. You can't see me, I can't see you."

"Mind the mosquitoes, young man," Veselov said. "Though it may be too hot for them still."

Veselov watched Andrew go. He bounded down her soft hill toward the wood's edge. Even with him far away, Veselov leaned in and whispered, "He is —"

"Her grandson, yes," Lane said, sipping the scalding tea. Veselov nodded. Sonya Young clearly hadn't given her the full picture. He wondered about the weaved tapestry of Young's secrets, how difficult it would be to track the particular threads each person might know. "Your employee record said you were in security. Is that right?"

"I was Sonya's private bodyguard."

That made sense — someone with whom Young felt safe, trusted with her life.

"She had a nickname for me," Veselov continued. "Nikita. Even though I am much taller. If she would have let me, I would have continued in her employ. I could have stopped..." Her voice trailed off, her eyes adrift in the horrors she imagined for Young.

Lane needed to bring her back. "Did she direct you to mail the will to Serena? Or did you do that on your own?"

Veselov sat upright. "It was her bidding."

"Why?" Serena cut in. She had been keeping an intent eye on Andrew, but now turned to Veselov.

"A year ago, she presented me with the will. I wanted to decline, but she had saved me, all those years ago, from..." She faltered. "From a bad marital situation."

"Who else knows about the will?" Lane asked.

Veselov paused for a moment. In her roaming eyes, he saw the machinations of an impending lie.

"Nobody. She trusted only me."

"Why did she want me to have it?" Serena asked.

"Shutting down the company... that was a thing she could not make public. She needed a person of no association with Youtopia Reborn. She needed—"

A shout from the yard cut Veselov off.

At the base of the woods, Andrew stood stock-still. Before Lane could react, Serena rushed out of the veranda and flew across the yard. She slowed when she neared Andrew, her hands gently coming down on his shoulders. They stood still as Lane approached.

In the trimmed grass before them, just on the wood's edge, a massive cluster of black and yellow snakes slithered in cramped commune. A black tarp lay next to them; Andrew must've lifted it in curiosity. Lane put a hand on Serena, backing her and Andrew slowly away.

"It's okay," Lane said. "Just plains garters. Not dangerous." He turned to Andrew and away from the snakes, to show they were harmless. "They won't hurt you."

Serena turned to Andrew. "You scared me shitless! That's your bad scream."

When they were clear of the woods, halfway back to the house, she asked Lane, "How do you know so much about snakes?"

"As a journalist, you learn a lot. More than you care to know."

"Like which snakes can kill you."

"Like that."

When they returned to the veranda, Veselov wasn't there. Their teacups sat in the saucer, whispering out their final wisps of steam. Everything felt too quiet.

Lane pushed the door to the house open a crack and peered inside. From some distant corner came Veselov's muted voice. Lane tried but couldn't make out the words.

He signaled Serena to stay put, then chanced a step inside. Then another. The house was aggressively modern: white and stainless-steel kitchen, sharp lines and thick faux-wood trim, no pictures on the walls, minimalistic décor. It felt less lived in than staged. Across the narrow living room, past an ornate fireplace, Veselov's voice traveled from a short hallway. Lane stepped further, soft on his feet, the hardwood floorboards threatening to herald his heavy steps.

"I could not tell you," Veselov said. "I did not expect her to show up here!"

Lane tipped his head around the corner. Veselov leaned against the wall, facing away from him. She stood near the door to her basement stairwell.

Lane's mind immediately flashed to the abduction video, to Young bound and tied. As farfetched as it seemed, Veselov became a sudden suspect—a former bodyguard enacting some sinister vengeance for being abandoned, for unrequited love, for some other unknown, insane reason.

"I can't do that."

Veselov half-turned. Lane ducked; she only needed to turn her head fully to catch him inside her house spying, to force their progress drastically sideways.

He tiptoed backward. He needed to get out. In his last glimpse, he spotted a cellphone in her hand.

"Even if I tried," he heard Veselov say, her voice coming closer. "I don't think I can."

As fast as he could move while remaining silent, he darted through the kitchen, slid through the veranda door, and shut it behind him.

Serena's eyes carried the ambivalent awe of a parent who knew her child had done wrong, and yet couldn't hide her deviant pride.

"You're crazier than me," she said.

"She's on the phone. Talking about us."

"Sheesh." Serena pulled Andrew in close. "Who with?"

"Don't know, but we need to find out. Whoever it is knows about the will, and might—"

The door shuddered. Lane stepped back as Veselov reentered. She had no phone in her hand, though her eyes looked hesitant.

"Everything all right?" she asked. Lane didn't realize she was asking about Andrew until she looked over at him.

"Yes, he's fine," Serena said. "Just too curious. Par for the course."

"Pack of garters," Lane added. "Under your tarp out there. Gave him a scare."

"I understand," Veselov said, turning back to Andrew. "For me, it was a fear of dogs. Your grandmother, she loved Great Danes—very large, gentle—yet I could never feel comfortable around them."

"Nicole," Lane said, stepping toward her. He was about to repeat a question in hopes of getting a different answer, hoping she might confess to her surreptitious call. "When Sonya Young went missing, did anyone contact you about the will? Does anybody else know about Serena and Andrew?"

Veselov turned from Andrew to Lane. This time, she did not hesitate. "We are the only ones. Until Sonya is found, that is probably best."

***

Saeed brought Ana a second cup of black coffee. She wrapped her fingers around the hot porcelain. Two blankets covered her shoulders, but still her body chittered, her muscles tensing and loosening, trying to regain the heat it imagined it had lost. The dim lights pierced her eyes, like the worst of her migraines. Saeed offered her sunglasses as her head throbbed with undulant waves of pain.

You are here, her mind told her body—Saeed's office in Youtopia Towers, floor-to-ceiling windows and hardwood floors and industrial air. *You are not there. You are here.*

Saeed's other hand blossomed open to reveal a small pill, coated bright red. "Naproxiphentanol. Everyone complains about the withdrawals. Some give the *worst-pain-I've-ever-felt* spiel. Ten out of ten on the Richter scale. A bit dramatic, if you ask me. Sonya designed this specifically to tone it down."

Ana hesitated, not wanting to pull her hand from the blanket, or take more drugs engineered by Sonya Young. The first was a paralyzing toxin unwillingly injected into her in North Dakota years ago. Then the KaliSerum from Saeed. Now this.

"I'll be fine."

"Thought you'd say that." He retracted the red pill.

Ana wasn't as certain as her voice sounded. She would be fine in the physical sense; the pain and shivering punished her, yes, but she could handle it. And she felt buoyed by their success. The Immerser girl provided a sketch clearer than any artist's rendering. For the first time they had a substantial, promising lead.

But *how* they achieved it had shaken Ana. Charlotte was there. She was real—as real as the febrile chills, the thrashing in her temples, the wool surrounding her shoulders. If only they'd had a moment together. If only there had been time.

Behind his glassine desk, before a litany of flatscreens, Saeed's eyes bounced across images of Ana's Intervention. None showed Charlotte.

Outside, a solitary red-tailed hawk descended, likely from the Tower's rooftop Terrace. It seemed to peer into the room, or perhaps at itself in reflection.

"What happened in there?" Ana asked.

Saeed shook his head. "Not what I expected, that's for sure." He spun a screen toward Ana, revealing the furious torrent when everything changed. With nimble finger taps, he progressed through the flashing light to the familiar beach landscape. He paused before Charlotte's appearance. "Not to Veronica's taste. Looks a helluva lot like our world."

Ana immediately recognized the place: the sloping curve of the beachline to their right, the pristine white sand. Beyond it all, too distant for her to initially notice, stood three palm trees in a perfect triangular pattern. Even farther, high-rise hotels stood in upright unison.

Haulover Beach: the place Ana and Paul, and then Charlotte, had vacationed every summer.

"It's my world," Ana said.

Saeed slapped his hands together. "I knew it! That's..." He let out a slow breath that morphed into a whistle. "That's so fucking cool!"

"How did it happen?"

"No idea. I designed Interventions to help establish the basics. Wheels roll, birds fly. ABC, easy as 123. Interveners are supposed to teach the Immersers how to build, not be the architects themselves."

"It was my Youtopia too."

He nodded. "Right here —" He turned another screen. " — when she grabbed your hand... Some connection that I never conceived. Not in my wildest." He turned from the computer screen to his phone with the deftness of a person constantly plugged in. "Oh, Sonya, you need to see this, doll face. The possibilities!"

Ana tried to sit straight. The blood in her body immediately flooded upward, spinning her head. Fireworks burst in her peripheral vision. She fought back vomit as Saeed dragged a feverish finger across his phone.

"Is that beach still there, I wonder?" Saeed said. "If we sent you back in, would —"

"Saeed," Ana said in the sternest voice she could muster.

"And the little girl... where'd she run off to?"

Charlotte, Ana's mind reflexed. *Her name is Charlotte.*

"If we could find her again. Study the way..."

No. Ana shook her dizzied head. She couldn't do this, not again. Saeed was here, in front of her, in an office on the highest floors of

Youtopia Towers. He was real. Charlotte—her Charlotte, from her memories, from her deepest desires—was not.

They had a lead. They needed to act.

"Saeed," she repeated. He finally shook his gaze from his phone. "We need to focus. We have a job to do."

"Damn. Right. The guy."

"She gave us his face. A full build."

"Yeah. Picture perfect." He ran a hand through his coarse hair. "I feel comfortable telling you this now: I thought we'd fail. Ninety-eight-point-seven-percent certainty. I haven't really thought past this point." He slid down into a slouch. "You're the former Fed. What do you do with that profile? Run facial rec, right? Get your matches. Cross-reference criminal records. We find the most obvious one and take a stab at him. I have the gist?"

"No," Ana said.

"Then what?"

Still softly shivering, she shrugged off the blanket and stood. "Engaging a child Immerser in her own Youtopia was dangerous, but a psychopathic hostage-taker? Even if we could ID him, we'd be insane to go knocking on his door."

"So what do we do?"

"We call the FBI."

***

With Veselov closed off, Lane insisted that they go, that they'd taken up enough of her time already. He knew he'd get nothing more from her, but they needed to know who she called—who else knew about the will. So, as Veselov moved to usher them out of the veranda, Lane asked Andrew if he needed to use the bathroom.

Serena squinted, pondering Lane's newfound paternal instinct. Andrew just shook his head.

"You sure?" Lane asked. "We need to find a hotel. Might be a bit. Better to try while the can is nigh." He crouched down and gave Andrew a wink. "At least that's what my dad always said."

Serena took Andrew's shoulders, her intuition clearly sensing something in Lane's unnatural insistence. "Lane's right, baby. I'll go with you." Then, to Veselov, "You don't mind?"

"Of course." Veselov stepped aside and opened the veranda door. "Down the hall. It is your second door."

As Veselov gathered the tea and cups, Lane ducked into the house behind Serena. On the counter just to his left, he spotted Veselov's cellphone. He snatched and pocketed it just before Veselov clattered in with the tray.

He slid around the kitchen table to close the door behind her. "I'll go after you," he called, hoping Serena and Andrew would be quick. In the meantime, he needed to distract Veselov from her phone's absence, and hope against hope it didn't ring.

"You have a beautiful home," he said. "How long have you lived here?"

Veselov set the tray near the sink. "Long enough."

"You like the area? Your neighbors?"

"No."

Her eyes roved the countertop. Hand in his pocket, Lane felt the weight of her phone like a stone threatening to sink him. Small talk would not work. He needed more time.

"You know," he said, "I don't usually tell people this, but... I was in Youtopia."

Veselov's eyes raised. "You were?"

"Almost two years."

She turned her attention to him. He had her. Not knowing how long a story he would need to tell, he started at the beginning: his knee, his journalistic endeavors in college, up to his parents' death. He described Youtopia with acute detail, things he'd forgotten, like his favorite vacation spot — an approximation of the Grecian Islands — and his favorite meals — a fried-egg-topped hamburger from a local pub. He described things FAR and Henrick had encouraged him to forget. Strangely, with Sonya Young's former bodyguard as an audience, he felt comfortable in sharing what happened to him, a healthy detachment. It happened. It was good. It just was.

Serena and Andrew returned as Lane reached his Reawakening. He smiled. "Coming back... well, I guess that's a story for another time." He turned to Serena, opening his eyes as wide as he could without startling her. "Looks like I'm up."

He was asking too much of Serena, for her to intuit what he needed of her. And yet, somehow Serena absorbed his peculiar look with a soft smile. She approached Veselov.

"Ah-*mazing* house," she said. "My little Andrew here couldn't keep his eyes off your library."

Veselov smiled. "Living out here... my books have become my company."

"You can relate, huh, Andrew?" Serena tousled his hair, a gesture he shrugged away. "Would you mind showing us some of your favorites? He's always up for recommendations."

"I have a first edition C.S. Lewis."

"Hell yes! Narnia, here we come."

As Veselov led Serena and Andrew down the hall, Lane sprung into the bathroom and locked the door behind him. He pulled out Veselov's phone, an older, all-black Android with no case and hairline cracks creeping from one corner. He awakened it, a desert landscape and the time alighting across the screen, praying it was unsecured, that she hadn't enabled retinal or worse. After all, she lived so far away from civilization. He found himself clenching and unclenching his right fist, an old free-throw superstition from his basketball days. He swiped up.

Draw unlock pattern.

"Shit."

He heard a loud laugh—Serena's—from the library. He didn't have much time. Swipe was better than biometrics or even a password, but still. He rushed to the mirror, holding the phone up to the sconce and seeing his only chance: smudges across the nine-dot pattern, a distinctive cross with a diagonal connecting the ends. From right to left the streaks were more prominent, suggesting she touched the phone on the right first. Thankfully, like most people, Veselov didn't clean her phone often. He would need to recreate her pattern from these traces.

He tried right to left, then across the diagonal and up, hoping for beginner's luck. The phone softly vibrated.

Incorrect pattern drawn.

He tried left to right with the same result. Up and down. Down and up. He held the phone again to the light, seeing now the traces of his own fingerprints across Veselov's.

"Damnit," he whispered.

He returned to the original pattern, cutting it short this time across the opposite angle.

The blurred screen dissolved, and her home screen appeared.

Lane's blood ignited, tingling all over, as though he was in the bathroom of a plane at some immense altitude. Immediately, he pulled Veselov's recent call history. The last number: no contact name, but a 414 area code. Milwaukee. He took out his burner phone and snapped quick photos of her call log, scrolling down a month or more, well past the abduction. Then he pocketed both phones, flushed the toilet and washed his hands. His face, the stubble and sleepless eyes, looked back at him from the mirror. He looked like an aberrant, errant version of his usual self, equal parts focused and deranged. He felt alive. He smiled.

The bathroom hinges squealed as he opened the door. Veselov still entertained Serena and Andrew in the library. Lane hastily stepped to the kitchen, replacing Veselov's phone not where she left it—not out in the open, where she would have noticed its absence—but along the wall, pressed against the backsplash tiles. Reasonable to think she would have put it there without much thought, that Lane and Serena were indeed as wholesome as they seemed.

But even if Veselov did suspect them, they would be long gone by the time it mattered. He got what they needed. And they were finally, finally, getting closer to the truth.

JOSEPH REIN

Chapter 11

Ana and Saeed stood just off the desolate runway. Ana wiped her brow, the unremitting morning humidity hanging on her like ill-fitting clothing. She was reminded of the Dominican, days upon days of inescapable sultry heat. There, at least, her job hadn't required a black suit.

The Intervention, the spikes and dips in her adrenaline, the lack of sleep the past 24 hours, had all left her feeling hollowed out, dehydrated. A metallic taste lingered on her tongue, a remnant of the three cups of cheap coffee she'd had since she called Bruce. Jittery in her fingers and chest, dizzy near her temples, she felt suddenly too old for this. She needed a clear mind. She needed sleep.

Thirty feet behind them, a pair of black BMW SUVs with FBI drivers flanked Ana's rental car. Saeed turned back to them. "You Feds always such creeps?" he asked. "They could at least introduce themselves."

"They're only here to drive," Ana said. "Here comes the headliner."

The jet arrived from the east, eight minutes ahead of schedule, its triple-engine roar playing like a forgotten song. Ana took in an unsatisfying breath of relief. The jet was likely sanctioned by the DOJ, the White House, maybe even POTUS herself. Bruce had commissioned the runway of a local farmer who doubled as an amateur stuntman. As the off-white, nondescript plane touched down, the wheels burning across the steaming asphalt and the stench of rubber pluming, Ana recalled similar planes at the end of the Villalobos case, as they closed in on the murderer. The plane brought that familiar thrust of urgency, an augury of the end. They were that close.

When the plane's stairs descended, two identical-looking, black-suited agents stepped out first, followed by Bruce. He flipped on a pair of dark sunglasses and circled his burly shoulders. When he saw Ana, he nodded like a parent greeting his wayward child. Never a small man, Bruce was now larger, fuller at the waist and jowls. His trim beard carried more salt than pepper. The younger agents trailed on his heels, their peppy steps shuffling behind him. Bruce introduced himself to Saeed first before turning to her.

"Downer. You ignored my orders."

"Look where it got us."

He offered his hand to shake. His body already glistened with beads of sweat. He appeared genuinely happy to see her.

"How is Leann? Life at home?" Ana asked.

"Leann's Leann." He adjusted his lapels, the fat Windsor knot of his tie. "Field office is thirty miles from here. Ride with me. Catch me up on Dominican culture." He nodded his head to the pair behind him. "Mr. Free can ride with Fox and Gibbons."

Ana slid into the black BMW. To her surprise, Bruce joined her in the back, navigating his girth without grace as he plopped into his seat. "AC up. Full boar," he said to the young agent in the driver's seat, though the fan already churned loudly, drowning out the radio and the agent's GPS.

Saeed's car jumped out before them, leading down the dusty trail.

"I don't know how you weaseled your way into Free's good graces," Bruce said.

"It's a long story."

"No matter how, I have to say it: hell of a catch, Ana."

Bruce stared out his window at a massive crop irrigation sprinkler that doused the knee-high corn below it, much of the water steaming up before even reaching the ground. Giving such praise made him uncomfortable, Ana knew. He looked away, which meant he was sincere. When he needed to reprimand, to chew someone up and spit them out, then he looked them dead in the eye.

"From the images Free sent us," Bruce continued, "we got a 99.6% positive match."

"It's him."

"It's him."

Ana nodded. "I don't suppose you can tell me who he is, being my catch and everything."

"Why do you think you're in this car?"

As if on cue, the SUV driving Saeed took a leftward turn, onto a back country road. Theirs continued forward.

"Free won't like that," Ana said.

"Who gives a damn what he likes. We got what we needed."

Bruce reached into the front seat and retrieved a black satchel holding multiple manila folders. One of them had the name *Arthur Mauer* hastily scribbled across the tab.

"Didn't know anybody still printed," Ana said.

"With this guy, the less we're online, the better. This is your eyes only."

The file contained legal documents, birth certificates and insurance papers, an op-ed written for a local newspaper in Nebraska.

"Mauer's seventy-seven years old. Lived outside Lincoln his whole life, where he—surprise surprise—farmed corn. He's the one infiltrating Reborn."

Ana found a handful of recent photographs of Arthur Mauer, all with him wearing a faded John Deere hat and a smile filled with several silver crowns. Only one photo was from Mauer's youth: a staged picture of him and a woman in an unnatural pose, a wedding photo perhaps. But Bruce was right: this man was undoubtedly the sandman from Veronica's Reborn. Or rather, from the Reborn she and Ana had shared.

"Seventy-seven, a farmer," Ana said. "He must have an accomplice."

Bruce reached over and shuffled through the documents to reveal photos of a younger man, mid-thirties. Behind them rested application documents for a Master's program in Computational Science and Engineering from MIT, multiple tables of contents of *Applied Physics Quarterly* dated in the mid-2010s, and then one, some years later, in *The Christian Science Monitor*.

"Goes by the Graduate in online circles, after that Dustin Hoffman movie. Thinks he's quite the lothario with older women."

In recent photos, all taken in small bars, the Graduate sat smileless and sullen. A white baseball hat donned his head. His eyes were narrow, his cheeks sunken. Only in an old college ID photo did his face seem vibrant. His eyes radiated an optimism washed away with the years.

"How'd they connect?"

"This kid apparently aced everything in school, but he was an outcast—rural kid from an unstable home in a sea of East Coast elites. Multiple misconduct citations. Problems with alcohol. Eventually, he dropped out. After that, he couldn't keep a job for more than a few months. When he moved back home, he started in on cybercrime. From what we can tell, he created hundreds of online personas to scam elderly women out of their pensions."

"Sounds typical."

"Until he met Mauer at a downtown dive called the Fat Toad. Mauer was fresh into Reintegration—chronic pain, lung issues from decades of smoking. Ready to drink himself to death."

"A perfect match."

"Seems they struck a deal: Mauer offered up his full inheritance, and the kid hacked him into the Reborns. I'd call it a con, but the kid genuinely seems to care for the old man. Mauer never had a son, a family. The kid never had stability. Heartwarming stuff, if they weren't criminals."

Bruce shuffled to another photo, this one from a perched security camera, of the Graduate sitting in a crowded shuttlebus. He wore the same white baseball cap, the same deadened eyes.

"He took one of the first Reborn Cradle tours," Bruce said. "Must've laid his groundwork in the closed loop then."

Ana turned to the other recent photos. In two of them, a woman roughly Ana's age hung on his shoulder. She seemed dressed the part of Mrs. Robinson, down to the fur coat and long cigarette. "She involved?"

"Not that we can tell. Just a fling that has lasted longer than the rest."

Ana handed Bruce the files. "This Graduate has a clear motive. He wants *Reborn for All*, so he abducts Sonya Young to force her to capitulate."

"And," Bruce added, "Mauer has the perfect middle-of-nowhere farmhouse to hide her."

Ana felt that tingling in her fingertips, her cheeks — the tinge of inevitability. "You'll bring him in then?"

"Our team's moving in within the hour."

Ana nodded. Even after all she'd seen, she could still be impressed by the FBI's speed.

"Before you ask," Bruce continued, "Yes, I'm going to let you watch. Because you made the catch. Because you were one of my favorite agents." He finally looked into Ana's eyes. "How many times do I have to say it?"

"The once is enough. Though for the record, I wasn't asking."

"With your goddamn eyes, you were."

They hit the highway north, away from Youtopia Towers and toward Milwaukee. Billboards gleaned with the broad smiles of car dealers and religious figures. The driver's GPS put their arrival at FBI headquarters, a discreet building on Lake Street, at thirteen minutes.

In the silence of the car, the cool air conditioning crystallizing the sweat on the back of her neck, Ana felt the raw excitement of the fact that, in less than an hour, they'd have their suspect in custody. *Her* suspect. The beginning of the end. The thought brought her, suddenly, back to Lane Samson.

Lane. She had given him little thought since they parted — rightfully so, as her solo pursuit had proved, yet it didn't need to be like this. She didn't need to shut him out the way Lonnie and Paul did to her. For retrieving her, for helping her regain her former self, at the very least she owed him something.

She opened her messages but saw nothing from Lane. Perhaps he was still in dogged pursuit of Serena, of the daughter that never was. Perhaps he had simply given up. Once the dust settled, Ana would give him the scoop, an exclusive interview. *Hey, sorry for the delay. But we got him,* she typed. *Watch the news.*

As her finger reached for the send button, she hesitated. She shouldn't send it—not until Mauer and the Graduate were in custody. Lane surely couldn't jeopardize the case, but there was no rush. The Feds would have them soon.

They exited on Harbor Drive, past Lake Michigan and the vast fields and concert stages of the half-disassembled Summerfest grounds. High in the sky, a hundred kites on endless strings battled the lake breeze.

"One thing doesn't add up," Ana said.

"I know what you're thinking," Bruce said. "How did the kid get Young out of her house?"

Ana nodded. It was reassuring that Bruce, after years of heading the division, still maintained his instincts. In the right circumstance, she and Bruce could still be on the same page.

"Cutting the cameras would be easy enough for him," Ana said. "He has the technical expertise to manipulate her systems. But could he abduct her without leaving a trace?"

"Her house is off the grid, built for secrecy. She's never let a single member of the press inside."

Bruce reached back into his bag, producing another folder with the initial police report filed by the LAPD Pacific Division. Photos showed the vast woods, the long driveway. The exterior of Sonya Young's house was almost entirely composed of reflective glass. The bedroom picture— the one splashed across the news—showed the red REBoRN FoR ALL oR REBoRN FoR NoNE message on the wall.

"Sixty-two hours," Bruce continued, "from the time she was last seen until the call from the housekeeper. If he knew her schedule—which he also could have hacked—he also knew he had time to clean up after himself."

Ana looked at the photo of the slanted words, painted like a child's signature. The Russian nesting dolls stood watch over the bed like eerie sentinels.

"What if Sonya isn't there?"

Bruce turned to her, and for the first time she saw, beneath his eyes, the dark half-moons, the wrinkle crease between his brow, the years of scowling now permanently etched.

"Have to be a hell of a coincidence," he said. "You know I don't believe in coincidences."

"Normally, neither do I."

"Then it's high time we bring the old Ana back."

***

Lane vacillated between dream and memory, between the perfect and the real—plush pillows beneath his head, Serena's leg rubbing against his. This time, when his eyes opened, he felt no fear.

The night before, they'd driven an hour past Veselov's house, Lane hoping that Andrew would finally tucker and his drooping eyelids would surrender. Fueled by an energy drink and a can of mixed nuts, Lane was ready to put as much distance behind them as possible.

Ultimately, though, Serena knew her son better: Andrew couldn't sleep while in motion. The boy had a hard enough time in his own bed — a function, Serena claimed, of his latent genius, of a mind too active for its own good. They stopped at a Holiday Inn Express and got another double queen. Serena cuddled with Andrew until he fell asleep.

Lane lay on the bed opposite, wired and fidgeting. He played a quieted Esperanza Spalding on his earbuds and tried to let his mind drift to the necessary recesses of sleep. Only when Serena joined him in his bed, when she placed a hand on his chest and entwined a leg with his, did everything finally unwind.

Upon waking, he didn't remember falling asleep, his dreams lifting away like a morning fog before the July sun. He felt no need to stretch or pump off pushups or ab crunches. He didn't care to check news sites, to stalk Bethany Fawkes. He felt clear, as he hadn't in a long time. He was here, in this moment. He was ready.

The clock read 9:33 a.m. Serena lay completely still, her mouth slack, deep in sleep. To his surprise, Andrew was not in his bed. He turned about the room and almost missed him, legs crossed in a corner chair near the window with a book between them. Headphones engulfing his small head, he read by the low light entering a curtain slit. The book appeared intentionally weathered, antique: *The Hobbit* by Tolkien.

Lane walked over to him and peered at the pages, expecting to see a graphic novel or at least some illustrations, but he saw only words. He tapped gently on Andrew's shoulder; Andrew's eyes scanned to the end of his sentence before looking up and removing his headphones.

"Good book?" Lane whispered. "I've seen the movies, but never got a chance to read it."

"Yes."

"Do you... does it all make sense to you?"

"You should read it. It's better than the movie."

"They always are." Lane knelt next to him. "Hey, Andrew, I wanted to ask you... You okay with everything we're doing here? With all this road tripping?"

Andrew thought for a moment. For his age, he seemed impressively careful of his own words. His eyes returned to the book. "Mom says we need to."

"I know, and I agree with her, but it can be hard sometimes, as a kid. When your parents say you need to do something."

Still staring into the book, Andrew said, with a nonchalance Lane hadn't seen in him, "I trust her."

Lane looked back to Serena, who hadn't moved. Suddenly, he wished his own mother were still alive. He wished Serena had been awake to hear Andrew, to understand how much her virtuoso son believed in her. Something told him she already knew.

He showered, shaved with supplies purchased from a front desk kiosk. When he finished, he leaned over Serena and gently pressed on her shoulder to wake her.

"Rene," he said.

She rolled to her side, her lithe arms stretching out above her head. Her palm oil smell rose off her pillow. "Laney, you bastard. I was having the most delectable dream."

"I know," Lane said. "But it's time to wake up."

While Serena showered and Andrew read, Lane took up his phone and called the one man who could help him trace the number from Veselov's phone.

When Quinn didn't answer, Lane video called, hoping it would signal his urgency.

"No," Quinn said when he saw Lane. His face loomed large in the videochat screen, his beard stippled with mustard from the sandwich he devoured. Behind his voice, the hammering guitar opening of "Back in Black" played through the phone into their hotel room.

"I haven't even asked yet."

"You're calling from a new number. I can only guess — new number means new hijinks means I'm six degrees of Kevin Bacon away from federal prison."

"Last one," Lane said. "I promise."

"Just like the last one was the last one." Quinn sighed. "You're going to owe me... something monumental, I'll tell you that."

"You name it."

Quinn stroked his beard. "A date. I want a date with your former boss."

"Millie?"

"Lane, my man, I like the cut of that woman's jib." Quinn flashed a smile mid-bite, bits of bread and meat between his teeth.

"We need this fast."

"Which is why you called me."

The video jostled, but then rested steady on Quinn's end. Lane saw his fingers type at a keyboard, his eyes roving an unseen computer screen. When the song ended, another AC/DC one began, an even louder rock ballad Lane couldn't place. Quinn said something that Lane missed.

"Can you turn the music down?" Lane asked.

Quinn half-giggled. "Sorry. Something about Brian Johnson's raspy voice, man. Zeroes me in. Grandpap *loved* them. He was one for the ages. I ever tell you —"

"Quinn. Focus. I'm sending you the number now. Just need a simple trace, like before."

"Simple. Ha." He went back to his laptop. His tongue lolled in his mouth as his fingers typed away. After a minute, he said, "Hot damn. That part *was* simple."

"You've got the trace?"

"No trace. But I've got the owner."

"Who?"

"The phone is licensed by none other than Youtopia Reborn Incorporated."

"Can you see who it was assigned to?"

Quinn quickly shook his head. "Hack Reborn's internal records? With all the eyes they've got on them right now? You jest, sir."

"What about the location? You can track it, right?"

A laugh came from behind him. Serena stood with her hair in a towel, Andrew at her side. Lane hadn't heard the bathroom door open. She wore the same tee and jeans as the day before, and yet, somehow, they didn't look mussed like Lane's clothes.

"And to think," she said, "you got after me for ditching our phones."

Lane turned to his phone again. Quinn's lips were pursed. "If you're gonna ignore me, the least you can do is introduce me."

Lane looked to Serena, who shrugged. Andrew retreated behind her legs as Lane flipped his phone to face her. She struck an immediate, alluring Madonna pose, and Quinn laughed from his end. In the way only Serena could, she had charmed a stranger in mere seconds.

"Spitting image, man," Quinn said as Lane flipped the phone back. "Don't know how you missed it."

"It's not exactly something you look for. Let's get back to tracking the number."

"On that: yes and no. A solid maybe."

"What's the problem?"

"Well, for one, the phone needs to be powered on."

"It should be. Veselov called it only yesterday. Likely the person on the other end is keeping it live in case she calls again."

"It's a start. But there'll still be some sizeable landmines I gotta sidestep. Harder than finding your girlfriend's T-Mobile." He raised his voice. "No offense!"

"Couldn't offend me if you tried, sweetheart," Serena called in response.

"But you could get it?" Lane asked Quinn.

"TBD, my friend. Tee. Bee. Dee."

Quinn's fingers played again. At the small desk in the hotel room, Serena dug through their gas station food leftovers, handing a bag of baked potato chips to Andrew.

Lane said to Quinn, "You can turn your music up now."

"Rock n roll." Quinn's hand reached out and the music blared.

Lane minimized Quinn and opened his news feed, looking for anything related to Peterson's assault. He again Googled Bethany Fawkes, for the first time hoping that she had something, that she discovered some nugget he could put together with his and Serena's discoveries, but there had been nothing since the attack—no mention of ongoing leads, police or otherwise; no interviews or statements from Reborn. And even though she and Peterson seemed to have a connection, Anabel Downer remained out of the spotlight.

Downer. Lane admitted to himself that he had lost her. Reaching out now was pointless. At the AAU basketball game—just over a week earlier but feeling so much longer—Millie told him he needed an FBI Agent. But instead of paving the path together, they had built entirely separate roads.

Still, he pulled the napkin with his numbers from his pocket. He typed her a brief message:

We're onto something. Can't go into detail, but... Serena is definitely Sonya's daughter. Got a lead on who sent the will.

He stopped. The deviant parts of his mind envisioned Downer swooping in, apprehending Serena and confiscating his entire path forward, taking credit for all the work he did to get here. His finger hovered over the send button.

Then a girlish shriek shot from his phone. He enlarged Quinn again, who flashed a beguiling smile.

"You got it," Lane said.

"Hook, line and sinker, baby!" Quinn called above the screeching song. "I gotta say, this is wild man. We're like Briscoe and Logan."

"Who?"

"Who, he asks! Only the most infamous pair of... you know what, forget it. If you don't know —"

"Quinn. Where is the phone?"

He turned down the music. "Thirty miles west of Milwaukee."

"You have an address?"

"Believe it or not, the number's an actual *landline.* Who even has those anymore?"

Lane's phone chimed: Quinn sent him the exact location on a Google map. Lane zoomed in on the pulsing red dot of the phone's location, taking note of roads and surrounding areas.

"Looks like a big plot."

"Yep."

"And the company owns it?"

"That's the thing. Check out the online specs — public photos galore."

Lane typed in the address. Quinn was right: a basic search pulled up photos of a spacious dining room interior with a massive rectangular table, a fireplace-laden library room, an outdoor gazebo staged for hosting events.

"A rental?" Lane said.

"That'd be my guess," Quinn said. "Might be for out-of-town bigwigs to stay when they're visiting."

"Companies have those?"

"The size of Mom's company?" Serena said from across the room. "Hell yes, they do."

"Smart and beautiful," Quinn said. "She is, as the adults would say, a keeper."

"Any way you can find out who's using the house?" Lane asked.

"Negative, Ghost Rider. Takes us right back to the whole can't-hack-the-company conundrum. And before you ask, it's can't, won't, don't want to try, wouldn't if I could. You pick."

"All right. I'll be in touch if we need anything else."

"Just dinner reservations for two, my man. July 29—there's a new moon coming in. My peak charm coincides with a new cycle."

"You're a weird guy, Quinn."

"All the way to the bank. Keep me posted."

Lane hung up and tossed his phone to the bed.

"He's something else," Serena said. She sat beside him. "I thought I was the only eccentric one in your life."

"You don't even scratch the surface." Lane took her hand in his. "Milwaukee here we come?"

She smiled. "We didn't come this far to stop now."

***

Seven black SUVs; a dozen-plus FBI Agents, part Nebraska local, part national; a DC SWAT team with AR-15s and fully body Kevlar: Ana watched it all on two large flatscreens, one a satellite bird's-eye of the wending country road leading to Arthur Mauer's house, the other a body camera affixed to one of the field agents. The bodycam jumped and jutted with the bumpy gravel road they traversed, its effect nauseating, like riding a virtual rollercoaster. Ana turned to the other screen and watched the SUVs march down the same road they'd been on for minutes now. Each country house they passed felt like the one: Ana had to fight the rising and fading tidal waves of phantom premonitions.

"How much longer?" she asked Bruce, who remained uncharacteristically silent. His eyes burrowed into the sky view, as though he could somehow, with his intense concentration, will the outcome. "Bruce. How far out?"

"Two miles." He broke his concentrated stare for just a moment. "They're storming. Brace yourself."

Ana returned to the screens. The procession felt slow, like a funeral, and yet based on the dirt their tires expelled and the steady movement of the camera, she estimated they were doing over seventy, a dangerous clip on such an unpredictable path. They flew through what seemed like endless, vacuous farmland until, suddenly, in a billowing hurricane of dust, they slowed.

The house was small, a ranch-style one-story without a garage. Battered shingles covered the rooftop. It was secluded, decrepit—the exact kind of place one might hide Sonya Young.

Bruce expelled a long breath. The leading SUV pulled dangerously close to a solitary tree and stopped. The others followed.

Ana turned to the bodycam, which shuddered and then twisted as the car doors opened.

The silent storm descended.

Ana watched from above as the rifle-donning SWAT team climbed the stoop to the front door. They parted for the two battering-ram-toting agents with graceful efficiency. The bodycam agent stood at a perfect mid-shot distance, the outline of his arms visible where he held his own pistol.

On a silent count, the battering ram rocked back and then violently forth.

The aging door splintered with ease, surrounding Bruce and Ana with shattering sound.

The SWAT team and FBI agents surged inward, a flood into the open dam. They shouted and identified themselves. The bodycam agent started forward as a huge German Shepherd with slathering jowls and dark black eyes bucked and gnashed at everybody entering. It took three agents to wrangle and subdue the manic animal.

The bodycam agent lingered near the entryway. Down the far hallway, SWAT members cased the rooms and shouted "Clear!" in bellowing voices.

Bruce leaned toward the screens and touched his communication earpiece with a steady hand. "Any contact?"

The bodycam agent entered the rectangular living room area covered in outdated veneered walls. Then he shifted left, to the kitchen where a mass of Russian nesting dolls lined the wall, disassembled and patterned like bar graphs. On the table, one brown, unfinished doll stood atop scattered newspapers littered with brushes and flecks of paint that eerily resembled blooddrops. The bodycam agent held on them for a moment, mesmerized.

Ana's body immediately arrested, taken back to all the horrific crime scene videos she watched and rewatched as a Special Agent—all the limbs abnormally folded on themselves, spatters of blood and unmoored skin. The Youtopia murderer in the Nest as she yanked the Senator's body from its tentacles, leaving him to die. The Villalobos children, awash in blood. She imagined Sonya Young's body the same, lying in this man's basement. If the Graduate and Arthur had fled, leaving Sonya dead, the Feds were already too late.

"Downstairs," Ana said. "Which door leads downstairs?"

Bruce didn't respond, and so Ana placed a hand on his arm. It was flexed, tense, his whole body wound up, a powder keg awaiting a fuse. His eyes were knife points looking down on her.

"Sonya Young," she said. "Check the basement."

Bruce turned back to the screen. "Anything in the cellar?"

A long silence followed. No one answered. The bodycam agent turned to the hallway, to the door leading downstairs. A broken padlock latch hung, shattered either by the SWAT members or the Graduate himself. Below, the cellar's dim light contrasted the sun's sharpness above.

Two steps in, the bodycam agent stopped. "Boss?"

"Talk to me."

"Guys below say it's clear. No sign of Sonya Young."

JOSEPH REIN

Interlude: Up a Long, Lonesome Highway

Time: Late morning.

At rise: The Graduate drives in the heat of the day. His small coupe respects posted speed limits as eighteen-wheelers and lunch commuters rattle by. Despite his thunderous heartbeat, his unsteady hands, he cannot rush.

See, in his passenger seat, his precious cargo: his Apparatus, unplugged and stacked with slapdash haste. It jars and grates, protesting every bump his coupe hits.

But that is not the worst. From the back, we hear pained groans — lying across the seat, head propped on all the pillows the Graduate could find, body under flannel blankets: there lies his most precious cargo.

His Arthur. How he suffers.

His coupe dings: low gas. Now it's the Graduate's turn to groan. No cellphone, no tech other than what rattles beside him, he must rely on the next gas station to appear. One mile passes. Two. Five. He wonders how many he has left. He cannot get stranded. He cannot draw attention.

In the ninth mile, a station finally appears. The attendant sits buried behind covered windows, face in his phone. Perfect.

With Glenda's lifted credit card, he fills.

All is silent, calm.

Until it isn't.

Hear the revving of a car engine, strong and fast. Hear the fate of another car approaching.

The Graduate's body seizes, his flight response widening his eyes, clenching his hands. His tank fills and fills: must be half by now. The choice plays out on the brittle landscape of his face — pull the pump, get on his way, and risk having to stop again in daylight... or let it run, and ignore the oncoming driver whose engine resounds monstrous in the hushed afternoon.

Arthur's body lies still in the back, grateful for the reprieve. The Apparatus sits a strange companion, but would this interloper even see it?

- 179 -

The trunk: no reason for anyone to ask to look.

The Graduate stands still, his lack of movement his answer. The gas churns into his tank.

He chooses wrong.

The roaring car, pulling to the island across, is an Iowa State Patroller.

The driver – a bulky, brutish officer with a full beard and sweat stains on his too-tight shirt.

The resounding thump of the Graduate's pump, finally full, portends the Patroller's exit from his cruiser, a mere island away.

The Graduate pulls the pump handle and rushes to replace his gas cap. His fingers fumble. Observe him looking, but not looking, at the Patroller, who is making a slow, curious path toward him.

The Patroller should pump his own gas, should stroll into the vacant, dilapidated convenience store. Why does he march straight at the Graduate?

PATROLLER: *(Wipes his forehead)* Hot enough for ya?

GRADUATE: *(Looks up, just a glance. Even so, sweat drips into his eyes. The gas cap won't twist on. Looks back down, cowering under the Patroller's aggressively humdrum stare)* Yes.

PATROLLER: *(Steps pointedly, perhaps hostilely. Approaches closer, this curious man carrying broad shoulders, a pistol, and the weight of the law)* What is that you've got there?

GRADUATE: What?

PATROLLER: *(Steps even closer now – to the hood of the coupe)*

GRADUATE: *(Shifts his eyes, frenzied, looking for something strong, something metal, something...)*

PATROLLER: Haven't seen one of these in years.

GRADUATE: *(Finally raises his eyes to the Patroller, hands still shaking, teeth gritting)*

PATROLLER: *(Paws the hood ornament)* An old Buick. My pop had one of these growing up. Don't see many of 'em around anymore.

GRADUATE: Don't see 'em. Yes.

PATROLLER: *(Nods. Stands with hands on hips, eyeing the Graduate with curiosity)* Remember coolant. These puppies tend to overheat in this weather.

GRADUATE: Coolant. Yes.

PATROLLER: *(Tips his cap)* Have a good day now. *(Turns back to his car, footsteps no less menacing in that direction)*

GRADUATE: *(Holds his breath — has been holding. Replaces, finally, the gas cap, rushes back to his driver's seat and grumbles the engine to life. Eyes the Patroller back at his cruiser — possible he's on his radio now, reporting the Graduate, calling for backup)*

GRADUATE: No. *(Hits the gas, flees — can't play it slow now. Pushes his speedometer to a desperate pace, willing the trip to its ultimate end...)*

JOSEPH REIN

Chapter 12

They cruised down Interstate 94 past Eau Claire, Wisconsin Dells, Madison. Serena was peculiarly quiet behind the wheel; for the first time since Lane arrived at her doorstep, she seemed uncomfortable. She fiddled with the radio dial. Her face was strangely active, her brow scrunching, her lips pursing with things she seemed unwilling to say.

"Everything okay, Rene?"

"I didn't want to say anything, but..." she said with hesitation. "I heard. Back at her house. When Andrew and I were in the bathroom." She gave a soft smile. "I had no idea."

Lane startled. His body felt suddenly heavy, as though he'd been holding an impossible stretching pose. He felt equal parts exposed, for Serena finding out like this, and ashamed, for not telling her himself. For being afraid of his past.

He looked back to Andrew, who watched them silently. Serena noticed Lane's uncomfortable glance. "Andrew, honey, why don't you listen to some music. We're almost there."

Andrew obeyed, sliding the headphones to his ears and leaving Lane with no more excuses.

"I..." Lane began. "I was just buying time with Veselov. Maybe some credibility. It's not something we're supposed to talk about."

"Even with me?" Serena asked. The question hung between them. "I gotta admit, this whole thing makes more sense. Why you're out here. Why it matters to you. But..." She rubbed a hand at her forehead. "What happened, Laney?"

She turned, and her dark brown eyes penetrated him. Lane immediately knew what she was asking — not what happened in Youtopia, but instead, the tougher question: what happened that caused him to Immerse, to need Youtopia in the first place?

"You don't have to say," she continued. "Unless you want to. You just always seemed... I don't know, solid. A straighter arrow than me, for sure."

Lane took a deep breath. Serena had told him everything. They were, inseparably, bound on this journey together. He might have loved her once, and might love her again. For all this, he needed to tell her the entire truth, including things he'd never spoken aloud before.

He recounted everything since they parted in college. His parents' death stopped him, but he pushed past the familiar barrier, the lock that entrapped the pain in his heart.

"I got the call on the last week of the semester. My father... the night before, he pulled all the carbon monoxide detectors, turned on both of their cars, and just slipped beside my mother in bed."

"Oh Laney. Oh God. I'm so sorry."

"Coming home, people looked at me differently. Sorry for me, sure, but... I don't know... like I was too much like my father. You find out pretty quick who really cares about you. For me, it turned out, not too many."

"I wish I'd known. I could've been there for you."

He nodded. "Me too. I dropped out of school. No job, few true friends. Not much other than my mom's life insurance money. A perfect future sounded a hell of a lot better than no future at all."

"What was it like coming back?"

He shook his head. "Harder... or not harder, just, I don't know... embarrassing." He touched the final remnants of the scab on his lip, the rough skin reminding him of those small pains and inconveniences that Youtopia had erased. "Suddenly, I wasn't just the sorry guy with the dead parents—I was the quitter. Everyone looked at me like I'd taken the easy way out, and I wasn't even sick."

"But you were," Serena said. "Youtopia was your answer for a whole mess of shit. So what? You made a choice. Who gives a flying fuck what they think!"

He looked in her eyes. Countless meetings with FAR, Midnighters and calls with Henrick, and never had it been put to him like this. From them, it was all Reintegrating with society, inviting the opinions and valuations of others, taking part. Serena just told them all to go to hell.

"When you showed me that will," Lane said, "I just... we need to make sure it doesn't happen, Rene. Shutting down Reborn would be a colossal mistake. I'd rather give this guy his way than to force those kids to Reintegrate, or worse."

"You really feel that way? Even after what Immersing did to you?"

"Those kids can't come back to the world. Even the ones without diseases, it's just..." He closed his eyes. "It's too hard."

When he reopened his eyes, Serena was looking directly at him.

"I don't know, Laney. Kids are pretty resilient." She smiled at Andrew, then reached a hand to Lane. "And even if you don't think it, you are too."

***

"You fucking ditched me!" Saeed pouted. He took a vociferous bite of a tofu burger, chewing with mouth wide. "I drove all that way just for the Feds to dump me back here? Total BS."

They ate delivered food in the subdued cafeteria of Youtopia Reborn. With tours canceled, staff minimized, a freeze on research and further Interventions, the place was a shadow of its former self, of the initial Youtopia halcyon days. Saeed and Ana ate like common employees on a common day, as though the Graduate hadn't just slipped through their grasp.

"Don't feel left out," Ana said. "You know what happened on my end."

Back at FBI headquarters, when Ana had asked to see the basement, she could sense that Sonya Young had been there. The camera jounced with each wooden step. The creaking stairs felt like they were under her own feet. The bodycam agent reached the basement floor and slowly turned the full 360 degrees. He caught all the angles. Freed of the possibility of an altercation, he became impressively aware of his job as videographer: a utility sink, a collection of boxes wet and molded, dangling singular bulbs cloudy from disuse. Three scattered agents took photographs with blinding flashes.

"Have him go again."

Bruce relayed the message, and the agent spun, even slower this time. Eerily, the camera's PPI matched that of the abduction video—it felt like an old, pirated VHS tape. Ana stared, searching for some clue to confirm her suspicion that this was it. "Three feet to his left."

The agent obeyed. From this view, Ana saw more closely the hidden southeast corner, the alcove beneath the stairs.

Then, in the flash of one of the camera bulbs, she caught it: the stain— Alaska-shaped, spattered on the wall, as clear as in the abduction video.

"Sonya was here."

Bruce turned to her. "You're sure?"

Ana directed the agent to the wall, explained it all to Bruce. "That's it."

Bruce shook his head. "Goddamnit. Sometimes I hate this job."

The ride from FBI headquarters back to Ana's rental car was somber. Bruce sulked in dejected silence. The agent behind the wheel proceeded with hands at ten and two, checked his rearviews with perfect posture, a picturesque model of driving habits. Ana felt the crushing weight of the empty basement, of standing in the lightning's latent electric charge, its aura, only for it not to strike. They were so close.

The driver pulled off the interloping highway interchange and headed toward the runway. Bruce spent most of his time on his phone, listening, talking in quick bursts.

When he finally hung up, Ana asked, "Anything useful?"

"Sweep says they fled not twelve hours ago. Half a day. That's how close we were." Bruce rubbed at his eyes. "Why do I feel like we're even farther away?"

"Because it's Youtopia."

"Lucky you're no longer a Fed. I'd have your ass for that kind of talk."

"No you wouldn't."

The car pulled onto the gravel road leading to her rental car and Bruce's plane. Instinctually, she wanted to plan next steps, to rebound by moving forward, but she knew Bruce could only go so far, that he'd broken protocol already by involving her. Her tip had played itself out, and unless she could bring something useful, she no longer bore a part. She was now a floater, an informant, expedient only in snippets.

When the car stopped, she said, "Find him. If Sonya Young's alive, she won't be for long."

"Don't I know it." Then, with all the gravity of recognizing the unstated obvious—that they might not see each other again for a long time, if ever—Bruce said, "Take care of yourself first, you hear? It's too late for me, but not you."

Despite his advice, on the drive back to Youtopia Towers, Ana's mind flooded with FBI protocol: Bruce would put out a national APB for any vehicles licensed to the Graduate or Mauer, though a half-day's head-start put them virtually anywhere. A team would swarm their small Nebraska town, interviewing anyone who might have known them. Ana knew how intensive and important such work was, to dig into every crevice and corner of a suspect's life, to pan through the dregs in hopes of finding the one small nugget of gold that could lead them to Sonya Young. But she also knew how time-consuming such work was. It could take days, if not longer—time they absolutely did not have.

Bruce's cyber team would take up the other angles, contact lists and call histories, traffic cameras and satellite footage. Flight records into Lincoln and Omaha, even Seward and Crete and other small municipal airports nearby. They'd check rental cars and credit card purchases. But

Mauer's house was secluded, miles from anything resembling surveillance. If this Graduate was smart—and signs pointed to yes—he would have covered his tracks.

Saeed finished his burger, licking spilled ketchup from his fingers like a child. "This burger is shit," he said, though the fact that he had devoured it suggested otherwise. He called out to nobody, "Can't we keep a single chef on staff? Are we so savage?"

Ana pushed away her sandwich. She considered her next move, wondered if she and Saeed had any other recourse. As she saw it, their only move would be for her to reenter Veronica's Reborn, but she didn't know what that would accomplish, or if Veronica was even willing. She and Saeed had undercut Kowalski once, and doing so again could lose Saeed his job, and bring her potential criminal charges.

She also recognized that her desire to revisit that space had less to do with the case than with the pull to see Charlotte, to feel her own Youtopia, to live the unreal. It was an impulse she needed to resist.

Then, as if in response to Saeed's taunt, the overhead lights of the cafeteria deadened. The space became eerily dark, illuminated only by emergency lights running in tubed tracks along the walls.

Saeed huffed. "What in the everlasting fuck is it now?"

Footsteps echoed down the hall. Ana slid from her chair, turned to the entryway, and pulled her gun.

Saeed pushed away from the table, his chair dragging heavy across the laminate floor, his face not showing fear but incredulity, his brow heavy with scorn. "What is going on here!" he shouted, before Ana could warn him.

She slid backward, to the tables nearest the kitchen, taking aim at the door.

Saeed stepped toward the entryway, angered and assumptive.

"Saeed," Ana said in a raised whisper, "Get—"

"Saeed?" The voice came from the hallway.

Saeed stopped and cocked his head. "Reddy?"

Into the cafeteria entryway stepped Rob Reddy, the one Board member Ana felt remotely pleased to see. He wore tattered jeans and sneakers and an orange hoodie, as casual as she'd ever seen him.

She lowered her gun. Her body still needled with adrenaline as he looked to her. She'd been on edge since Bruce arrived on his plane—since she'd touched down in Chicago with Lane. The feeling wouldn't stop, she realized, until the case was solved.

"I'm supposed to give you word," Reddy said. "We're going dark."

"Thank you, Captain Obvious," Saeed said. "Didn't think to consult me on the decision, did you?"

"Dark?" Ana asked. "As in, you're shutting down?"

"All operations outside of the immediate," Reddy said.

"Meaning everything except the Cradles," Saeed added. "Oh, the kiddos will still be in there, but we'll have no Oversight, no way to Intervene. No way to know if we even should. Hope the kids truly are all right, because we just sent them up shit creek."

Reddy looked away. He shifted his weight from one leg to another. His body language spoke of contrition, even as he relayed the Board's official edicts.

"The situation with Daniel is..." Reddy trailed off, letting his silence finish the sentence. He nodded at Saeed. "You messed up, Saeed, letting her Intervene when it was clearly inappropriate. Illegal even."

"You're leaving out one important part, Bobby," Saeed said. "The part where we almost caught the bastard because of it."

"Well, if you actually had, we might not be talking in the dark. The Board has decided that, unless Sonya Young's will is discovered — if there truly is one — all executive decisions will be theirs."

"The Board," Ana said, "or Kowalski?"

"The Board." Reddy squinted at her. "The risk is too great."

"What if the Board is the risk?"

She thought too late to exclude Reddy himself from this accusation. His face soured. He might have sympathized with her once, but she'd pressed him, and everyone had limits.

"You will leave the premises," he said. "You too, Saeed. Until further notice, this building is locked down."

Surprisingly, Saeed agreed to leave without a fight, without sarcastic quips about Reddy or his loved ones. He waited until entering the elevator with Ana before speaking.

"Gotta tell you," he said, a mischievous grin on his face, "that was fun to watch. Bobby Brady back there never gets the heat. His superiors do the heavy lifting while he plays the virtuous kid brother."

They descended the Tower, Ana realized, perhaps for her last time. Outside the building, a patch of thick, dark clouds loomed in the west, carrying with it bursts of sharp wind — an impending storm.

"This lot looks creepy when it's empty. The whole fucking building, man, like a giant funhouse mirror." Saeed pulled a vape pen and took a long drag, the unnatural light of the pen glowing. "Forgive me my weakness."

Ana should've made for her rental car, and yet something Reddy said stuck with her: *other than finding Sonya Young's will...*

Like a shocking herald, Ana's phone buzzed, a text from an unknown number. Its author didn't introduce himself, but everything about it read Lane.

> *We're onto something. Can't go into detail, but... Serena is definitely Sonya's daughter. Got a lead on who sent the will.*

Ana tried to piece it together. *We're onto something... definitely Sonya's daughter... who sent the will.* Lane wrote to her as though she was part of some conversation they never had. Or more accurately, that she excluded herself from. If any of his ramblings had taken him closer to the case, closer to the Graduate, without Ana's help, he was better than she thought — and also in immediate danger.

Ana dialed the number — ten rings until it went to an automated voicemail. She texted, throwing in extra question marks to signal her urgency.

> *Where are you???*
> *You might be in danger. Check news.*

After a minute without a reply, Saeed obnoxiously sucking away on his vape pen, Ana could wait no longer. She pulled up and dialed an old number, one she hadn't called since the first Youtopia case. As always, he answered immediately.

"You were part of the sting, weren't you?" Sergio Morales said by way of introduction. He was her favorite tech specialist from her Fed days, and the one person willing to do her a favor.

"You know I was."

"Ha! The rumors were true. Bruce must've had a hemorrhage working beside Anabel fucking Downer again."

"He was pretty magnanimous, all things considered."

"Getting soft in his old age. But hey, aren't we all."

"Sergio, I—"

"Need a favor. Of course you do. I'm surprised it took you so long to call. Offended even."

Ana imagined Sergio on the other end, in his Florida home, fingers handling the papers of one of his hand-rolled cigarettes. Saeed stood looking at her, his mind trying to piece together the situation with only her side of the communication.

"I'll do it," Sergio said. "On one condition. Don't you dare feed me some Ana Downer BS about how this is the last time."

"It is the last time."

"What'd I just say?"

Ana gave him Lane's new number. As he typed, he whistled a vaguely familiar tune. One of the older Board members exited the third Tower, looked their way, then walked in the opposite direction.

Between vape pulls, Saeed said, "Surprised she didn't stomp over and—"

Ana held up a finger. Sergio's whistling went quiet, suggesting he had Lane pinpointed. "You still up near the Towers? He's close."

"How close?"

"Stone's throw. Sending the coordinates."

Her phone buzzed; Ana looked to it. As she did, Saeed stopped mid-inhale to look over her shoulder, smoke unnaturally seeping from his nose like a dragon.

"Anything else?" Sergio said, but Ana looked to Saeed, whose boyish face widened in confusion.

"You recognize the address?" she asked Saeed.

"Of course. Loaner McMansion number five. I'm a number three guy, myself."

"Who's in five?"

"Same person as always."

***

As they pulled up to the wrought-iron gate, extensive home security signs lining the driveway like decorative lights on either side, Lane sent the message. He felt somewhat relieved of his guilt for keeping Downer in the dark, but this was his lead, his life, and he was about to get farther without her than he ever did with. For that, he wouldn't apologize.

The gate had no visible keypad or intercom system. Serena looked at him and shrugged. "One last barrier, I guess," she said.

"I'll check it out."

Lane stepped from the car. Beyond the gate, the driveway narrowed and curved upward. All he could see otherwise were the browns and summer greens of dense, overgrown woods.

"Can I help you?"

The woman's voice startled him. It came from a minute, camouflaged box affixed to the gate.

Lane leaned toward it. "Hello?"

A brief silence, then the voice said, "Press the button when you speak." It sounded vaguely familiar, like a former teacher, or a game show host from his childhood.

Lane searched until he found a taupe circular button on its side. "My name is Lane Samson and —"

"The reporter."

Lane dropped his arm. A long moment of silence followed. Then came a rumbling sound, like the high call of impending thunder. The pavement quaked as the gate opened.

He returned to their car, to its tepid air conditioner. The driveway felt intentionally long and unkind. At the end should've stood some massive estate, a castle, something more at home in Beverly Hills than Wisconsin, but instead they found a plain — though large — Colonial with overhanging eaves and brick siding. Bright yellow shutters bracketed rows of windows. The woman stood in the open doorway, one hand against the robin's-egg-blue door and another on her hip. Without makeup, hair in a simple ponytail, she looked nothing like the only time he saw her in the hallway at Youtopia Towers, and even less like the persona she exemplified on video — Jeanne Haskins.

When Lane stepped from the car, Haskins said, "I didn't expect to see you again, young man." Her throat sounded scratchy, as though she fought an unseasonal cold. "Thought you might be chasing the story down in Nebraska."

"Nebraska?" Lane said.

"You don't know? Honey, check your news feed." Then Haskins's face changed as she looked beyond Lane to the car. He watched her formality melt away. "My good lord in heaven. It can't be."

Haskins vacated the door. She paced into the driveway, her eyes affixed, almost bumping into Lane as she passed him.

"It's really you," she said to the car. "You're here."

Serena slowly exited. Haskins eyed her as though meeting royalty. Without asking, Haskins took Serena into a prolonged embrace, the smaller, older woman hanging on with an unearned familiarity.

For her part, Serena returned the hug with grace. When they broke, she gazed into the backseat. "Come on. It's okay."

Andrew shuffled out. Lane watched Haskins, this time reacting with her whole body, as though an immense but bearable, almost pleasurable weight landed atop her shoulders. Her hands quivered. "Her grandson."

"Andrew," Serena said.

"Oh, Lord above," Haskins said. She moved forward, but Andrew retreated behind his mother. Thankfully, Haskins caught herself and spared him an attempt at an awkward hug. "You so remind me of my Oscar — his hair, his mannerisms. A little genius, just like you must be."

Andrew slid farther behind Serena, breaking Haskins's reverent stare. Haskins turned to Serena. "Nikita must have told you to come here."

"She did," Lane lied.

"If you would believe it," Haskins continued, "I hadn't heard from her in years." She leaned her head to speak to Andrew. "Your grandmother kept secrets, some closer than I could ever have imagined."

"What did Nicole say to you when she called?" Lane asked.

"She was frightened. Afraid for herself, and for you. I asked her to keep you there, until I could come myself and help, but you found me instead." She took Serena by the hand. "Come inside. We have so much to catch up on."

She took Serena's hand. Andrew clung close to his mother. Lane followed the three of them across the threshold into the Reborn rental. The entryway was florid, enchanting, a throwback to an older era. Haskins led them to a small living space off the entryway with upright, cushioned chairs. For a rental unit, the place had many personal touches, seasonal table runners, real flowers in vases, and a digital picture frame that cycled photos of a young Haskins with her son Oscar.

"This is practically a second home for me," Haskins said. "I'm from Kentucky, before this all. Can you imagine? I know, my accent is completely gone."

Instead of inviting them to sit, Haskins continued through the dining area. It too held various mid-season flowers in full bloom, the bright orange tiger lilies spilling out like angry tongues.

Haskins abruptly stopped and turned to Serena. "I can't believe you're here! I have so much to tell you about your mother. Things she wanted to say but never could."

She led them to a kitchen with bay windows and a dinette with Craftsman chairs. From speakers embedded into the walls, Israel Kamakawiwo'ole softly beckoned them over the rainbow. Beneath the sound, Lane caught a mechanical hum from another room, some sound akin to the drumming of a sump pump.

Haskins halted near a glass display case. She opened the door and pulled from the top shelf a brass Great Dane figurine with stoic, intent eyes. "Most of these came from my pupils, the ones I assisted in Reintegration." She petted the head of the statue as though it were alive. "This, though... this was from your grandmother, Andrew. She was always more compassionate than people knew."

Haskins extended the statue out. Andrew stood still. He looked ready to accept the Dane, to grasp the hind legs masked by Haskins's hands. But though she offered it, Haskins seemed suddenly reluctant to give it up.

The song cut. The whirring noise from the other room filled Lane's ears. He eyed the display case, the other small gifts: a crystal paperweight, a triangular Rubik's Cube, an American Girl doll that eerily resembled Haskins herself.

Then he saw, resting on the bottom shelf, almost buried behind the others, three separate, handcrafted Russian nesting dolls.

"Rene," he muttered, just before a gong sounded out. His vision flashed white. A high-pitched whistle followed, in his right ear. His hand cupped blood.

A man flanked him, short and skinny and a white baseball cap atop his head. Like a confidante, he held Lane's shoulder. But then his other arm swung some blunt object again, squarely to the back of Lane's head.

Lane's knee tremored. His head pounded. His legs gave way. He was falling.

His head collided with the hardwood floor.

Everything went black.

***

An eerie moan. Whispers. In one ear, Lane heard a rhythmic Max Roach drumline. No, not whispers: someone spoke clearly, with conviction, her voice frantic.

His mother? No: Lane was no child. His mother was dead. His head throbbed, singing its own dull tune, his neck stiff, his body chilled. His throat burned with bile.

He opened one eye, then the next. Dim light. Wall studs ran from floor to ceiling, bracketing pink insulation. A metal storage shelf hovered above him. The concrete floor, cold against his cheek, pooled with his own blood-tinged saliva. The copper taste coated his throbbing tongue. He must have bitten it while falling. His head stung with countless knifepoints of pain.

"I tried," the voice said, clear and direct but behind him, to someone else. "Now *they* show up *here*? You know what needs to be done."

The voice: Haskins.

Someone had knocked him out, had dragged him to whatever corner he lay in. Seismic pain rippled in his hips, shoulder blades, ankles. He wanted to raise his hand, to wipe his mouth, to touch his head and assess his wounds, but his hands were bound.

Something also told him he shouldn't move, that his only advantage was his undetected consciousness.

"The first time, you caved so easily! Some killer outsmarts you for a month, and what do you do? You pull me out!"

A smack, skin thrashing skin. A prolonged, muffled whine followed.

"You pull... you pull Oscar out. And what happens? He *dies* because of your cowardice. All those Reintegrators who committed suicide? They died because *you* were weak."

Lane breathed, low and slow, keeping his eyes closed. He needed to focus on her voice, on what he could hear. Footsteps on the concrete. Toward him? His whole body throbbed with adrenaline. No, the steps, four, five, six, moved across the room.

A muffled voice rose, a squeal, a plea for help, and in it he recognized something familiar. A sharp tenderness. Serena.

"You have a chance to make this right," Haskins called. "I never wanted to hurt anyone. Certainly not the daughter you hid from us all."

Lane exhaled a breath, and the room went silent. He heard the thunderous beats of his own pulse. Haskins knew he was awake. The thin man, whoever he was, stood nearby, ready to strike him in the head again.

He couldn't do this. He couldn't do this.

He heard Haskins's voice lower to a near-whisper. "It's too late for Mr. Nebraska and his old man up there. They're onto him. He needs to be... expended. But me? I will still get what I deserve, one way or another."

The central air unit kicked in, the churn and hum cutting into the silent room. It snapped Lane's mind into focus. The thin man was somewhere upstairs. They'd dragged him downstairs, into the basement storage room. Haskins was acting recklessly, out of desperation.

He could do this. He needed to find a way.

His mind traveled about his body, feeling past the pain and wounds, shutting out the central air's whirl and his heartbeat. They had pulled his arms above his head, affixed his wrists together around a steel shelving unit with something thin and sharp. A zip tie. His ankles were folded one over the other. With the slightest movement, he flexed the toes of one foot, tensing his ankle and calf, but felt nothing. His hands were bound but his feet were free.

If he could somehow break the zip tie. If Haskins left, even for a moment, he could spring up and release Sonya Young and Serena and Andrew. He could rescue them. He could find a way.

"Daniel is in a coma because of you," Haskins said, her voice cutting through the fan. "*Look at me.* Do you even care?"

Lane reopened his eyes. Hands in a prayer position, he slowly slid them apart until the tie hit his thumb's lowest knuckle. Tight, but not without give — hastily bound. He looked to the shelves for tools or stored jars or bakeware or seasonal decorations, anything resembling a weapon. Somewhere directly behind him, in the adjacent corner of the room, Young was gagged and tied. Cross-corner, Haskins hovered over Serena and Andrew. How far away, he couldn't be sure: maybe ten feet. Maybe less.

"And what about the Immersers? *The children I never had,* you loved to say. That man upstairs? He'd kill them all if I let him."

Serena's gagged mouth cried out, and was met with another smack.

Lane's body involuntarily shivered. He chanced a painful tug at his hands. If only Young could distract Haskins — a confession, an agreement, anything to get the attention off Serena. Just give him a chance.

"No, you don't really care for them either. Just like you didn't care for Oscar. Or me. You stole our perfection from us. Oscar can never get it back. But I can. I *will.*"

More cries. This time, they continued.

"This is where we go from here. I take care of our friends upstairs. After what you've been through, I'm sure you won't be sorry to see *that.* Tonight, we'll dump them into Lake Michigan on our way to Reborn, where you'll Immerse me. *Permanently.* I never want to see you or this world, ever again."

A gaping silence. The zip tie sliced into Lane's wrist as he tugged farther. It cut into his outer hand, bled — he would lose skin.

"It's your job to keep your family and Mr. Reporter here quiet. Whatever you want to say happened to *you,* I don't care. You're the genius. You'll figure it out."

If he could only slip past the first joint, up the thumb line. The plastic edge stretched sharp as a blade. If he could only...

"If you pull me out again, I will tell everything. Make your life hell. Yours, and theirs."

More silence.

What was Young doing? Why wouldn't she buy him time?

"No? Then here's what we do instead. I kill you all right now. Everyone except sweet little Andrew. By the time anyone knows what's happened, we'll be long gone. Russia. The Middle East. Somewhere they'll *never* find us."

Serena groaned, a sound far worse than physical pain.

Lane's eyes welled with tears.

"Don't worry. I'll love him as I would have loved Oscar. The way *you* never let me. And you can watch it all from hell."

Lane risked a tug. It slipped the first knuckle. Just a little more. His thumb and pinky finger were numb, the rest of his hand on fire, but one last pull, like the fast thrust of a Davis saxophone blare...

"We'll start with Seren—"

Lane heaved. His hand shot free. He shoved himself to his feet. The blood loss dizzied him, his first steps wobbly but true. His spotted vision blurred.

Haskins held a knife; she pulled it from Serena's arm. Her eyes lit in rage.

Lane locked hand over fist as he rushed, lunged, brought his arms down with all the force he could muster.

Haskins ducked and thrusted the knife in desperation.

His thigh locked, combusting with pain, but his balled fists connected with Haskins's shoulder, the shudder reverberating up his arms. He brought them down again, this time to her head. His throat burned as he let out a scream.

Beneath him, Haskins went limp. Her body folded.

Lane reached up again, but her head crashed against a pipe extending from her water heater. Within seconds, blood pooled.

Lane hovered over her, his leg soaked in the marriage of his and Serena's blood. He breathed heavy. His limbs burned.

Haskins's bleached blonde hair hid her face, her eyes—the same woman from the instructional video at the Minneapolis Cradles, the sympathetic woman in the hall of Youtopia Towers.

It was her, the whole time.

And now she was dead.

Without warning, the dam of adrenaline holding back his pain broke open. He could barely catch himself from falling. He smacked one hand against the concrete, trying to transfer the howls in his leg. He could not black out. Not again. Not now.

A muffled shout brought him back. He looked up.

Sonya Young. Alive. Her hair was gnarled like in the abduction video.

This couldn't be real. It was surreal, in the exact opposite way of Youtopia—a perfect nightmare.

Young's eyes burned with an urgency that sobered Lane. He hobbled toward her, leaning on his good leg, and pulled the gag from her mouth.

"We need to stop her bleeding," Young said, her voice deep and firm. "Now."

Lane struggled with the zip tie binding Young's arms to a metal support beam. He searched for something sharp, but then lowered his head and chewed through it with his teeth, the blood from his mouth leaking onto Young's chafed wrists.

Once freed, she rushed to Serena, tore the shirt from her body, and fashioned a tourniquet just below Serena's shoulder. She then turned to Andrew, her grandson, his face wet with tears, and looked over his body, assessing for wounds. When she found none, she placed a tender hand through his hair, just behind his head. They locked eyes. Young simply nodded.

"He may have heard," she said, turning to Lane. "Stop your own bleeding, then stay with them. Protect them."

"We need to call the police."

"She will have destroyed your phone." Young's eyes roved Haskins's shelves, the various supplies there. She grabbed a common screwdriver and a short length of utility rope. "Do not leave their side."

"You sure about this?" Lane asked.

"My certainty does not matter." Her face was unflinching. Something about her assurance, her uncanny poise, instilled confidence in Lane. "If he comes through this door, kill him."

Young rose, her back straight and chin high. She stood a foot shorter than Lane, more, and yet she seemed a giant, not someone incapacitated for nearly two weeks.

Lane needed to feed off her strength. As she slipped out of the storage room, he limped over to Serena, whose sobs were muffled by her good arm. "It's okay. We'll be okay." Then, to reassure himself as much as her, "I won't let anything else happen to you."

Serena's eyes rose in blind bewilderment about how it had come to this, how any of this was happening. Andrew stared at his mother, his eyes fixed on her battered arm. He might've been in shock. All of them. This was nothing for anyone to see, let alone a child.

For a strange moment, Lane considered all the Reborn children, their unconscious minds directing them to uncharted, imaginative, haphazard, yet ultimately safe spaces. Places that offered comfort and joy. Here, Andrew had been thrust into traumatic abduction because of those very children, because his mother was the biological child of Youtopia Reborn's creator.

Lane used his own shirt to stanch his bleeding leg. Then he slid behind the door, a sliver of the basement visible through the open crack.

He grabbed the only thing he could find, a spare light bulb that would hopefully shatter in the thin man's face. Above them, he listened for footsteps, for the thumps and bangs of an altercation. His own heartbeat pulsed in his ears, and underneath it a distant, arrhythmic drum of a deep bass. The opening of that same slow Max Roach number played in his head — his drubbing headache, set to his father's music.

But no: he truly heard the beat. It revved up. Pounding footsteps. Young and the man. They fumbled in a stomping dance until all went silent. Behind him, Serena released a pained breath.

More silence — somehow, the worst silence yet. A minute passed, though it could've been much more. It could have been mere seconds.

He anchored himself to an exposed stud, trying to blot out his leg's scalding-hot pain. How long could he obey Young's order? Serena's arm, his leg... Nobody else knew they were here. Minutes passed, and Lane wondered if he was condemning himself and Serena — if, after coming so close to escape, they would ultimately bleed out here.

Suddenly a door slammed shut.

Lane's whole body flexed. He nearly fell again. He envisioned the thin man's beady eyes as headlights, his mouth the monstrous grill of a truck careening toward them. Whatever physical strength Lane had painstakingly amassed in the past minutes — since starting this journey, since Reintegrating — felt depleted. His anxiety cascaded over him, plunged his mind into that shaky plane between reality and his fears. He could no longer trust what he saw.

The footsteps approached. A person flashed through the door crack, too close for him to see. He raised the bulb, ready to smash it in the thin man's face.

The man flew through the door with a gun in his hand.

Lane's anxiety unleashed in a scream as he brought his own hand forward.

The man easily knocked Lane's hand away. In the brief second before the bulb shattered on the ground, Lane feared the gunfire, the deafening sound of his own demise shattering his ears and his world.

Instead, the gun lowered.

Lane's eyes unblurred. All his adrenaline released in a guttural exhale as he saw the person in front of him: not the thin man at all, not Sonya Young.

Tears flooded his eyes as he realized they were saved, as he saw standing before him, impossibly, Anabel Downer.

What Really Happened That Day

A Huntington Weekly Beacon Exclusive Interview
Millie Monroe, Senior Editor and Correspondent
August 26, 2026

***

*Before we begin, a note: Though Lane Samson needs no introduction, I must note that he is a former colleague, a friend, and one of the best men I've ever known. He is also a hero, even if he would never say so. The following interview is unedited.

***

So, Lane. How are you feeling?

I'm okay. I mean, not really. <*Nervous laughter*> Shaken up, I guess. Like I've seen behind the veil. It's not pretty back there.

What do you mean, the veil?

So... you imagine the world a certain way. You think things like what I just went through can't happen to you. And then they do, and... It's just a different perspective. Not a good one.

The world is worse than you expected.

Yeah. And I wasn't that high on the world to begin with. <*Laughter*>

You saved the day! Sonya Young is alive because of you.

I suppose. If you're asking, am I better off now than I was before... I guess to some degree the answer would be yes.

How about physically? Is your leg healing?

Let's just say I'm not making runs at the YMCA courts any time soon. But they tell me it'll heal with time. Like most things.

Okay, onto the questions everyone wants to know. Let's start at the beginning. What interested you in the Sonya Young story?

It was this huge, crazy thing. The Bermuda, as we called it—a story so big and unexpected it sucks up everything else. Better question would be, what didn't?

When looking for help, why did you seek out (former FBI Agent) Anabel Downer?

Other than your suggestion? <*Laughter*> When you think about it, it's obvious. She had previous experience with Sonya Young and Youtopia. She knew the right people. She got us immediate interviews, led the FBI to their biggest break. The real reason Sonya Young is still alive? It's her.

Don't be so modest!

I just happened to be in the right place at the right time. Or wrong, depending on how you look at it.

About that: how did you end up at the doorstep of Jeanne Haskins?

A few reasons, I guess. I'd love to say journalistic instinct, but it was mostly just dumb luck.

You drove all the way to Wisconsin on a whim?

I'd met Haskins briefly at Youtopia Towers. We had a connection, both being Reintegrators. Now that association doesn't feel so great. We already have enough stigmas, some so bad I don't even want to name them. Add this to the list.

You're not her, Lane. Nobody is saying you are.

No, I get that. But I'm taking us on a tangent here. I didn't answer your initial question. What a bad interviewee! <*Laughter*> The real reason I went to her was: I was out of ideas, caught on the outside looking in. I thought Haskins could somehow bring me back into the loop. Unfortunately, I had no idea how right I was.

Could you describe what happened that day?

...

I know it might be difficult.

I'll say this: Haskins was over her head. She wanted Immersion into Reborn, to escape back into her perfect cocoon without consequence. Her hacker accomplice might've believed in *Reborn for All*, but for Haskins it was all a ruse. She only wanted it for herself. Luckily, I was able to escape my bonds. Young and I fought back. And Haskins... well, no point in dwelling on that any further.

You seem sorry for her, even after all she did to you.

I'm not. I don't think I am. A person willing to scorch the earth for their own gratification is unforgivable. We have to think outside of ourselves, if we're ever going to survive. We have to get out of our own heads.

A strong anti-Youtopian sentiment, I would say.

<*Laughter*> I guess so. It's a dangerous game Youtopia plays, offering perfection. Give it and then take it away, and this <*expletive deleted*> happens.

I don't know what Sonya Young will do from here. We've only conversed through lawyers, and contrary to all the rumors out there, no, we are not dating. If she decides to throw in the towel permanently this time—put Youtopia out to pasture—I wouldn't blame her.

You think they should shut down Reborn?

No, I don't think so. She would have to release the children. She'd risk another Haskins fiasco. It's... we're in a *Catch-22* here because, either way, there are just too many things that can go wrong. And with Youtopia, for some reason, they always do.

JOSEPH REIN

Chapter 13

Fall arrived on a single October day. A cloudless eighty degrees acquiesced to overcast mid-fifties and crisp wind. The overnight chill made waste of sunflower and begonia swan songs. As he drove, Lane slowed to pass the recent landmarks of his life, the Weekly Beacon office, Q&C Entertainment. Then deeper into his past he strode — the woods where he drank his first beer at fourteen, the mini-golf complex where he landed his first job. He lingered at his middle school basketball court, the loose-hanging rims replaced with double-thick, bright orange monstrosities. Then, finally, hesitantly, he slunk down the street of his childhood home.

He hadn't passed it since Reintegrating. Most of the homes were built in the 40s and 50s, before Lane's parents were even born. Theirs rested on the corner, behind the sycamore tree into which he had deeply carved his initials, at the end of the driveway where he had burned out innumerable pairs of shoes playing pickup. His parents' house. His home.

The exterior looked nothing like Lane remembered, the color darker, the décor rustic. In the middle of the driveway, a young boy sketched with sidewalk chalk. Lane watched him for a moment, feeling a nostalgia he rarely indulged. But, he supposed, this happened when you left with no intention to return — when you finally said goodbye.

He stopped at a gas station and exited the car with care, his leg emitting a dull ache from his wound. What a fool he'd been, arriving at Haskins's door with no clue as to what truly lurked inside. Of course, to the outside world, in the version he sold to Millie, he was the valiant hero. Just after Millie's article hit, even Bethany Fawkes had reached out. Lane expected something of a professional anger — jealousy even — but after all, she had sent him an earnest, solicitous message wishing him a fast recovery and commending him on his bravery.

Bravery masked in recklessness. Recklessness and bravery. Anymore, Lane couldn't tell the difference, if there was one. Anymore, he wasn't sure it mattered.

As he fueled up, he dialed the number for the Fort Wayne rehab clinic. He knew Henrick wouldn't take his call, but he'd call every day until he did. When Lane had first returned, calling Henrick's cell to no answer, he'd feared the worst. After a little digging, he discovered that Henrick checked himself into Fort Wayne shortly after they'd spoken. He wanted no visitors, especially those from FAR, which Lane respected. Still, Lane called every day, knowing that one day Henrick would change his mind. Today was not that day.

Finally, he texted Millie, attaching a photo of him with gas pump in hand and a stupid grin. *Off to see the wizard,* he captioned, which he hoped would make her laugh. He was glad he gave her the scoop — at least the parts he could give — instead of keeping it for himself. For the story, she'd received the modest promotion to chief editor she'd always wanted. As for the offer from the IndyStar, which Lane himself had always wanted, Millie parlayed that into better pay and benefits with the Beacon. Her ambitions were startlingly simple, enviable. She wanted to stay in Huntington, wanted the life she had achieved, and little more.

When their interview had ended, Lane's head swooning from heat and painkillers, his leg playing its familiar painful tune, Millie stood and kissed him on the forehead, like a parent seeing a child off to college. Or simply as a friend, grateful for their time together.

"Can't thank you enough for this," she said.

"Don't worry." Lane had smiled. "I'll turn it into something yet."

And he did, though not in the way he'd expected. In the immediate aftermath, he rejected interview requests and news appearances. With his insurance money and severance pay, he bought takeout Chinese and binge-watched TV he hadn't known existed. He didn't know where to go, or what to do, but it didn't much matter. His leg was healing; he was recovering.

Then, one day, an email solicitation from Quinn, of all people, brought clear the idea for his future.

> *Dude! Got a guy in Chicago who does true crime podcasting. Killer stuff. (Hahaha) Last cast got 20K listens. Told him I know you, and he wants to do the Sonya Young abduction. $$$. Name's Tramel. CONSPIRACY CRACKDOWN is the pod. Check him out.*
>
> *Oh, and if you do it, 10% finder's fee to yours truly.*
> *Q*

Lane's immediate reaction was revulsion. He deleted the email without even Googling the podcast. He had already told Millie what he wanted to say. Any more investigation seemed a temptation of fate.

In his hospital bed, while he'd been lying in agony with his leg wrapped so tightly he couldn't feel his foot, as his head swooned in oxymorphone and the fog of his trauma, before the police could even question him, a slew of Youtopia Reborn lawyers entered his room and pressed representation. They promised damages, protection from legal liability. They decried the potential of a court-appointed attorney, who would know nothing of the case. They, on the other hand, were prepped since the minute Sonya Young went missing. They would be on his side.

Initially, he hesitated. Even in his fugue state, he was skeptical. And yet, in the back of his mind lingered the realization that, at some point, the police or FBI or some other entity with the ability to punish him would question why he drove from his Indiana home to Minneapolis to North Dakota and then, finally, to Wisconsin. They would see his numerous, suspicious phone calls to Quinn. They would put him to trial, prod and probe. They would bring the heat of consequence, a heat he wasn't sure he could handle.

On the other hand, he also knew his signature on Reborn's dotted line meant that his version of the story must match their own, that Young's wish to keep Serena out of it entirely must become his reality. What began for Lane with a nighttime voicemail and a reconnaissance trip to the Dominican Republic—a journey for the *truth*—would be far from this new reality.

But what was truth, after all? To his clouded mind the truth felt periphery, smoke and mirrors. That the public know the full story was a journalist's idealistic, improbable pipe dream. The truth ruined people's lives. It could ruin Serena's. He would sign any paper assuring that she would never find herself in that situation, ever again.

No, Lane would do no more interviews, least of all this Tramel's podcast. He would let this particular trauma die out.

But the name Lane Samson, he knew, was very much alive. By becoming a player in the story, he had gained cultural cachet with a brief window of opportunity. Though he wouldn't speak of his own crime drama, people might still follow as he spoke on others.

I know this type of situation, he imagined himself saying with Orson Welles severity. *It's even worse than it seems.*

And so arose *The Fast Lane: A True Crime Podcast.* With a heavy dose of seedling money from his damages, and Quinn's editing help, his first episode bloomed to thousands of followers overnight. Initially, he trod familiar territory—Ed Gein and Jeffrey Dahmer were easy sells with his newfound Wisconsin connection—but teased his burgeoning followers with insider angles they'd never before heard. "Get it here and only here," he ended each episode. "I should know. I've lived in the Fast Lane."

The podcast also opened him up in other ways. Contrary to FAR's preachings, to his conception of himself, listeners generally appreciated when he brought up Youtopia, his Immersion. After dozens of attempts, he finally built up the courage to remove his socks and take a snapshot of his Immerser number tattoo—S402051, on the unattractive bottom of his foot—and post it to his podcast's Instagram page. It immediately garnered the most likes he'd ever gotten.

But the best part of podcasting—aside from the advertising royalties—was that it rewarded him for the deep-dives that brought him to the waters of journalism in the first place. He could roam, could explore archives and interview people with fascinating, if fantastic, stories. He was no longer tied to Huntington, to his former self.

His apartment proved easy to pack up: kitchen utensils and unwanted clothes in donation boxes, unused condiments and cleaning products in the trash. He wiped layers of spilled protein powder from his countertop crevices, spackled the few holes in the walls. He left little trace that he'd ever been there.

Once everything was packed, he dialed her new number. The Minneapolis area code brought Lane a small comfort. He was returning, but also starting anew. He didn't know where this road would lead him, but for the first time in a long while—since his Reintegration began—he felt comfortable in the uncertainty. It was time to embrace the unknown.

"Laney, you old dog," Serena said. "What ace you got up your sleeve this time, big boy?"

He smiled, the sound of her voice the jazzy tune he'd long waited to hear.

"Get ready, Rene," he said. "I'm heading your way."

***

Ana approached Sonya Young's estate, where awaited two armed guards in full Kevlar. Their faces portrayed a mix of boredom and, beneath it, intrigue at Ana's arrival. She counted at least three cameras, two apparent and one not, trained on her. Hundreds of others must've been scattered about the premises, a new army of surveillance connected to different live feeds and power sources. Same with the security guards, up and down the driveway like Secret Service Agents locking Sonya up as tightly as the President herself. Ana knew Sonya would not make the same mistake twice.

Once Haskins had been revealed as the catalyst behind the abduction, the pieces fell into place. Her clandestine closeness with Sonya came to light. So too came her connection to Arthur Mauer, through her fledgling Reintegration program. Her motive—to return to her perfect life, where her son Oscar still lived—explained her contrived agog attitude toward Reborn. A Reintegrator, who had her perfect life ripped from her and her son, now devoting her life to help others achieve it? It was as unlikely as Paul choosing Ana's happiness over his own. If her first stint with the Youtopia Feeds had taught Ana anything, it was that, no matter how philanthropic people seemed, they would ultimately revert to rapacious, self-seeking behavior. If Haskins couldn't have Youtopia for herself, then nobody could.

Ana only wished that Haskins had survived. She wanted to know how close Haskins and Sonya really were, how much of herself Sonya revealed. Did Haskins know that Sonya authored Youtopia's first demise? That Oscar's death was one of Sonya's many secret burdens? Ana could ask Sonya now, but that would require breaking their unspoken truce. It would mean unearthing the skeletons between them Ana would rather leave buried.

The first guard, a man in thick sunglasses, perused Ana's passport. He chomped pink bubble gum, the kind Charlotte always wanted but Ana never allowed, never trusting her not to swallow it whole. He blew a prismatic bubble that popped and stuck to the stubble above his lip.

"She's waiting for her, man," the second guard said. He was early twenties, a hand on the pistol at his hip. "Just let her through."

The first guard handed back her ID and pointed to her suitcoat. "You'll need to leave your gun."

He was good: Ana thought she had concealed it well. "No chance."

The guard huffed. He turned from her and spoke through an earpiece. They waited until he finally received the go-ahead. With a resigned smile, he waved her through. "Be prepared. We're the first of many."

"I expected as much."

Twice more she was stopped before she could exit her car. Sonya's home—no Youtopia Towers but a marvel itself, made almost entirely of

JOSEPH REIN

pearlescent glass—looked even more perplexing in person than in
magazine and online photos, the reflective walls casting tall trees back
out onto themselves. It had the feel of timelessness, of mirrors reflecting
mirrors. Of eternity.

And yet the Graduate—with Haskins's help—somehow broke in
and pulled Sonya out, leaving only the traces they wanted: Russian
nesting dolls and *REBoRN FoR ALL oR REBoRN FoR NoNE* splashed
across her bedroom wall. It seemed impossible.

When Saeed had revealed Haskins as the Reborn house inhabitant,
Ana ran to her rental car, leaving Saeed at the foot of the Towers.
Something was off, and she'd feared the worst. The house was twenty
minutes away, but Ana pressed the gas, her pace accelerating from
simmering to torrid, ninety-five-plus on the freeway. She weaved,
tailgated, laid on her horn when necessary and received the same. Off the
freeway, she ignored stop signs. The gate protecting the property was
dubiously open. She snaked the long driveway, saw a small coupe that
couldn't have been Haskins's. Lane, and maybe Serena. They were still
here.

The front door stood slightly ajar, sounding her instincts. Someone
had entered or exited in haste. Beyond that innocuous blue door lay
something insidious. Ana's hands quivered on her wheel. As she pulled
her gun, she realized the obvious: she needed far more than herself. She
needed to call Bruce, 911, local PD. She needed everyone behind her.

Just as she reached for her phone, a figure stalked into the doorway.
Ana opened her car door, ready to leap behind it for cover.

The figure limped out. Though dirtied and pale, starved and
bloodied, she kept her shoulders erect, her head high, projecting, through
it all, her regal air.

Sonya Young.

When they converged, Sonya seemed unsurprised to see Ana, as
though all the strange twists of fate that brought them both here, together
again, were unexceptional.

"Serena and her son were never here," Sonya said, before Ana even
knew of the events inside—before she even knew of Andrew. "They've
suffered enough. We must allow them their lives."

Ana surged past Sonya into the house, through the foyer and into the
kitchen, where the Graduate's splayed body spilled fresh blood from a
head wound. In an adjacent room, Arthur Mauer lay hooked up to the
elaborate, octopus-style contraption that the Graduate used to hack the
Reborns. His veins a deep crimson-purple beneath feathery, pale skin, the

corners of his lips crusted with phlegm, his eyelids half-closed and fluttering, he dreamed. Ana felt a small moment of remorse for the man, who could only find relief by stealing a child's fantasy. But a larger part of her wanted to rip the plugs from his arms and torso and temples, to shake him awake and force him back into the torment he and his accomplice had created.

She moved down the stairs. Sonya didn't follow, standing instead in the doorway like a guard defending her castle. In the back storage room, she found Lane, Serena, her son, and the curled corpse of Jeanne Haskins.

Her mind swam as she tried to assure Lane, as carefully as she could, that they were safe. Both Lane and Serena needed medical attention. Ana needed to call in the police and an ambulance. She reached again for her phone.

Then, at Serena's side, her son slid and nestled his head into her stomach. They folded into one another as only mother and child could.

Ana felt the fierceness of the boy's embrace, bringing back a memory she'd forgotten. The final Fourth of July they'd spent together, at, of all places, Haulover Beach. Charlotte, sensitive to sounds, spent the entire evening wrapped in Ana's lap, a blanket over her head despite the sticky heat, her arms clinging to Ana's midsection. Paul tried to coax Charlotte out, to berate Ana — *She's getting too old for this* — but Ana simply let Charlotte hold on. *Anything you need*, she whispered. *I'm here for you.*

Sonya's plea came to Ana's mind: *They've suffered enough. We must allow them their lives.* That meant protection from the press, from scandal, from the constant barrage of paparazzi and writers. Andrew needed a chance. Keeping him out of this horror was the only way he would have it.

And so, for a second time, Ana had perpetuated Sonya Young's lie. But this one felt different. Ana had not been coerced. It was not to Sonya's, or Paul's, benefit. She had a choice this time, and she had chosen Serena and her son, Sonya's daughter and grandson. She'd chosen life for them.

Ana finally passed the full security and entered Sonya's home. A slender female assistant in a powder-blue blouse ushered her through the expansive entryway. Open, vast, each space had the untouched feel of a showroom. In the living area, three black Great Danes rested near the glass wall in picturesque poses. One with graying hair around the eyes and muzzle saw Ana and stood, as though it recognized her, as though it welcomed an old friend. Ana heard the clack of the assistant's heels echo on the hardwood and turned to follow.

They passed more security detail on their way to the house's octagonal center, where Sonya had built a wide arboretum with exotic South American flora. The two-tiered doors closed behind them with audible suction. Humidity hung thick in the air. The assistant led Ana through boggy ground, her heels sticking until she peeled them off, all the way to the farthest end. There, Sonya stood looking at a thin-trunked, festooning tree speckled with pinkish white blossoms. Erect, stolid, she showed no sign of having spent weeks trapped in a madman's basement. No sign she'd ever been the victim.

"Cinchona," she said. "My grandmother was fond of its bark, for various maladies — a salve for wounds, for reducing varicose veins. Neighboring villagers would walk for days at a time to visit her." She placed a tender hand on the tree, as though touching a child. "Like so many things in this world, they are now endangered."

"I didn't peg you as a family person."

"We are all human. Susceptible to the same weaknesses."

Ana stepped closer. Part of her wanted to reach out to Sonya's shoulder, to offer condolences. She had, after all, undergone a great trauma — abduction, near-starvation, torture — but the instinctual, guarded part of Ana felt the hair-raising nerves of their encounter from years ago. She expected the black-donning Nikita to pounce from behind a tree and incapacitate her. This could all somehow be a trap, a game of Sonya's devising. She instinctively reached for her gun.

"I am grateful to you," Sonya said. "For once again taking up my case."

"I wasn't the one who saved you."

"Do not be so modest. The Lane Samsons of the world do not thrive without people like us. You played an integral part. For that, I am indebted to you."

Ana bristled at this. As a woman Special Agent, she had spent her entire career learning how to gain an advantage, to stay a step ahead. But a debt from Sonya Young felt like a detriment, not a boon — something that would loom over her like a lurking storm cloud.

"I just want to understand," Ana said. "Some things don't add up."

"Such as?"

"How did they get you out of this house?"

"You have no doubt read the report."

"There are no real conclusions."

"But your job, Miss Downer, is to investigate, to deduce. So, what do you think?"

"I think you have an underground tunnel somewhere, a secret escape route. Something Haskins knew about."

"A tunnel perhaps out of this very arboretum."

"It would be the logical place."

"And if such a tunnel exists, you would like to see it." Sonya's eyes pierced Ana.

Ana suppressed a shiver in her shoulder blades and said, "No, just knowing it exists is enough."

"Any other curiosities?"

"The will. Why would you shut Reborn down?"

"You must understand, I never desired that outcome. Youtopia Reborn is, as you know all too well, incredibly delicate. Susceptible to corruption. The very notion of transparency — their insipid tours and the like — created many vulnerabilities." She reached out to a thin tree and slid her fingers along its bark. "You have seen what they wished of my creation. Mr. Free, the insufferable Board of Directors. Even Daniel." She shook her head with visible regret. "The Interventions, the research teams... these were only the beginning. They would turn my children into test subjects. Reborns would be mazes, and Immersers their mice." Sonya clasped her hands before her and said, "No, it has to be me. Me and no one else."

Ana nodded, almost in agreement, though behind Sonya's idealism, she recognized the glaring mask of egotism — Sonya believed, as all narcissists did, that only she was suitable for the task.

"Instead, you would entrust your whole empire to a biological daughter you've never acknowledged as your own."

"You are wise enough to recognize why I separated myself from Serena." Sonya sighed. "Still, you have hit upon my greatest regret, Miss Downer. I was young and exceptional. I had a choice. I am still unsure as to whether I chose correctly." Her lips tilted upward, as close to a smile as Ana had seen from her. "Andrew has his grandfather's look, in his eyes and cheekbones. One day he will inspire the world."

"Did Haskins know about them?"

Sonya looked back to the tree. "No. Though many times, I considered telling her. I have the regrettable tendency to trust bright, inquisitive women. Those I might call friends. With you, my instincts were correct. With Jeanne, they were not."

"I wouldn't call us friends."

Somewhere within the small ecosystem behind them, a thicket ruffled as though caught in a breeze. Ana heard a soft slithering, something like a snake.

She took a quick step away from Sonya.

"Nothing here will harm you," Sonya said. "You are safe."

The assistant arrived with tea neither Ana nor Sonya had asked for. Sonya took hers. Ana held up a hand to decline. Sonya placed her teabag onto a miniscule spoon and dipped it into the steaming water. She circled the spoon, the tip tinkling against the cup.

"If we are not friends, then let us remain professional," she said. "I believed Youtopia suitable only for children. You and I are perhaps the only ones who truly know why. But this... *incident* has caused me to see that our imperfect world will not accept that. Adults are far too selfish to accept a greater good for their young and not themselves. As long as Youtopia is exclusive, those without access will rebel."

"You're serious?" Ana said. "After all this, you plan to reopen Youtopia for everybody?"

"I have seen the footage from your Intervention," Sonya said, a small, genuine smile forming on her lips for the first time. "A certain altercation happened. Explain it to me."

"It was... Veronica grabbed my hand and —"

"Not that," Sonya interjected. "The events that immediately followed."

Ana's mind jumped to Charlotte, to the sand and sun. To how *right* everything felt.

"Explain the experience to me."

Ana gazed downward. "I don't think I could, even if I wanted to. I'm not sure I do."

Sonya stirred the teabag a final time. Daintily, with great care, she fished it out. She then strangled the teabag with its own string, dripping the dregs into the cup. The process was practiced, ritualistic. It made Ana wonder how Sonya ever lost control. It seemed impossible it would ever happen again.

"I will admit," Sonya said, "I was truly surprised by your Intervention. After contemplation, however, it all made perfect sense.

"Intervention was conceived unilaterally — as a singular current of influence, from Intervener to Immerser — but that is not how our minds operate. Every interaction in our daily lives represents an opportunity to shift, to transform, to color the life of another — but we will also, inevitably, be colored by that same experience."

She smiled a final time at Ana. "We would have discovered it eventually without you, Miss Downer. That does not, however, diminish the fact that you were the first. Our pioneer. The commencing step of our next and final phase.

"What you did in Veronica's Reborn has opened the door for so many possibilities. They are truly infinite."

THE END
...but please keep reading for our Bonus Content.

Acknowledgements

This book, like all books, exists because of the help of so many others. I am eternally indebted to all those who knowingly or unknowingly supported its creation. This goes to all the authors of the utopian and dystopian fiction that influenced my early thinking on this series, and to the countless speculative, sci-fi, and futuristic authors and filmmakers who spurred my imagination as I wrote.

Thanks to the University of Wisconsin–River Falls—in particular, my students, former and current, whose talent and sheer drive amaze me on a near-daily basis. To former instructors and mentors of mine: David Treuer, Liam Callanan, Jonis Agee, Gerald Shapiro, and countless others. To Kevin Morgan Watson, for recognizing the value in my short fiction. To Kelsey Kaufman, for her diligent line edits and enthusiastic support. To Dave Yost, the best reader (and writer) I could ever hope to know.

Thanks to Dave Lane (AKA Lane Diamond), an excellent editor, and Kris Norris for another beautiful and haunting cover.

To my parents Bill and Barb: my deepest gratitude, for never saying I couldn't or shouldn't. This book is for them, and also for my kids, Colette, James, Johnny, and Olivia, who each day simultaneously keep me young and age me considerably. And finally, it is for my wife Jessica, my best friend and my most avid reader, for accepting this compulsion of mine and giving me the time and space to nurture it. None of this is possible without you.

About the Author

Joseph Rein is the author of the short story collection *Roads without Houses* (2018), which was nominated for numerous literary prizes. His short fiction has appeared in over twenty journals, magazines, and anthologies worldwide, and has twice been nominated for a Pushcart Prize. He is also a screenwriter and critical essayist. His second feature-length film, Who Killed Cooper Dunn? (2022), was featured on Showtime and other streaming platforms. He wrote, produced, and acted in multiple other short festival films, and has two feature-length projects in pre-production. He is currently a Professor of Creative Writing at the University of Wisconsin-River Falls. When not writing or reading, he can be found hiking with his wife Jessica, playing cribbage, or recovering from various small injuries inflicted by his four children.

For more, please visit Joseph Rein online at:
Website: www.JosephRein.com
Facebook: @JosephReinAuthor
Instagram: @joseph_rein1
X (Twitter): @joseph_rein1

What's Next?

Watch for the third book in this series to release in late 2025.

YOUTOPIA INFINITY
Youtopia – Book 3

Finally, the perfect worlds of Youtopia can be shared with loved ones, allowing Immersers to live out their dreams together... until those dreams become nightmares.

Youtopia has reached its culmination in Infinity, a shared mindspace that offers collective perfection. Within the system, however, lurks a mysterious presence — the Harbinger — who warps perfection into the perfect killing grounds.

As Youtopia creator Sonya Young chases the Harbinger, the FBI knows it has only one place to turn: former Special Agent Anabel Downer, who will seek to unlock the mystery and finally overcome the company that has come to haunt, and define, her life.

More from Evolved Publishing

We offer great books across multiple genres, featuring high-quality editing (which we believe is second-to-none) and fantastic covers.

As a hybrid small press, your support as loyal readers is so important to us, and we have strived, with tireless dedication and sheer determination, to deliver on the promise of our motto:
QUALITY IS PRIORITY #1!

Please check out all of our great books,
which you can find at this link:
www.EvolvedPub.com/Catalog/

Thank you!